On Lill Street

On Lill Street

Lynn Kanter

Third Side Press
Chicago

Cover art copyright © 1992 by Riva Lehrer
Cover design by Riva Lehrer and Midge Stocker
Interior design and production by Midge Stocker
  Text set 11/12.5 Sabon

Printed on recycled, acid-free paper in the United States of America.

Library of Congress Cataloging-in-Publication Data

Kanter, Lynn, 1954–
    On Lill Street / Lynn Kanter. — 1st ed.
      p. cm.
    ISBN 1-879427-07-9 : $10.95
    I. Title.
    PS3561.A4905 1992
    813'.45—dc20   92-28048
                                                             CIP

This book is available on tape to disabled women from the Womyn's Braille Press, P.O. Box 8475, Minneapolis, MN 55408.

Third Side Press, Inc.
2250 W. Farragut
Chicago, IL 60625-1802
312/271-3029

First edition, September 1992
10 9 8 7 6 5 4 3 2 1

For Pam

With special thanks to Karen Kanter

THE HOUSE ON LILL STREET

Margaret counts the cartons crowding her living room floor and clutches her forehead in despair. She cannot imagine how she accumulated so much junk. She cannot envision how she will pack it, move it, merge it with the artifacts of another woman in a new apartment that she must learn to call home.

Margaret slumps in her favorite chair and wonders if she should make Gwen move in with her instead of the other way around. But that makes no sense. Gwen's sunny Upper West Side apartment is three times the size of Margaret's at half the price.

Besides, square footage is not really the problem. Margaret knows that; Gwen knows that. All Margaret's friends know what her problem is. Even strangers who write moronic self-help books know what Margaret's problem is. She has an Armored Heart. She dares not Love Too Much. She is Afraid to Say Yes.

The fact is, Margaret is over forty years old, and she has never lived with anyone. Not exactly. Not since Lill Street.

Margaret wanders among the cartons and squats beside a dusty box marked "Chicago." She pulls off the cracked packing tape and opens the flaps. A faint odor escapes: old newspapers. Margaret sifts through a few clippings, sets the delicate yellowing strips beside her on the shiny wooden floor. She sees the corner of a photograph, slides it out from underneath some files, gently dusts it against her sleeve.

The woman in the photograph is short and thin, with long, straight brown hair pulled back into a braid. She's wearing patched blue jeans, a faded denim jacket, and a black t-shirt emblazoned with a green women's symbol that encloses a fist. Her grayish-blue eyes gleam with revolutionary fervor. She is a

*true foot-soldier of the women's movement, and every inch of
her body proclaims it.*

*Margaret studies that picture and she's embarrassed not by
the militant stance, but by the sweet, foolish smile of that younger
self who had so much to learn.*

*Over the years, she has heard many times about the alarming
image she presented on the morning when she first met someone
from the house on Lill Street. People who meet Margaret now, in
her mellow and ample middle age, scoff at the idea that Margaret
could intimidate anyone. But when she recalls that winter day,
she is not so sure.*

She had been at the tail end of a trying week. On Monday
she had worked late into the night polishing a story for
Feminist Times, the monthly newspaper where she held a
part-time job. Tuesday Margaret had submitted the piece to
the editing collective, only to find that they had decided not to
use it until next month's issue or perhaps the one after that.
The following morning they assigned her to interview a famous
feminist whose first book had just been published.

Weeks earlier the editing collective had received an advance
copy of the book from the feminist's press agent. But the book
disappeared from their cluttered office, as small items were apt
to do while the collective's vision was focused on larger things.
And without the author's smiling visage shining up at them
from the glossy front cover, the editors forgot to assign a
reporter to the story until two days before the woman was due
in Chicago.

Margaret spent Wednesday frantically searching for a copy
of the book. After much phoning and fretting, she finally
reached Deborah Stern, the manager of an alternative
bookstore located in the venerable suburb of Oak Park.
Deborah said she had taken her copy home to read, but would
be glad to bring it to the store the next day.

It was more than the icy hour Margaret had spent on the
elevated train that made her tremble that morning as she
stamped the snow off her boots and waited for Deborah
outside the locked doors of Lucia's Books. She had always
been a slow worker. Now she would have just twenty-four
hours to read the book, type up her notes, complete her
research, select her approach, and prepare her questions.

Then she had to consider the important issue of what she
would wear. What would look professional, yet not too

straight? What would make the statement to famous feminist
Lillian Green that she was dealing with a sister, but one who
wanted real answers to real questions—not the glib retorts that
so tickled the New York media establishment? Moreover, what
was clean?

A tall woman came striding toward Margaret, her curly
blond hair tossing in the wind, a large leather book bag slung
over one shoulder of her green down jacket. "Hi! Margaret?"
she called out.

"Yes. And you're Deborah?"

"Right-o," the woman sang as she unlocked the door and
ushered Margaret in. Deborah tossed her bag behind the sales
counter and hung her coat on a wooden peg attached to the
wall. "Take a look around. I'll be right with you," she called
over her shoulder as she moved through the store with a
smooth, athletic walk, flicking on light switches as she passed.

Margaret's sunglasses fogged up in the warmth of the store,
and she stuffed them into the pocket of her navy blue parka.
Lucia's Books was rectangular, with windows filling one long
wall. The other three walls were lined with unpainted pine
bookshelves. Sunlight reflected off the multi-colored book
covers, making the place bright and cheerful, despite the gray
paint on the walls and the black plastic floor that looked like a
giant Lego® toy. Bean bag chairs hunched in the corners,
creating cozy reading areas. The central area of the store
featured homemade display tables of various heights and
lengths. Hand-printed signs hung from the ceiling to designate
such sections as Biography, Nature, and Third World.

Margaret was just heading for the section marked Lesbians
and Gay Men when Deborah emerged from the back room,
carrying two ceramic mugs. She pulled a Thermos® out of her
bag and poured.

"Here." Deborah slid a steaming mug across the high,
formica sales counter. "I'm about to make you very angry, so I
thought I'd try to appease you with some coffee. Besides, you
look cold."

"I am cold. What's the problem?"

Deborah gripped her own cup as if for courage. "I forgot
the book."

"What?"

"I left it at home. I'm really sorry. I forgot all about the
book until I saw you standing here. I really feel terrible about
it."

"I can't believe this!" Margaret passed her hand over her eyes. "I was counting on that book."

"I know," Deborah said humbly. "I'm sorry. I'd run home and get it for you, but I can't close the store."

"Where do you live?" Margaret asked. "I'll go get the book myself."

"Well, I'm not exactly sure where I left it."

"Great. That's a big help."

"Look, I know you're mad, but let's sit down like humans and figure something else out." Deborah handed Margaret a tall wooden stool from behind the counter.

Grudgingly, Margaret leaned against the stool and glared down at her coffee.

"How about if I mail the book to you?" Deborah offered.

Margaret shook her head. "I'm interviewing her tomorrow morning."

"Well, all the other bookstores must have copies. I'll call around and find one."

"I already called. Nobody seems to have one. I don't understand it. Why would her press agent set up an interview if her book hasn't been released yet?"

"It must be released if I've got a copy. Usually we're on the bottom of the list. Hey, I know!" Deborah hopped off the stool in her enthusiasm. "Why don't you call her press agent and ask her where you can get one?"

Margaret looked at her boots, dripping slush onto the clean black floor. "I can't. She sent a copy to *Feminist Times* and we lost it."

"Oh." Deborah's eyebrows drifted down like two parachutes. "Look, can you meet me here at six? Then I'll take you to my house and give you the book."

Margaret calculated quickly. That would mean an hour on the el to get home, another hour to get back here at six, and a third hour to get home again—all for a book the editing collective had held in their hands and had collectively lost. "I don't know what to do. I need the book, but I can't afford to spend half the day commuting—I have to do some library research on Lillian Green."

"Perfect! We have a good library just a few blocks from the store. I'll meet you there a little after six."

Margaret hesitated. "No, I'll come back here. Then if I don't show up, you'll know I found it somewhere else." She gave Deborah an embarrassed smile. "Sorry I bit your head off."

"No. I'm the one who screwed up, so I'm the one who should be sorry. And I am." She uncorked her thermos. "Have one more for the road."

"Thanks," Margaret said. "This isn't Nescafe® or Taster's Choice®, by any chance, is it?"

Deborah gave her a strange look. "No, it's Colombian."

"Oh." She took a sip. "It's just that I don't drink Nestlé® products. You know, because of the baby formula."

"Baby formula?" Deborah looked amused, as if she expected Margaret to make a joke.

"Yes, you know, the immoral way Nestlé markets their baby formula in third world countries, even though the women can't afford it and don't have good water or refrigeration. But Nestlé gets them to try the formula, and then their own milk dries up, and they have to keep using it."

Deborah stared, her mouth slightly open.

"There may be an international boycott soon," she finished lamely.

"Of baby formula?"

"No, of Nestlé products. Also Stouffers® and all the other companies that Nestlé owns."

"Oh, my God," said Deborah. "I'd better stock up on chocolate chips."

Margaret made a show of blowing on her coffee to cover her confusion. Was this really the limit of Deborah's political conscience, or was she joking? Or was Margaret out of line to lecture a stranger about what kind of coffee she should buy? But surely it was her responsibility as Deborah's sister not only to fight against her oppression, but to help her avoid oppressing others. Wasn't it?

Deborah took a key out of her pocket and turned on the cash register. "So, are we friends, or do you still want to cut my heart out with a carving knife?" She punched a few buttons and the machine made some churning noises and spit out a receipt.

Margaret laughed. "You have a lurid imagination."

"Too much television."

"Well, I guess I'll see you at six. Thanks for the coffee."

Margaret zipped her coat and stepped outside. It was one of those rare bright days that reminded her that even in Chicago, even in the middle of January, there was such a thing

as nature. Of course, she wasn't actually in Chicago, so that
could account for it.

Suburbs, she knew, were not to be trusted. They were only
for the parasitic middle class, who took sustenance from the
city during the day and went home each night to their color
TVs. That sort of life led to complacency, which led to a vested
interest in preserving the status quo, which led to goddess
knew what kinds of horrors—husbands and children,
probably. But despite all she knew about suburbs, here she was
enjoying herself as she ambled past large, old homes on her
way to the library.

As Margaret spread out her notebooks on a table in the
sunny central room, she felt the cocoonish silence of the library
envelop her. It was a pleasant feeling, warm and relaxing, and
she let herself slip into a daydream: this was her neighborhood
library. *Feminist Times* hung on the wooden rack next to the
Chicago *Sun-Times*, the *Tribune*, and the *Daily News*.
Margaret knew all the staff and they knew her. Each week
closing time would find her with her elbows on the tall
wooden check-out desk, chatting quietly with that cute,
red-haired librarian. The lights would flicker and, with a wave,
she'd clasp her stack of books to her chest and head for home.

But there the dream ended, because she was a person who
had no home.

She had a place to live—a studio apartment in the "gay
ghetto" of Chicago's north side. But the landlord had informed
her that the rent was going to double in two months, making
the apartment well beyond her reach.

Perhaps a better way to describe her state would be to say
that she didn't belong anywhere. When she was a senior in
high school, her parents had settled in Bloomington, Indiana,
where they taught at the university. But she had grown up in a
series of comfortably shabby rented houses near, but not in, the
prosperous sections of a half-dozen Midwestern college towns.
Her parents tried to decorate each new house to look as much
as possible like the one they had just left. Waking up the first
few mornings in a new town was like stepping into a
nightmare where everything was familiar but ominously awry.

On moving day, Margaret, her parents, and her younger
sister would converge on the kitchen the moment the movers
left. They scurried around like a well-trained theater crew,
cleaning, unpacking, and organizing. Their tradition required
that regardless of the condition of the rest of the house, the

family had to sit down that first night to a dinner of her father's homemade spaghetti. The large pot of sauce simmered peacefully, surrounded by the chaos of half-emptied cartons, homeless piles of kitchen towels, and dishes wrapped in newspaper. It was as if only the mingled aromas of tomato sauce, onion, and garlic could drive out the claims of earlier tenants and make the house truly theirs.

When she thought of those moving days, she could picture her parents perfectly: her mother with her nondescript brown hair, so much like Margaret's, tied up in a red bandanna, her soft gray eyes squinting in concentration as she double-checked her mover's list against the numbered cartons; her father in his stained blue workshirt and his worn khaki chinos, a screwdriver sticking out of his back pocket, his caramel-colored hair falling over his broad forehead as he leaned down to taste the bubbling sauce.

But she had not seen them since the June day three years ago when she had graduated from college and declared that she was a lesbian. They gave her two choices: renounce her lesbianism and seek therapy, or never come home again. She chose the latter, and the family station wagon drove back to Bloomington with the back seat empty.

Margaret stood frozen, watching her college world disperse into a hundred happy homecomings, her childhood explode in a spray of gravel as her father rocketed the car away from the campus, the East, and anything that would remind him of her. Just before she left, her mother managed to dash off a check for $1,000. Margaret could still see that check, and the way her mother's handwriting had suddenly become as shaky as an old woman's. She wanted to save it forever, but in the end she had to cash it.

She was alone then, alone as the moon on a starless night. Her whole body felt numb, like a stubbed toe in the instant between impact and pain. Margaret sold everything she could to undergraduates—the books she had planned to cherish, the quilt she and her mother had discovered at a rummage sale, the tape player her father had given her for her twentieth birthday. Then she took the bus to Chicago. New York was closer, but she didn't have the courage for that. Margaret had grown up in the Midwest, and Chicago seemed challenge enough.

Those first few months she felt like a ghost. Strangers looked through her as if she were invisible. Sometimes she tried to talk and no sound came out; sometimes she spoke aloud and there was no one to hear.

She found a job at a small community newspaper, chatted with her colleagues, made jokes, ate lunch. But no one really knew her. If she failed to show up for work one morning, she thought it might be days before anyone noticed. Even then, they would not know who to call, who to console over her disappearance. How could they, when they did not realize that she had already disappeared?

Later she tried and failed to make a home for herself with *Feminist Times*. She worked part-time for the paper, which meant 30 to 40 hours a week for slightly under $4,000 a year. She worked hard on her stories, was a decent copy editor, and didn't mind typing up other people's work. Yet she did not feel accepted by the editing collective.

The collective was comprised of four women, chosen by secret ballot and a complicated method of job rotation. On the surface, the collective was a veritable UN of different ethnic types from various backgrounds. Yet a more monolithic orthodoxy of political opinion would be hard to find. Margaret didn't mind, however, because she agreed on most matters. And she knew exactly why they distrusted her.

First of all, she was a writer. Margaret did not believe that being a writer necessarily disqualified one from working for a newspaper, but she was practically alone in that opinion. The editing collective felt that every woman had a right to express herself in the pages of *Feminist Times* in whatever way she chose. If Margaret's work showed more style than others', she was acting in an elitist manner, trying to monopolize the means of communication at the expense of women who had not enjoyed the same privileges of social class and education.

Second, she had been to Vassar. This was considered either shocking or pitiable by the women she knew.

Finally, she was writing a book and had an actual contract from a small women's press. *Feminist Times* was an outlet for those who had been denied a voice in the patriarchal press, not for people who could speak out elsewhere. The fact that Margaret's contract was with a feminist press and not a straight publisher was the only margin that allowed her to stay on staff.

The 1970s were strange and thrilling times to be a young lesbian feminist, charged with energy and faith in the future. The Stonewall rebellion was taking place as Margaret received her high school diploma. While she was choosing a major in college, the Equal Rights Amendment was passed by the House and Senate after fifty years of struggle. During her first three years at Vassar, she was deeply involved in a sort of underground railroad that helped women from other states get legal abortions in New York. Before she graduated in 1973, the Supreme Court decided *Roe v. Wade*, and abortion became legal across the land.

The women's movement had found its voice, and she was a part of it. Perhaps certain sacrifices were required of her in return, but she never saw them as such. For Margaret and most of the women she knew, the revolution was their life, and even revolutions have rules.

They could eat no meat or processed foods. Bourgeois urges, such as the desire to go out to dinner and to the movies, were to be strenuously fought. If they did succumb, they were obliged to comment constantly on the sexist behavior taking place around them and therefore could not have a very good time.

Certain types of clothing—jeans, overalls, t-shirts, flannel shirts—were allowed. Other types of clothing were taboo, a way of adhering to stereotypical notions of femininity and beauty.

Some of them had once had "good" jobs, or could have gotten them, but chose not to. To have lucrative jobs meant they had sold out to the male business world. To work for the women's movement was a privilege in itself, and they did not ask to be paid market wages on top of it.

Margaret watched the white winter sun cross the library's picture window and disappear. She prepared for her interview and dreamed about her future, and the day passed pleasantly, more pleasantly than she had imagined it could.

When she got to Lucia's Books a little before six, she was shocked to find Deborah on her hands and knees in front of the "Science" section, wiping blood off the floor.

She dropped down next to her. "Are you all right?"

"I'm fine," Deborah replied with a grim little smile. She had removed her bulky sweater and was wearing a black t-shirt, which revealed strongly muscled arms that wouldn't be fashionable for at least a decade.

"What happened?" Margaret glanced around at the customers who browsed unconcernedly among the stacks.

"A kid came in here and got a nosebleed, and her
father—you know, one of those new, involved dads?—just
stood there and let her bleed." She gave the floor a vicious
swipe with her bloody rag.

"Why didn't you force him to clean it up, or just throw
them both out?"

"Because it was my kid and my ex-husband." She looked at
Margaret and sighed. "Come on, let's go." Deborah stood and
dragged Margaret up with her. "Let me get rid of the gore and
I'll meet you in front."

They talked about books and writers on the way to
Deborah's house, walking quickly because of the cold.
Margaret was impressed by how knowledgeable Deborah was,
both about mainstream writers and about the new feminist
writers who were just beginning to publish. When she
mentioned this, Deborah laughed.

"I work in a bookstore. The pay's terrible, the benefits are
worse, and the only reason I do it is because I love books.
Naturally I'm well-read."

Margaret was just beginning to wonder how far Deborah's
place was and why one of her suburban friends couldn't have
picked them up in a station wagon when Deborah turned into
a driveway and said, "Here we are."

She balked. "You've got to be joking." The house was a
four-story Victorian with two large front porches and a vast
front yard. Light glowed from every window, and Margaret
could have sworn she smelled a wood fire. Apparently she had
drastically misjudged both Deborah's politics and her income.

"Don't worry." Deborah gave her arm a little tug and
started walking toward the house. "We only rent."

She led the way around the house and through a back
door, which opened to a narrow, dimly lit staircase. "There's
my apartment." Deborah nodded toward a half-open door on
the first floor as they began to climb the creaky stairs. "Charles
and Cindy live on the third floor. Mrs. Rogers lives in the attic
apartment." They had reached the second floor landing, and
Deborah paused with her hand on the doorknob as if she were
about to unveil a treasure. "And this is Arden's apartment."
She flung the door open.

They stepped into a foyer, really a white hallway enclosed
at the far end by a milky glass door. The sudden light and
warmth dazed Margaret after the long cold walk. Peering
through the glass door, she felt as if she had stepped into a

dream. She could make out a large room, one end flickering with firelight, and the indistinct forms of several people. She heard music, laughter, and conversation, but the sounds were muted and rounded, as if they had traveled a long way under water before reaching her.

Deborah pulled off her boots and opened the glass door. The room leaped into clarity, revealing a group of people talking and laughing. A few of them looked up momentarily, like animals disturbed at a watering hole, but immediately went back to their party.

All alone, tending the fire, stood a woman who somehow seemed to be the nucleus of all this activity. Her strong profile was barely visible from the doorway. Her back was turned toward the others in the room. Margaret looked at her and was pierced by a sudden hunger to belong in the circle of light this woman created.

She heard a strange sound in the room, like a low buzzing, and realized it was male voices. One of the men unfolded himself from the sagging blue couch and ambled over to them, wrapping his arm around Deborah's shoulders. He was tall and trim, with a medium-length Afro, a thick walrus moustache, and sweet brown eyes shining behind gold wire-rimmed glasses.

"This is Paul, my current heartthrob," Deborah said, returning his hug. "This is Margaret."

"Nice to meet you," he said in a quiet, rumbly voice.

"You too," she murmured, suddenly shy.

"Honey, you left our front door open," Deborah said.

"I know. It was so cold in our apartment I hoped some of the heat from upstairs would sneak into our place."

"Is that what they taught you at MIT—that heat falls?"

Margaret jumped. It was the woman from the fireplace, standing practically at her elbow. The woman was smiling, despite her sarcastic question. Covertly Margaret noted her thick chestnut hair, the deep matching lines that bracketed her mouth like parentheses.

"Arden, behave yourself," Deborah chided. "We have company."

"Yes, I can see that." She turned her smile on Margaret and extended her hand. "Hi. I'm Arden McCarthy."

She was not much taller than Margaret, so when they shook hands Margaret could look directly into her deep-set hazel eyes. She felt again with an odd pang that someday she

wanted to mean something to this woman. "Margaret
Osborn," she replied.

"She's with *Feminist Times*," Deborah said. "She's here to
pick up that copy of Lillian Green's book, which I think I left
here last night."

"You did. It's in Joe's room. He was probably reading it to
find ammunition for his theory that feminism is just a
diversion to take people's minds off important issues."

"Yeah, like saving the whales," Deborah laughed.

Paul turned to Margaret. "Don't you think the ecology is
important?"

"Sure. But I'm more interested in saving women's lives than
whales'."

"But feminism isn't a life or death issue," he argued, his
mild expression unchanged. "It's a reformist movement
designed to provide business opportunities and symbolic civil
rights to white middle-class women. Not that I don't think they
deserve those things. I'm a feminist myself—we all are. But
you've got to admit it's hardly the most pressing issue of our
time."

Margaret stood frozen, blood pounding in her head. When
she heard pronouncements like that she wanted to kill. Not
just refute his argument, but completely destroy him, his ideas,
and his self-esteem.

"You've been hanging around Joe too much," Deborah
said with irritation. "I'll go get the book."

"Oh, come on." Arden had taken a step closer to Margaret,
so they stood side by side facing Paul. "Didn't we have a fight
about this very subject just last week? Let's think of something
else to do tonight."

"I'm not baiting you," Paul told Margaret pleasantly. "I'm
interested in your opinion. What do you think?"

Struggling to remain impassive, she doled out the words. "I
think you are completely mistaken."

He was about to respond when Deborah re-entered the
foyer and shoved him sharply with her hip. "Paul, go play with
the other boys," she ordered, and he did. She handed Margaret
the book. "And I bet you thought black men had higher
consciousness."

Margaret blushed. She had been thinking exactly that.

"Hey, Margaret, do you remember an article in your last
issue about how men are learning to give lip service to

feminism so they don't have to make any real changes in the way they relate to women?"

"'Co-opting the language of liberation.' I wrote it."

"We had a big blowout last week about that article. No wonder Paul was ragging at you," Deborah cackled. "He had to sleep on the couch over that one."

Arden gave Margaret an appraising look. "Why don't you stay and have a drink?"

She hesitated. "No thanks. I've got to get home and read this book."

"Yeah, she's interviewing Lillian Green tomorrow."

"Well, good luck."

"Arden, I'm using your car to drive Margaret to the train."

"Okay. See you later, Margaret." Arden turned away to join the others, closing the door behind her.

"Who were all those people?" Margaret asked as they bounced along in Arden's red Honda.

"Well, let's see. You met Arden. She lives with Joe, who you didn't meet. He was sitting on the couch. Charles was the one screwing around with the stereo. He lives upstairs. Cindy lives upstairs too, but not with Charles. She works at the bookstore. She was sitting in the corner, reading the paper out loud to Leslie and Sue, who don't live there but who went to school with us."

"Does Arden always have that much company?"

She seemed surprised. "I suppose so. It's not really company, just the people we grew up with, plus a few friends and lovers. We hang out at Arden's apartment because—I'm not really sure why. We've always gotten together at Arden's place, even when we were kids. Habit, I guess."

They had reached the station. "Thanks for the ride. How much do I owe you for the book?"

"Just return it when you're through."

As Margaret jostled home, clutching Lillian Green's book and keeping a wary eye on the other passengers, she kept mulling over the evening's events. Why was she so drawn to Arden and her group, and yet so disturbed by them?

The kind of fuzzy liberalism they espoused revolted her. Sure, there were lots of causes in the world, but it was possible—in fact, it was *necessary* to identify the issues that were important to you and to fight for them exclusively. How could Arden and Deborah call themselves feminists if they didn't know that? Although now that she thought about it, they hadn't called themselves feminists; Paul had.

And that being the case, how could she now be wishing she were still in that warm, noisy apartment, laughing with Cindy as she read "Dear Abby" aloud, and tasting just a tiny bite of the meat she had smelled cooking for dinner? What was happening to her, she wondered in horror. Was she getting soft, or just lonely?

Early the next morning she arrived at the downtown hotel where she was to meet Lillian Green. Her head buzzed with nervousness, lack of sleep, and the dozens of questions she had prepared for the interview.

What was Lillian Green like, she wondered as the mirrored elevator made its stately ascent. What would she be doing— polishing up a speech, going over plans for a top-level strategy session, calling Gloria Steinem for a lunch date? Margaret tugged her jacket into place and knocked on the door. "It's open," the famous voice called.

She was ironing. She had set a tiny portable ironing board on the dresser and was pressing a blouse with a tiny portable iron. She was in her mid-forties and had short, blond hair shot through with silver, intense blue eyes, and a thin, sculpted face with prominent cheekbones. Margaret wondered if she'd used her travel iron to put that sharp crease in her gray corduroy slacks.

"You must be Margaret Osborn," she said, smiling, and offered a hand with long, manicured fingernails.

"And you must be Lillian Green."

"I guess I must be." She waved her over to the bed. "Have a seat. Please forgive this housekeeping, but I'm due to make a speech in Indianapolis tonight, and I didn't think I'd get another chance to get my clothes ready for the next few days. Want some coffee?"

"No thanks." Margaret took out her reporter's notebook and set a tape recorder on the dresser.

"Don't put it there unless you want to record the sound of my iron." Lillian picked up the recorder and put it on the bedside table.

"Thank you," she said, blushing. So much for her image of cool professionalism. "How long did it take you to write your book, Ms. Green?"

"Call me Lillian. The actual writing took me two years, but I'd say it's taken me twenty years to learn enough so I'd have something to say in a book. Not that I've been exactly silent," she joked, alluding to her prominent career as a public speaker and organizer.

"What would you say is the major theme?"

"I think that's something for the reader to decide. I know what I meant to say, but it's up to each reader to determine what, if anything, the book says to her. What do you think the theme is?"

Margaret hesitated. "Well, that women need to share our failures as well as our achievements. And that sometimes our failures are not really failures at all, because the tasks we set for ourselves are so difficult that accomplishing any portion of them is a success in itself."

Lillian laughed again. "Wonderful! You see, each reader sees what she needs to in the book, just as each woman finds what she needs to in feminism. And when enough people have the same needs, that's when a movement forms." Lillian carefully folded her blouse and spread another on the ironing board.

The interview continued sedately for half an hour as Margaret conscientiously covered the groundwork. Finally she felt ready to move on to more challenging questions. "Until now you haven't been known as a writer. Did you have any, uh, editorial help with this book?"

"Oh, yes." Lillian sprayed some starch on a sleeve. "Good Lord, I called every writer I know and begged them to look at the manuscript and offer suggestions. I know a lot of writers, and they all had a lot of suggestions." She looked up keenly. "But if you mean a ghost writer, no."

Margaret scribbled furiously, even though the tape recorder seemed to be working for once. "How did you decide to go with a mainstream publisher rather than one of the feminist presses?"

"That was a tough decision." Lillian pushed a button and a blast of steam shot out of the iron. "The women's presses are wonderful, but like everything else in our movement, they're short on funds. I wanted women to have easy access to my book, and I thought that a major publisher would put some

money into advertising it—regardless of its literary merit—in
order to capitalize on the fact that I happen to be a 'name'
right now." She said the word with a wry smile. "I made a deal
with my publisher that the book would be released to women's
and alternative bookstores first, so they would get the initial
benefit from the publicity. The big guys get it just a day or two
later, but every little bit helps."

So that was why Margaret had had to go to Lucia's Books
to find a copy. She looked at Lillian Green with new respect.

"Why did you ask? Have there been some rumblings about
treachery in the women's community here?"

"Well, a little bit. I mean, we kind of wondered," Margaret
mumbled.

"Is there anything else you kind of wondered about?" she
asked with a sigh.

"Sort of. How do you justify staying in an expensive hotel
like this when the money could be put to much better use
within the movement?"

Lillian studied the younger woman for a moment. She set
the iron down and sat beside her on the bed. "Let me explain
something to you, Margaret. My publisher pays for this hotel
room. But even if I had gone with a publisher that couldn't
afford to put me up in good hotels, I'd pay for it myself. Do
you know why?"

Margaret shook her head.

"Because I'm tired."

Margaret had stopped taking notes and was simply staring
at Lillian. She wasn't sure if she had angered Lillian or not, or
whether that mattered in the pursuit of good journalism.
Lillian's words were harsh, but her tone was so kind that
Margaret was confused.

"How old are you, Margaret? Twenty?"

"Twenty-four."

"Well, I'm forty-five. When I was your age, I didn't
understand this either. So let me clarify it for you, and maybe
it'll save you some of the trouble I went through." Lillian
reached across her and turned off the recorder.

"Margaret, we don't have to prove to anybody that we're
good feminists. If I'm able to do my job better when I've had a
good night's sleep, then I'm going to make sure I have a
comfortable bed. When I'm on the road, that kind of comfort
is even more important.

"I've paid my dues, just as you're paying yours now. I've had movement jobs where I worked my buns off and got nothing for it but criticism." Margaret nodded. "I bet you know a little about that," Lillian said. "And I've had times when I've lost people who were important to me because they thought I'd gone overboard or they didn't like the principles I was committed to."

Tears stung Margaret's eyes as she thought of her parents turning their backs on her and hurrying toward their car.

"I suppose you know a little about that, too," Lillian added more gently. "But here's my point. You know what you believe and what you can contribute. If anyone—even a sister—doesn't like the way you live your life, that's her problem. Your only problem is to figure out what you need in order to do your work. If that's a good bed, or $30,000 a year, or just a word of praise every now and then, well, that's what you've got to have and that's all there is to it."

Lillian stood, picked up her blouse from the ironing board and flattened it against her chest. "I think this'll look okay on TV, don't you?"

"I think it'll look fine."

She unplugged her iron. Margaret took that as a cue and rose to leave. "Well, thank you for your time. Would you like me to send you a copy of the article when it comes out?"

"Yes I would. But why don't you stay for a few minutes? Give me a chance to ask you some questions."

"Sure, I'd love to."

"Good. Don't mind me while I finish packing. Do you work full-time for the paper?"

"No, only part-time."

"And you don't make a dime, right?" She laughed.

"Well, I do make something. It's not much, but it lets me earn a living in the women's movement."

"And what do you do the rest of the time?"

"I'm writing a book."

"Wonderful! Have you found a publisher?"

"Yes. Women's Words, in Boston."

"Oh." Lillian looked up suddenly from the sweater she was folding. "Do you have a written contract with them?"

"Sure. Why?"

"Oh, no reason. Did you get an advance?"

"Yeah." She grinned. "A hundred and fifty dollars. But it's my first book and I'm really excited about it even though I probably won't make enough to pay for the typing paper."

"Well, I don't know, of course, but all my writer friends tell me it's a good idea to keep in touch with your publishers. Frequently. In writing."

"Well, I will then. Thanks for the tip."

Sliding open the top dresser drawer, Lillian efficiently removed the clothing and tucked it into her suitcase. "What's your book about?"

"It's an experiential study of sisterhood at work. I interview different women's groups and analyze the way they make decisions and create power structures."

Lillian poured herself a cup of coffee and sat next to Margaret again. "Sounds like it would be fascinating to read but difficult to write. Do you have a background in sociology?"

"Well, no. The research is anecdotal."

"What's the book called?"

"I don't have a title yet. I'd love to call it *Sisterhood is Powerful*, but that's already been taken, and after that every title I think of sounds wishy-washy."

Lillian laughed. "I'll tell Robin when I see her." She took a sip of coffee, grimaced, and put the cup down on the floor. "This stuff's deadly. So what did you do before you worked for *Feminist Times*?"

"I wrote for a small neighborhood newspaper. It was a pretty good job, actually, except that I kept getting assigned to write articles like 'The Manly Art of Controlling a Conversation,' and 'An NRA Christmas.'"

"As if anyone would want to read stories like that. I know, don't tell me, they do." She studied Margaret in a way that was kind but impersonal. "Twenty-four years old. Do you have any family here?"

"No. My sister Jane's in school in Wisconsin. I get together with her every couple of months. Our parents live in Indiana."

"What do they do?"

"They both teach at Indiana University."

"I imagine you had some wonderful dinner table conversations. They must be very proud of you."

Margaret heard an odd, strangled sound. Then she realized it was a sob fighting its way out of her own throat. Not now! she thought, holding her breath. Not in front of Lillian Green, of all people. But it was too late. She was crying—not weeping decorously, but bawling with loud, hoarse sobs, clutching Lillian's bony shoulders, and feeling her arms around her. This went on for a week or two, it seemed, although it must have been just a few minutes. Finally Margaret pulled away, grabbed a tissue off the bedside table, and managed to compose herself. She turned back to Lillian and her eyes widened in dismay. Here she was on assignment to interview the famous Lillian Green, whom she had admired practically all her life, and what did she do but blubber all over Lillian's clean blouse, which she had probably ironed with her own hands just before Margaret showed up. "You're going to have to change your shirt."

Lillian burst out laughing. "I'm sorry, Margaret. I'm not laughing at you. But what a thing to say after all that!"

"No, I'm sorry. I don't know what came over me. I never cry like that, especially with someone I don't know, and here I am trying to interview you, and I acted like such an ass, and I'm really very sorry." She shoved the tape recorder into her backpack. "I should go now. I'm sorry."

"Oh, Margaret, sit down," Lillian commanded in a tone that reminded Margaret of what a powerful organizer she was. "Are you okay now?" Margaret nodded. "Then what was it? No, tell me. Is it your parents?" She nodded again. "What about them?"

"You said they must be proud of me, and they're not. They despise me."

"But why?"

"Because I'm a lesbian. The day I told them they said they never wanted to see me again, and they haven't."

"So they cut you off? Just like that?"

"Just like that."

"Amazing." Lillian leaned her chin on her fist.

"What's so amazing about it? It happens all the time."

"Good Lord, the wounds we inflict in the name of love." Lillian shook her head. "Margaret, believe me, the loss is theirs, not yours. I know it's hard for you to feel that now, but it's true. You'll see." She checked her watch, sighed, fastened her suitcase. "Are you going to be all right?"

Margaret nodded.

Lillian squeezed her arm. "You've given me something to think about. Thank you."

"I'm sorry about your shirt."

"Oh, it'll dry." Lillian took an envelope out of her big leather brief case, slipped a $10 bill into it, laid it on the dresser, and marked it 'For the Maid.' She smiled at Margaret. "One of the most underpaid and undervalued jobs in the pink collar ghetto. That's how I started out—cleaning motel rooms in Lake George, New York."

What a woman, Margaret thought as they walked down the long, carpeted hallway toward the elevators, so strong and wise and thoughtful, yet funny and tender and beautiful at the same time. She was infatuated with Lillian: not in an individual way, but in the way that she was infatuated with all women and with the women's movement in general, for all of their strengths and foibles. Maybe she would call her book *Sisterhood is Wonderful.*

Whatever she ended up naming it, Margaret would write the best book that had ever been written. She would make this woman proud. Lillian Green and her mother and the editing collective and all the women she had ever loved or would ever love—she would make them all proud.

Margaret did not, as it turns out, make all of them proud.

There were women she angered, women she frustrated, women she bored. There were women in whose eyes she found delight; some of them she pleased and some she pained.

There were women like Gwen, who shared her nights and asked for her days. Each of them she disappointed. Even now, kneeling among her moving cartons, Margaret herself does not know if she is equal to Gwen's faith.

There were women she wanted but could not have. There were women she had but could not keep. And there were a few— a shining few— whose love she held on to throughout the long years.

Not many, perhaps. But enough.

THE JOB INTERVIEW

"What do you call this?" Margaret slammed down the latest edition of *Feminist Times*.

Mei Ling signed the check she was writing, entered the amount in the register, and looked up. "I call it a pretty good issue."

"Where's my Lillian Green article?"

"It isn't in there. That's why it's a pretty good issue."

Letitia entered the workroom from the small editing collective office, closing the door behind her. She perched on top of the heavy wooden table where Mei Ling was working. "Sit down, Margaret."

"No, I won't sit down. I want to know why the hell my article wasn't printed, and who made the decision."

Mei Ling smiled at her. The smile transformed her face: the hollows in her smooth cheeks deepened into dimples; her brown eyes melted like chocolate; her thin astringent eyebrows softened into curves. It was too bad Mei Ling was so good-looking, Margaret thought, because she could be one cold woman.

"The editing collective made the decision, Margaret. Our votes are secret and we don't mix personalities with politics. That's what keeps the collective process pure. You know that."

Margaret smacked the table. "I don't give a damn about your Girl Scout code. I want to know what happened to my interview."

"Girl, that was no interview," exclaimed Letitia. "That was a love letter."

"What are you talking about?"

"Baby, you didn't ask her any of the hard questions."

"Like what? I asked her about the hotel room."

Mei Ling snorted. "Yeah. She says she's tired and you believe her."

"Is it so inconceivable to you that after fifteen years of struggling for women's rights she may in fact be tired?"

"So what? So she's tired. I'm tired. You're tired. We're all tired."

"I am not tired, except of your bullshit."

Letitia ducked her head and picked at one of the colorful patches on her overalls. All Margaret could see of her was a dozen short, thick braids. "Margaret, you didn't ask her if she's a dyke," she mumbled, embarrassed to have to point out something so obvious.

"What has that got to do with anything?"

From under heavy brows, Letitia exchanged glances with Mei Ling. "It's got everything to do with everything. Don't you believe that the personal is political?"

"Of course I do, but—"

"There's no but," Mei Ling interrupted. She closed the checkbook and snapped a rubber band around it. "Our readers will want to know if she's a lesbian, and if she is why she hasn't come out publicly, and if she isn't how she can call herself a feminist when she's blatantly collaborating with the enemy. Those are the most important questions, and you didn't ask any of them."

"Look . . ." Margaret turned away from them, searching for patience in the peeling paint and bright posters on the wall. Choosing her words carefully, she began again. "This woman has written a good book, an insightful book, a book that empowers other women. She's spent her life organizing and inspiring women to choose their own directions. I talked to her about her work and about her book. I didn't think it was relevant to ask her who she fucked."

Mei Ling looked up sharply. "Women don't fuck," she began.

"We make love," all three recited in unison.

"But Margaret," Letitia said, a conspiratorial twinkle in her dark eyes, "didn't you wonder?"

"Of course I wondered. I always wonder. I see a woman on the street and I wonder if she's one of us. That doesn't mean I'd ask her that in an interview about an entirely different subject."

"That's the problem." Letitia shook her head. "You don't understand that it's all related."

"No, you don't understand. It wasn't relevant." Margaret sat against the edge of the table. "Besides, I don't think she is."

"Why not?" Mei Ling asked avidly.

"I just don't think so."

"Kid, just 'cause she didn't go for you doesn't mean she's not a dyke," Letitia laughed.

"Come on," Mei Ling coaxed.

"I'd tell you, but I don't want to see it in the next issue of the paper in place of my story."

"Whose side are you on?" Letitia demanded. "Hers or ours?"

"I thought we were all on the same side." Margaret jumped to her feet and whirled to face them. "You know, that's what's wrong with the editorial policy of this paper. Everybody has to toe the line in every little way, or she's a traitor to the movement. I don't approve of feminists relating to men either. But what if Lillian Green is straight? Does that in any way diminish the good she's done for women?"

They stared at her as if she'd gone mad. "Hell, yes," Letitia finally replied.

Margaret picked up her jacket and backpack from the floor. "I'm leaving."

She pulled on her coat and bounded up the stairs that led out of the newspaper's basement office. "Hey, Osborn!" she heard from the bottom of the stairs. "Wait up." Letitia trotted up the stairs and slid around her to block the front door.

"C'mon, you can tell your big sister Letitia. What makes you think Lillian Green is straight?"

"Well . . ." she stalled, eyeing the door handle.

Letitia leaned against it and folded her arms.

Margaret shrugged. "She has really long fingernails. Manicure, nail polish, the works."

"Gross." Letitia stepped aside and, with a gallant gesture, opened the front door. "Don't worry, kid. Maybe next month we'll come up with a couple of choice assignments for you."

"I hope so."

Why do I put up with that shit, Margaret asked herself angrily as she stood swaying on the el. Why don't I tell the editing collective to take their paycheck and their party line and go straight to hell?

Her vehemence faded slowly, like a blush. She knew the answer: the collective could replace Margaret far more easily than she could replace them. If she wanted to write for a women's newspaper, *Feminist Times* was the only one in town. And the women on the collective weren't so bad individually; they were only tough, well, collectively. When these women got together they could be demanding, unpredictable, capable of grinding disapproval and blinding spurts of warmth. A family, in short.

Margaret now thinks she could write a monograph about all the foolish things she has done in order to belong. She remembers putting up with outrageous behavior from obnoxious bosses. She remembers explaining away the transparent alibis of a straying lover. She remembers listening to the muffled, otherworldly laughter of distant audiences as she waited in empty theater lobbies for friends who were incessantly late.

Margaret opens her living room window and looks three stories down at what will soon cease to be her street. She wonders if she is about to make another, more drastic, mistake. She watches a woman in shorts trot past the building, towed by six panting dogs. On the corner she sees two black men wearing green knit caps. The tall man is playing a steel drum, the short one an accordion. The song they are collaborating on is the theme from "Exodus." This is why she lives in New York.

She loves Gwen unreservedly, but that does not mean Margaret knows how to be a good partner. That does not mean that by moving in with Gwen she is not commencing on yet another doomed attempt to recreate what she never had in the first place.

The winter light was fading as the train rattled its way into the suburbs. She hoped to see Arden again, and she hoped that Deborah would ask about the interview so at least she'd get to talk about Lillian, even though no one would ever read her article. But when she finally reached the house on Lill Street, what she found there made her forget all about Lillian Green.

Three squad cars, their blue lights flashing, sat haphazardly on the street and lawn in front of the house. At least there's no ambulance, Margaret thought as she ran up the long driveway. A small crowd had gathered behind the house, staring at the back door as if it were a curtain about to go up. The door was flanked by two cops, one male and one female, looking cold but stoic in their butch blue leather jackets. Margaret made her way slowly through the crowd, pushing past the brightly colored down jackets and catching snatches of conversation. "I knew something strange was going on in this house." "Have you heard what's happening?" "I hope it's not the old lady..."

She went up to the woman cop and tried to look harmless. "I had an appointment to return this book to a woman who lives here. Should I go in, or can you see that she gets it?"

At that moment, the door opened. A hand reached out, grabbed Margaret by the sleeve, and pulled her inside. As she stumbled over the step, she heard the cop laugh. "Guess you can go in."

Margaret squinted in the dim hallway. It was Arden. "Are you all right?" Margaret asked foolishly, since Arden was obviously fine.

"Everyone's okay. Deborah's upstairs."

She followed Arden up the narrow steps. "What's going on?"

Arden gave a resigned sigh. "Nothing, believe it or not. It all happened hours ago."

"Then what are the cops doing here?"

"Beats me. Must be a slow day for them."

The living room looked tremendous without a crowd of people. Faint blue light from the squad cars pulsed in the black windows. Paul sat alone in the dusk, slumped into a chair and staring at the cold ashes in the fireplace. He merely nodded in response to Margaret's greeting.

"Margaret, want a drink?" Deborah called from the kitchen. "Beer, Coke®, a little Nestlé's hot chocolate?"

"A Coke would be good, thanks."

Deborah bustled in and set a beer next to Paul, who ignored her. She deposited the other drinks on the glass coffeetable and clicked on a lamp. The three women sat on the aging blue couch.

"So what happened?" Margaret asked Arden.

"Do you remember Cindy, who lives upstairs?"

She nodded.

"Well, her apartment and Charles' apartment are filled with all the old furniture that Mrs. Rogers can't fit in her place."

"Some of it's *schlock*, but some of it's very good," Deborah interjected.

"Who's Mrs. Rogers?"

"She owns this house," Deborah replied.

"And where does she live?"

"On the fourth floor, in the attic apartment," Arden said.

"Where all madwomen belong," added Deborah.

"Is she mad?"

Arden shook her head. "Just . . . eccentric."

"And tight-fisted to the point of lunacy. Or perhaps you think she's merely frugal?"

"All right, she's crazy. But only about certain things. Besides, I'm sure she grew up very poor."

"That was sixty years ago. Time to get over it." Deborah took a swig of her beer.

"Anyway, when Mrs. Rogers got home this afternoon, she went to talk to Cindy about something."

"I wonder what it was," Deborah mused.

Arden rolled her eyes. "The rent, of course. What did you think she wanted to discuss with Cindy, grooming tips?"

"Forgive me. I forgot that you and Mrs. Rogers are best buds. Naturally you'd know what was on her mind at any given moment."

"Try not to lose your head like that again," Arden said primly.

"I will."

Margaret felt like she was watching a tennis game, as the narrative bounced back and forth. "So what happened?"

Arden took a sip of her drink. "When Mrs. Rogers knocked on the door, it swung right open, and the apartment was empty. No Cindy, no clothes, no furniture, nothing."

"Mrs. Rogers must have had a heart attack," Deborah said gleefully. Arden shot her a look of reproach. "Sorry, Arden, but when you have a landlady who tells you exactly how many inches of garbage you're entitled to put in her trash can each week, you tend to feel a little smug when she gets smited."

"But don't you see that this time she's getting punished for her generosity? She could have kept all that furniture and made Cindy fend for herself."

Deborah shrugged. "Where would she put it? Her apartment's so crowded there's no room to move. That's why Cindy and Charles got the furniture in the first place, not because Mrs. Rogers was feeling generous."

"Did Cindy steal any of Charles' furniture?" Margaret wondered.

Deborah shook her head. "Only her own. In fact, Mrs. Rogers is up there right now with a policeman and her lawyer, drafting some document for Charles to sign."

"Talk about a waste of time," Arden scoffed. "Cindy and the furniture are gone with the wind, and she's making poor Charles sign his life away. Charles, who won't even take a Coke out of the refrigerator without permission."

Deborah stretched her long legs onto the coffee table. "I hope Joe gets home soon so he can check the contract before they make Charles sign it."

"Is Joe a lawyer?"

"Yes."

"Where does he work?" Margaret inquired politely, expecting to hear another tale of storefront attorneys making the Law work for the People.

"Downtown," Arden replied. "For Continental Bank."

"He's changing the system from the inside," Deborah explained with mock earnestness. Arden elbowed her sharply in the ribs, making Deborah squeal. At the sound, Paul roused himself from his gloom long enough to send her a withering glance. Deborah threw him a kiss in response.

"Paul is very depressed because Cindy was black," she explained.

"Cindy still is black," he retorted. "Don't use the past tense just because she took some beat-up furniture. Besides, you always get upset when you hear about someone Jewish doing something wrong."

"That's only because it happens so rarely."

Paul's laugh came out like a snort, as if he had been fighting to keep it in. Deborah was very appealing, Margaret thought, with her easy manner, her smiling brown eyes, her curly blond hair bouncing when she laughed. But if someone were truly upset, her incessant light-heartedness might be hard to take.

"Yeah, but think about it." Arden leaned forward, elbows on her knees, both hands holding back her smooth chestnut hair. "We've all been robbed. You hired her for the bookstore, invested all that time and training, and now that's wasted. We got to be friends with her, and now that's gone too. And we've all known each other for so long, we're not good at letting new people in." Arden looked directly at Margaret, who couldn't tell if she was warning her away or inviting her to try.

"We weren't that close to her," Paul pointed out. He turned his chair to face the women.

"No, but we might have been if she weren't so busy bringing home a new girlfriend every week," Deborah replied.

Margaret took a sharp breath. "You mean she was a dyke?"

"I wouldn't exactly call her gay," Arden said judiciously. "Maybe bisexual would be more accurate."

"Maybe omnisexual would be even more accurate," Paul added.

"Let's face it, she screwed everything that moved and a few things that didn't," Deborah concluded. "Don't get me wrong. I liked Cindy, but I never met a human being more intent on getting laid. There've been lots of nights when Charles had to stay on our couch because he couldn't sleep through the racket coming from Cindy's room. I don't know how Mrs. Rogers avoided hearing it. Her bedroom's right over Cindy's."

"Unless she enjoyed hearing it," Arden suggested.

"Spare me." Deborah made a nauseated face.

"Well, didn't any of you ever say anything to her?" Margaret demanded. "I mean, sure, her love life is none of your business, but if it keeps you awake at night..."

"What would we say?"

"I don't know."

Arden shrugged. "Well, it's too late now."

Deborah sighed. "I just hope Mrs. Rogers doesn't rent the apartment to one of her creepy nephews."

"She can't," Arden reassured her. "The last one got married a year ago, and the apartment's too small for a couple."

"You know, one of these days you two are going to meet someone that you didn't grow up with, and you might actually like them." Paul took off his wire-rims and set them on the table, in the middle of the puddle spreading from Deborah's bottle. "You talk about 'letting people in' like this is some exclusive country club. This is just an apartment house, and you're just a bunch of old friends who got set in their ways."

Deborah kicked him lightly. "You're only talking that way because we let you in even though you're a Negro. But don't get too cocky; you're still on probation."

He laughed and grabbed her foot. "We've been living together for three years. When do I get off probation?"

"When I say so."

All this hetero horseplay was making Margaret uneasy. "Well, I've got to go now. Deborah, thanks for lending me the book." She picked up her jacket.

"Oh, come on, don't you want to see the exciting *denouement?*" Arden demanded. "Stay and have dinner with us."

"Yeah, stick around," Deborah echoed.

"I can't, but thanks anyway."

"Okay. That's twice now you've turned me down. You have to promise to stay next time." Arden turned a dazzling, disconcerting smile on Margaret, who stammered her agreement.

She couldn't stop thinking about the group at Lill Street as the train hurtled her into the half-sketched landscape of the city. Who were they but a bunch of straight, middle-class liberals? Yet she was drawn to them. She liked Deborah and Arden. There was a sense of largess about them, something she had occasionally felt from happy couples: content in their self-made family and their material comforts, they radiated a warmth in which Margaret felt invited to bask. It seemed clear that they had something she wanted. What was it?

"You need to have your head examined," her friend Alice announced as they strolled across the Wacker Drive bridge early the next morning, with the glinting river and the awakening city spread out before them.

Alice was an editor for UPI, working the 11 p.m. to 7 a.m. shift. They had met at a lesbian writer's conference when Margaret first moved to Chicago and had become close friends. Later they sidled into a romantic relationship, decided they liked it better the other way, and sidled back out of it. Now the two got together every few weeks for a combination dinner/breakfast when Alice got off work.

They always went to The Classic, their favorite downtown delicatessen. It was crowded at every hour of the day and night; the cooks, cashiers, and waitresses constantly yelled across the dining room at one another; and customers were generally treated as if they were annoying the staff, who had really important things to do. But they loved the place. It had good food, a great location, and an atmosphere of pure anarchy. Besides, where else could Alice get a beer at seven o'clock in the morning?

"I know you think I'm nuts to want to see them," Margaret continued the conversation after their food arrived.

"I don't think you're crazy to want to see them. I think you're crazy to worry about it." Alice spread mustard evenly on her rye bread. "I mean, they just asked you to stay for dinner. It's not a major commitment."

"I know it's stupid, but I keep thinking maybe it's not right to initiate friendships with people who aren't committed politically. Yet when I'm with them, I have this feeling of . . . I don't know what to call it, a feeling of lightness."

"Margaret, you really are a moron." Alice bit into her corned beef sandwich.

Margaret slapped cream cheese on a bagel and waited. Alice could be acerbic, but she was rarely wrong.

She took her time chewing, then patted her lips with the flimsy paper napkin. "First of all, that feeling of lightness you refer to is called 'having fun.' Remember that? You probably used to do it before you became so politically correct."

A waitress whizzed past their table, grabbing the mustard and the basket of tiny jellies and jams. The words, "You through with these, hon?" came wafting back in her wake.

Alice topped off her beer glass, watching the foam rise. "Second, you have the hots for Arden."

"I do not," Margaret exclaimed, feeling color climb to her face.

"Oh, really?" Alice looked at her with a lopsided grin. "What's wrong, isn't she smart enough for you?"

"That's not it."

"No sense of humor?"

"Her sense of humor is all right."

"So what's she do for a living?"

"I have no idea. She may work in a massage parlor, for all I know."

Alice shrugged. "We are everywhere."

Margaret set down her cup hard, sloshing coffee onto the table. "I told you, she's not one of us," she insisted as she mopped up the spill.

"Yet." Alice smiled again.

"She's straight. She lives with a man. He's a lawyer for Continental Bank, for christ's sake."

"Good, maybe he can get you a loan. You could buy yourself a condo next month when your lease is up."

Margaret rolled her eyes to the ceiling, and then realized she had seen Arden do the same thing the night before.

Alice leaned back and lit a cigarette. "You know, you didn't used to be so prejudiced." She signaled the flying waitress for another beer. "Everyone was straight once. Hell, I was married when you met me."

"But I didn't know it. You were at a lesbian writers' conference."

"I was just slumming."

"Okay, maybe you're right. Maybe she's a dyke in training, just waiting for someone to show her the way. But it's not going to be me."

"Fine. Here's another perspective. Why don't you see if you can get that job?"

"Which job?"

"The one at the bookstore. You'd love the work, and I'm sure you wouldn't make any money, so you wouldn't have to compromise your principles. You could schedule the newspaper work around a part-time job, couldn't you?"

"Well yeah, but—"

Alice put her head down and buried both hands in her thick black hair. "Oh, Margaret, you're so good at saying 'but'! You like these women, they're a relief from the 'more correct than thou' crowd you hang around with, and maybe you could get a pleasant job in the bargain. What are you afraid of?"

Margaret hesitated. "I don't know."

"You want my opinion? I don't care, you're getting it anyway. You're too hung up on being a good girl. You were a good daughter and a good student. Now you're working at being a good lesbian feminist. Just lighten up and be yourself. You'll be fine."

"I think you ought to get out of journalism and become a shrink."

"No thanks. One medical practitioner in the family is enough."

"So how is Laura?"

Alice's crooked grin lit up her face. "She's doing great. She's just been offered a place with some obstetricians and nurse midwives who have a group practice in Rogers Park."

"Tell her congratulations from me. Hey, maybe we should have a surprise party for her."

"Are you kidding? She would kill me, and you too. I can see the headlines: 'Lesbian Murder Spree. "I hate surprise parties," says alleged mass murderer.'"

Margaret had to laugh, watching Alice draw the headlines in the air above their littered table. "So you two are still happy."

"Still happy," she agreed.

"What's it been now, almost two years? This must be some kind of a record for you."

"Except for my eight-year marriage," Alice said drily.

"Oh, right. I keep forgetting about that."

The waitress rushed over, scribbled a total on the check, and slapped it on the table. "You girls finished? We got some working people waiting for seats." She hurried away.

"And what are we, the idle rich?" Alice demanded as they struggled into coats and scarves. They left the steamy restaurant, gasping at their first step into the winter air.

"Look at all the working people," Margaret declared as they waited for an opening in the stream of pedestrians hurrying past.

"Yes, and you'd better join them. I have to get home and catch a little bit of *Good Morning America*. Puts me right to sleep." They gave each other a quick hug, and Margaret made her way to the *Feminist Times* office.

There she found in her mailbox a notice saying that due to a temporary shortage of advertising revenue, everyone's paycheck would be a little smaller this month. The paper's financial condition was expected to improve next month, and the burden was being shared equally by all staffers. Anyone who felt the need to discuss the situation in a non-confrontational manner was welcome to bring her concerns to the editing collective.

Margaret felt a quick clutch of fear. She was barely managing on what she earned now. How could she survive with less?

There was no use fighting the facts. She needed more money. Perhaps Alice was right and she could work part-time at Lucia's Books. But that would not pay much and would require the expense and inconvenience of a long commute. On the other hand, she thought of what she might have to do to get a job that paid more: buy new clothes, shave her legs, sell

herself in job interviews, call some man "sir." She phoned
Deborah.

"Sure, I'd like to talk to you about it. Come over for dinner
tomorrow. We'll be at Arden's." But Deborah was always so
friendly there was no way to tell if she was really interested in
hiring her.

Friday night they gathered in the dining room at the rear of
the apartment. It was a pleasant, airy room, painted white,
with windows overlooking the snowy back yard, framed prints
on the walls, and a low wooden sideboard underneath the
windows. The table was covered by an Indian cotton cloth,
and all the plates matched. Margaret had not known many
people who had such complete table settings, at least not since
Vassar. She sat at one end of the rectangular table, between
Arden and Deborah.

"You know, I just realized that everyone here has some
connection with Lucia's Books," Deborah proclaimed.

"This ought to be good," Arden said.

"No, it's true. Charles used to work there part-time."

"No debate there," Charles agreed in a low, soothing voice,
like a disc jockey on an easy-listening station. He had hair the
color of freshly-made taffy. His smile began slowly in mild blue
eyes behind large tortoise-shell glasses, then meandered down
to his lips. "Now how does everyone else fit in?"

Deborah pointed to each person with a fork filled with
string beans. "Well, Margaret's here to talk about the
high-powered executive position that Cindy recently vacated.
Paul and I officially met at a party given by the former
manager of the bookstore. Joe has owed us $66.00 for seven
months, which puts him in Lucia's Book of World Records for
deadbeats."

"Go ahead, humiliate me in front of company," Joe said
good-naturedly as he sprinkled parmesan cheese over his
spaghetti. "It's good for my character."

"Relax," Arden told him quietly. "I already paid it."

"What a sweetheart. Thanks. I'll pay you back." He
squeezed her arm and returned his attention to dinner.

"Arden, that was your connection," Deborah exclaimed
indignantly, as if Arden had ruined her punchline. "You're
inscribed in the Lucia's Book of Benefactors."

"Tell me, Deborah, if Arden hadn't spilled the beans—no pun intended—how long would you have let me sweat it out?" Joe inquired.

Deborah crumbled the crust from a chunk of French bread. "Indefinitely, I think. You corporate types have no idea how much we little people crave power."

Margaret could not keep her eyes away from Joe. He was perhaps the handsomest man she had ever seen, with his curly black hair, bright blue eyes, and two huge dimples that appeared whenever he smiled. There was something mesmerizing about him, and she soon realized it was the way he ate. He was like one of those machines that swallows whole trees and reduces them to sawdust.

"Pass the spaghetti, will you, Paul?" Joe sopped up the last of his sauce with a piece of bread. "What is this, a new recipe?" he asked Arden.

"It's marinara sauce. The same as usual, but without the meat."

"I thought something was missing."

"You didn't seem to notice the first time around," she laughed.

"I was too hungry."

Deborah leaned toward Margaret. "He's mean when he's hungry."

"Get off his back," Paul reproved her.

"Don't pay any attention to the boys," Arden instructed Margaret. "They're normally very tame. Tonight they're showing off. I think it might be for you."

"Arden and I try to be understanding," Deborah added. "You know how men are at the mercy of their hormones."

"They seem normal to me," Margaret mumbled, completely at a loss as to what they were talking about or how she should respond.

"More wine, Margaret?" Charles offered.

"No thanks."

"Come on, loosen up." He winked as if he were trying to send a secret message, and motioned for her to send over her glass.

"So what do you do for a living?" Joe asked her.

"I'm a writer."

"I know, but what do you do to support yourself? I thought most writers have to do something else for money."

"You're right. I work for a newspaper called *Feminist Times*."

"Oh, sure. Arden, you read that, don't you?"

"Religiously," she said, and crossed herself.

"Joe, you know that paper," Paul grinned. "It's mother's little helper. Deborah and Arden quote it when they can't win an argument by themselves."

"Cute, Paul." Deborah patted his arm.

"So technically, you're a journalist," Joe continued. "Not a writer."

"I'm also writing a book." Margaret took a gulp of wine, grateful to Charles, who must have seen that the inquisition was about to begin.

"Good for you," Deborah exclaimed. "I didn't know that."

"What's it called?" Arden asked.

"Well, it doesn't have a title yet."

"Then what's it about?"

"It's about power structures within the women's community."

"That ought to be a short book," Joe said. "No, really," he protested in response to Arden's glare. "Women don't have any power, which is the basic problem feminism's trying to address. Right?"

"That's one of the problems we're addressing. But my book analyzes the ways women use the power we create within our own communities and our own political systems."

The room fell silent for a moment. "Are you going to look for a publisher when it's finished?" Charles asked finally.

"I've got a publisher. Women's Words, in Boston. I don't know if you're familiar with them—"

"Sure I am. They published an anthology called *Fightin' Words* last year. We get a lot of requests for that book."

"You do? Where?"

"I work at the local library."

"I love that place!" Margaret gushed. "I mean, I spent some time there once, and it was very . . . pleasant. You must have a fun job."

"Yeah, it's great," he laughed. "You spend $12,000 and years of your life in graduate school so you can make $8,000 as a librarian. But I like it."

"Man, if we all got stranded on a desert island, we'd be in deep shit." Paul pulled off his striped tie and draped it around Deborah's neck, where it clashed loudly with her alpine sweater. "Not one of us knows how to do anything really useful."

"You do, honey," Deborah said loyally.

"Yeah, there's a lot of call for electrical engineers in the wilderness."

"But at least you know how to build things and repair them. You could invent some machine to rescue us."

"What useless occupation do you have, Arden?" Margaret asked.

"I'm a translator. I work for a small publishing company. Sometimes I freelance too."

"Really? What language do you translate?"

"Mainly Russian."

"So you don't lie awake nights worrying about the cold war."

It was not much of a joke, but Arden laughed anyway. Her laugh was a cascade of descending notes. Margaret imagined it could pull smiles from strangers as the moon pulls the tides.

"No, I figure I'll be all right either way."

"She knows a lot of other languages too," Charles said proudly.

"Do you? Like what?"

"Oh, a few Eastern European languages. Polish, Serbo-Croatian, you know."

"Well, I'm impressed."

"Don't be. It may sound exciting, but for the most part it's underpaid drudgery."

"Just like most jobs," Charles added cheerfully.

"But back to writing." Joe crossed his fork and knife on his empty plate. "If so few writers can make a living at it, then you must be better than most."

"No, I just have a lower standard of living. Besides, I'm in the process of looking for another job," she replied, glancing at Deborah.

"And just think how talented Arden's mother must be," Paul grinned.

"Oh no, here we go again." Arden wearily rested her head in her hands.

"Is your mother a writer?" Margaret asked.

"Sort of."

"You must have heard of her. She's famous," Deborah added.

Margaret stared at Arden. "Mary McCarthy? You mean Mary McCarthy is your mother?"

Before Arden could answer, Deborah hooted, "It's Sallie McCarthy, the famous romance novelist. You know, *Love's Lingering Lust* and *Passion in the Palace*. Don't you ever go to the supermarket?"

Margaret must have looked startled, because Joe smiled confidentially and said, "I know what you're thinking. You're thinking Arden's mother must be very rich. But Arden can't get her hands on any of it. It's all in an irrevocable trust until she's twenty-one."

"How old are you?" she asked Arden.

"Twenty-nine."

"But she still won't touch a penny of it," Joe added sourly.

"That's not what I was thinking, anyway."

"Well, what were you thinking?" he prodded.

She felt her face grow red as everyone looked at her. "I was thinking that it must be, uh, kind of embarrassing for Arden."

Arden leaned over and patted her hand. "Bless you. Everyone else around here seems to think it's a big joke."

"I wish you'd take it seriously enough to accept some of the money she's always offering you," Deborah said. "That way you could take us all to Europe, or at least buy out Mrs. Rogers so we wouldn't have to put up with her nagging."

"Yeah, and then we could all quit our jobs and mooch off Arden for the rest of our lives," Paul said.

"Gee, what a good idea. Excuse me while I go call her."

"Don't you get along with your mother?" asked Margaret.

"Sure. We're very close, in a long-distance kind of way. It's just that money's not a big issue between my mom and me. She taught me to be self-reliant, and I like to live on what I earn." Arden stood and started to pick up her empty plate, but Joe grabbed it from her.

"Sit down, Arden. We'll do this. You and Deborah made dinner." He glanced at Paul and Charles, who rose to help him.

"Arden, sit down quick and look grateful," Deborah whispered urgently. "We've got to reinforce this behavior whenever it occurs." She turned to Margaret. "So, about the job in the bookstore."

"Yes?"

"It's between twenty and thirty hours a week, the hours are variable, and it pays fifty cents more than minimum wage. Since you'd only be part-time, you wouldn't get any benefits, but you're not missing much in that department anyway. Are you still interested?"

"Definitely."

"Okay, the job's yours."

"Just like that?"

"Why not? I hate to hire people. And I hate even more having to fire them."

"Don't give that a second thought." A smile spread across Margaret's face.

"But there's one thing I have to tell you," Deborah said.

"What?"

"There's no Lucia."

"What do you mean?"

"The owner. His name is George. He's a doctor with offices on Michigan Avenue. The store is a tax write-off for him."

"So you see, Deborah's whole life is based on a lie," Arden said sadly.

"Was there ever a Lucia?"

"Legend has it that there was once, but George divorced her years ago."

"So I'd be working for a man."

"Yeah, but you'd only see him once a year or so. He comes in every Christmas Eve to distribute little gifts to his serfs. The rest of the year he's downtown doing nose jobs, so you'd mainly be working for me."

"Which is probably worse," Arden warned.

"Well, don't you want to see any references or anything?"

"You returned my Lillian Green book without turning down any pages, so you seem to have some respect for books. I know you know how to read. My main concern is that my employees be fun to work with. So far you're a little stiff, but I think you'll be okay. If you want to, you can start on Monday."

"I want to," Margaret answered, grinning.

"All right," Deborah smiled and shook her hand.

The men came trooping in, carrying a coffee pot, mugs, and a plate of brownies.

"I didn't hear much water running out there," Arden said.

"All the pots were so dirty, we thought they needed to soak for a while," Joe replied.

Charles handed everyone a dessert plate. "What were you ladies up to out here?"

"I just hired Margaret to take Cindy's job."

"Good." Paul squeezed her shoulder. "I know it's a load off your mind, Deborah."

"That's for sure." She reached for a brownie.

"Congratulations, Margaret," Charles said with his sleepy smile. "Guess this means we'll be seeing more of you."

"I hope you're right. I didn't see that in the contract."

"Oh, it's in there," Joe said in an edgy, joking voice. "You've got to learn to read the fine print."

Margaret looked up at him in his handsome lawyer suit, as he broke off half of Arden's brownie and popped it in his mouth. "Hope you're right," she said again, and realized suddenly that it was getting late and she was far from home.

GOING TO HEAVEN

Working in Lucia's Books was like going to heaven. All day long Margaret was surrounded by books, thousands of them, and all of them free.

Each day before work she strolled down the street, watching white-aproned workers arrange produce in the window of the family-owned grocery store, or gazing into vacant storefronts and imagining them reincarnated as women's printing presses and lesbian resource centers.

Out of the corner of her eye she could see Deborah striding closer, her just-washed hair frozen into icy ringlets. Humming under her breath, Deborah taught Margaret all the arcane secrets of Lucia's Books, from taking the cash register through its daily routines to piping classical music through the shop's ancient sound system.

Margaret had thought that bookselling was mainly a matter of learning the stock, pointing customers to the right shelf, and ringing up the sale. Now she discovered there was quite a bit more to it.

Mind reading, for example. It was amazing how often a customer would ask, "Can you suggest a good book for my brother-in-law?" Or Margaret's favorite, "Do you have that book that was in the paper, you know, the one about the girl and the guy?" Eventually she learned to identify the book in question from the flimsiest of clues.

Of course, she had the usual duties of any retail worker: answering the phone, writing up orders, ringing up sales, rearranging stock. But for Margaret, the most exciting job was checking in the new books.

She'd hear the rumble of a truck, the sigh of air brakes. The trucker would honk the horn, and she and Deborah would run out. It was against union rules for the drivers to unload their cargo, so they'd hunch in the cab filling out paperwork while the two women hustled the heavy book cartons off the high truck bed and into the store, their breath coming out in steamy puffs. This must be where Deborah got her strong arms, Margaret thought.

It was a treat for Margaret to click out her knife blade and slice open the cardboard boxes to see what treasures they contained. Unfortunately, the first time she did this she also sliced the covers on the top layer of paperbacks.

"Don't worry about it," Deborah said. "I should have warned you not to cut too deep, but you were having so much fun I didn't have the heart. Next time you'll know."

One fact turned a job at Lucia's Books into paradise: employees were encouraged to read all the books they wanted. "Here's how management sees it," Deborah explained. "The more you read, the more you'll be able to recommend books to the customers. The more books you recommend, the fewer tummy tucks George will have to perform. So as long as the customers are taken care of and you've fulfilled my every wish and command, you can read to your heart's content. Just don't underline anything."

Many mornings, while the customers browsed, Margaret and Deborah perched on high wooden stools behind the counter and read. Quiet wrapped the room, textured by the turning of pages and the occasional squeak of Deborah's felt-tip pen as she circled a review in *Publisher's Weekly*. The shop was warm, the silence soothing, the coffee strong, and Margaret was perfectly content.

"This reminds me of winter nights when I was a little girl," she told Deborah. "My sister Jane and I would be sitting at a card table in the living room, doing our homework. My mother would be on the couch, with books and papers strewn all around and pencils falling between the cushions. She had a little table on wheels, like the ones they use in hospital rooms, and she'd be leaning over it, scribbling notes onto index cards. My father would be at his big desk, working on a paper and relighting his pipe every ten minutes. You know, I was probably in fifth grade before I realized that other kids' parents didn't have homework."

"Your parents teach?"

"Yeah."

"You must miss them a lot. You describe that scene the way my great-grandmother used to describe the old country, only without the accent."

Margaret shrugged. "Well, sitting here with you sort of reminded me of it."

It would have been inconceivable to Margaret, that quiet morning, to imagine that she would once again share a winter evening with her parents and sister. But it was true.

The time came when she sat on the carpeted floor of her parents' house, legs outstretched, back pressed against the familiar old couch, her right elbow resting on her sister's knees. Jane's head tilted against the back of the couch, her eyes scanning the ceiling, her nervous hands turning over and over the worn throw pillow in her lap.

Their mother leaned over the card table, peering with her now permanent squint at a complicated jigsaw puzzle. Their father sat as usual at his great desk, browsing through The New Yorker, *an unlit pipe hanging from the slightly slack corner of his mouth that was the only sign of his small stroke.*

The conversation was trivial, effortless. No one argued, wept, threw out recriminations. No one mentioned the wasted years. Everything was just the way it had always been, and of course, nothing was the same.

Little Jane, with her pigtails and big, gullible eyes was gone, replaced by this sleek, impatient woman who seemed to be always on the verge of flying off somewhere else. Margaret herself was middle-aged, hiding in her heart an icy granule of anger that no warm feelings could dissolve. Their parents were smaller, slower, only human after all.

This was a revelation to Margaret, one she had to learn anew each time. We all lose our childhood families, and Margaret lost hers twice. Somehow the firm, high-minded adults of her youth had given way to these searching, uncertain individuals exactly like herself, only more weary.

Late in the afternoon, as Margaret and her boss totalled the cash drawer to prepare for the night shift, Deborah invited her over for dinner.

"I'd like to, but I have to go to a staff meeting for the paper tonight. But listen, do you like poetry?"

Deborah made a "sort of" gesture.

"Well, Tess Gallagher is reading some of her work at Northwestern tomorrow night. Would you like to go?"

"I don't know. Is she one of those lesbo poets who make all the straight women leave the room?"

Margaret laughed. "Do you think I'd invite you if she were? Shame on you, Deborah. You've got some of her books right here in your own store." Margaret slid a book off the shelf and tossed it to her.

"I'll commit it to memory tonight so I won't embarrass you." Deborah stuffed the book into her leather bag. "Would you mind if someone else came along?"

"It depends," Margaret said cautiously.

"I think you'll like her. It's Arden."

"Oh, okay. I didn't think you were the type of woman who had to drag her boyfriend everywhere, but you had me worried."

"Oh, ye of little faith."

"So how long have you known Arden?" Margaret asked, counting out dimes.

"Since I was four."

Margaret wrote the total on a slip of paper and began to count the nickels.

"And how long have you known Paul?"

"Five years." Deborah scooped the pennies out of the cash register, spread them on the counter, and with incredible speed swept them two by two into her open palm. "Margaret, you're very transparent." She marked her total on the paper. "You're wondering why Arden and I don't drop the lugs we live with and move in together."

"Well, yeah. It seems so obvious."

"It would save us a lot of rent money. Unfortunately, I'm just not made that way. Sometimes I almost wish I were, but I'm not."

The cow bell on the front door clanged sharply. A tall woman wearing a black wool coat rushed in, accompanied by a blast of cold air. All that was visible of her face was a pair of large square glasses, which fogged up instantly. A heavy scarf covered her from neck to nose, and her hair was hidden by a black wool beret. She plopped a Marshall Fields shopping bag on the floor in front of the counter.

"Elaine, is that you?" Deborah asked. The woman nodded and began to unwrap her muffler. "Good," Deborah said. "I was afraid we were being robbed."

Elaine unbuttoned her coat, stamping her feet and shivering. "It's fucking freezing out there," she gasped, belying the elegance of her maroon wool suit and white silk blouse.

"Elaine, this is Margaret. She's going to be our new Cindy," Deborah said.

"Nice to meet you." Margaret shook her hand.

"Let's trade hands," Elaine offered. "Yours are nice and warm, and mine are frozen."

"Mine will be frozen soon enough."

"If she ever gets out of here," Deborah added pointedly.

"I'm hurrying, I'm hurrying." Elaine grabbed her shopping bag and flounced to the bathroom in the back of the store.

"Elaine works here a couple of nights a week," Deborah said loudly, "if you want to call it work."

"I heard that," Elaine called from the bathroom.

"I wanted you to," she shouted back. "Actually, I like her a lot," Deborah continued in her normal voice. "She works for a PR firm downtown during the day."

Elaine emerged wearing corduroy jeans and a sweater, her dress clothes folded inside the shopping bag. "I don't know why you tell people these terrible things about me. I work very hard here." Immediately she dropped onto one of the stools, put her feet on the counter, and opened a book.

"Right," Deborah laughed.

"Hey, Margaret," Elaine stage-whispered, "we'll have to get together sometime and gossip about Deborah."

"I'll look forward to it."

"Elaine seems like a good person," Margaret commented to Deborah as the door whooshed shut behind them.

"Face it: when you work at Lucia's, you're in with the in crowd."

"Lucky me," Margaret smiled, and she meant it.

At the poetry reading, she kept sneaking glances at Arden, who was listening intently, a small smile crossing her lips every now and then. In the half-light of the auditorium, Margaret could see Arden's clear, candid eyes and the deep smile lines around her mouth. But she saw something more: an inner quiet, an air of self-possession that both intrigued her and made her envious. She felt as if Arden knew a secret that

Margaret had been longing to learn all her life. Yet she had no idea what it was or how to discover it.

Margaret shook her head abruptly, eliciting a questioning look from Deborah. This is stupid, she told herself, folding her arms across her chest. She settled back to give her full attention to Tess Gallagher, but at that moment the house lights went up and the poet left the stage for an intermission.

"Is this when we buy the popcorn?" Arden asked Margaret.

"No, this is when we wander around the lobby making brilliant comments to one another."

"That sounds like hard work," Deborah said. "I think I'll stay here."

"Me too."

"Well, I'm going. I like to eavesdrop." Slowly Margaret made her way across the crowded lobby. On the edge of the room she noticed a stocky, red-haired woman studying a littered bulletin board. Something familiar about the set of her shoulders and the tilt of her head encouraged Margaret to call timidly, "Joanie?"

The woman turned and stared for a moment, and then a grin broke across her freckled face. "Maggie? Is that you?"

They hugged each other, laughing. "I can't believe it!" Margaret said. "I haven't seen you since you moved to California."

"I can't believe you recognized me," she replied, holding her at arm's length. "That was in the sixth grade. Hey, you turned out all right."

"You're not bad yourself." Margaret tousled her thick wavy hair. "How could I forget this carrot top?"

"You should talk, Maggie. Looks like you haven't cut your hair since we were the stars of Mrs. Epstein's homeroom."

She laughed. "No one calls me Maggie anymore."

"Same here. Joanie went out with training bras." Joan gave her braid a tug and Margaret noticed she was wearing a silver ring engraved with two women's symbols entwined.

"Joan, you're a dyke!"

"Is it that obvious?"

"Only to another one," she grinned.

"This is wild," Joan exclaimed. The lobby lights started blinking. "Oh, shit. Listen, I'm here with some friends, and we're going dancing at the Lavender Menace after the reading. Come and join us."

"I can't tonight. But let's get together tomorrow. What's your number?"

"This is going to be fun," Joan whispered at the door. "Don't tell me there's no such thing as karma."

"Tess Gallagher's really good," Arden concluded later, as they shuffled out of the auditorium with the rest of the crowd. "I'll have to get hold of some of her books."

"I know just the place for you," Deborah yawned. "Hey, let's go somewhere for a little nightcap."

"How about the Tenth Street Cafe?" Arden suggested.

"Oh, you always want to go there."

"That's because I like it." Arden unlocked her car. "Besides, I'm driving, so I get to be the boss."

"Arden has the easiest time finding parking spots of anyone I've ever met," Deborah claimed as Arden expertly backed into a tiny space in front of the restaurant. "Did you notice how that car pulled out just as we approached? She must have a parking angel that sits on her shoulder and gives her directions."

"Wrong," Arden replied. "I *am* the angel. And parking spots are the only reward I get for my pure and pristine life."

"Sad but true," agreed Deborah, and they both laughed.

"I don't get it," Margaret said. "What's so funny?"

In the rearview mirror, she could see Arden give her a long, studying look. "Ask me again later, when we know each other better."

A young woman in designer jeans and a tuxedo jacket led them past other diners to a dark wooden table, gleaming with a thick plastic finish. She handed them menus, lit the candle in the center of the table, and lightly touched the back of each chair, as if in homage to the vanished tradition of tucking in the ladies. Grace Slick's voice snaked out from overhead speakers, demanding "Don't you want somebody to love?"

"So, Margaret, " Arden began, "what did you think of the poetry reading?"

"Poetry isn't my strong point. You seemed much more engrossed in the reading than I was; what did you think?"

"But suppose you were assigned to review it for *Feminist Times*. What would you say?"

"I would say no. Send somebody who's more into it. Like you, for example. What did you find so fascinating?"

"Do they let you choose what stories to write?" Deborah asked.

"Not really." Margaret smiled, picturing the shocked faces of the editing collective if she turned down an assignment.

"All right, then we won't allow it here," Arden pressed. "What did you think of the reading?"

"Well...I liked her imagery, especially the images about nature. Also, I was impressed with her stage presence. It must take a lot of courage to face an audience and read your work out loud."

"You know, I've never liked poetry much," said Deborah, twirling a wine glass between her palms. "Paul is always running in with some book and saying, 'You've got to read this poem.' And then I read it and my reaction is, 'Yeah, so?'" She took a sip. "I guess it's not so much that I don't like it as that it doesn't say anything to me."

"Right," Margaret agreed. "And that makes me nervous, because I think the poet and her intended audience must be much smarter than I am."

"And that's coming from a person who's writing about power structures within the women's movement," Arden pointed out, "a topic that speaks to everybody."

Margaret was about to take a sip of her beer, but Arden's comment made her laugh into her glass, spitting foam across the table.

"That was mature," said Deborah.

Margaret mopped up the table as Arden dabbed at her sweater. "I'm sorry. It was an accident. If I'd meant to spit at you, my aim would have been better."

"So what did you think, Arden?" Deborah asked. "As usual, you pin us down and then you slither away."

Arden opened her mouth to answer, but suddenly her attention was drawn behind their table. Her eyes widened and her lips closed into a thin, straight line. Deborah and Margaret twisted around to see what she was staring at.

Joe stood in the entrance to the restaurant, his hand resting on the waist of a petite blond woman. She seemed much younger than he was, or perhaps it was her colorful clothing and bright makeup that made her look like a young girl playing dress-up. She gazed up at him, he grinned down at her, they pantomimed an animated conversation. Slowly his head

turned toward Arden at their distant table. He gave her a
sickly smile as a waiter led them to another room.

There was a certain inevitability to the scene, Margaret
thought, a balletic symmetry. Something had pulled Arden and
Joe to this restaurant tonight. Something had prompted each of
them to glance up at the only moment during the entire
evening when they were clearly visible to one another. Was it
the fates making a little mischief, or was there some force
unknown to Margaret that announced to long-time couples the
very presence of their mates in a crowded room?

"We both like this place," Arden said quietly. "I should
have thought maybe he'd bring her here."

"It had to happen sometime," Deborah agreed. "You two
are such creatures of habit, you were bound to run into each
other on date night."

"So what was I saying?" Arden asked. "Oh, about the
reading—"

"Wait a minute," Margaret interrupted. "I don't mean to
pry, but don't you want to talk about this?"

"If it makes you feel better, Margaret," Arden replied with
her teasing smile. "I've already talked the subject out. We have
what you'd call an open relationship."

"Yeah, Joe's free to see other women and Arden's free to let
him," Deborah said angrily.

"What about you?" Margaret asked. "Are you free to see
other people?"

"Of course. But the occasion hasn't really presented itself,
or at least I haven't been all that interested when it did."

"Well, doesn't it bother you that he does? Listen, tell me
the minute I step out of line with these questions."

"Don't worry, I will."

"We've done this conversation to death, but I still don't
understand why you stay with him," Deborah said. "I mean,
Joe's a nice guy and all that, but what's the point?"

"I have a history with him. We have fun together, but we
have fun with other people too. He has his room and I have
mine, and it's still comfortable and convenient. When that
changes, maybe the situation will change."

"I have a history with Richard too," Deborah countered.
"Christ, I have a daughter with him. But when it was over, I
left."

"We all make our choices, Deborah," Arden said mildly.
"This one is mine."

"Well, I don't like it."

"Then it's a good thing you didn't choose it."

"Don't you miss sex?"

"Not everyone is a hot-blooded young Jewess like you, you know."

Deborah laughed. "Well, if you don't want to talk about it . . ."

"Oh, come on. I've been sharing my innermost feelings with you since we were kids. I told you about everything from my first period to my last orgasm."

"Yeah, but they both happened in the same year."

"You mean you and Joe are just roommates?" Margaret demanded, trying to hide her astonishment.

Arden nodded. "That's not how we planned it, but that's how it turned out. Now I think it's your turn to spill your guts. How come you haven't introduced us to your latest honey?"

"I'm between honeys right now."

"Then tell us what happened to your last one." When she hesitated, Arden gave her a chastising frown. "Fair is fair."

"She left me."

"Really, why? Listen, tell me the minute I step out of line."

Margaret laughed. "If there's one thing I hate, it's to have my own words quoted back to me."

"We're waiting, Margaret."

"Well, she, uh, she said I was no fun anymore." The words, which had sliced through her heart when she first heard them, seemed bald and bland now.

"How long ago was this?"

"About a year."

"How long were you together?"

"Ten months."

"Not exactly a lifetime commitment," Arden commented.

"Remember, she's a lot younger than we are," said Deborah.

"I don't see what that has to do with it," Margaret bristled.

"You will."

The waitress came over, and Arden placed an order. Margaret tried to demur, picturing the tab mounting, but Arden gave her a peculiar smile with one eyebrow raised and said, "This round's on me. And I'm drinking coffee, in case you were concerned about the ride home."

"I wasn't worried."

"By the way, where do you live?" Arden asked.

"In a little studio on the north side. Not too far from here."

"You notice she's never invited us over," Deborah pointed out to Arden.

"We'd probably have to take a test for political correctness to get in, and she didn't want to embarrass us."

"I wouldn't do something like that," Margaret protested. "It's only a short questionnaire."

"Well, don't bother quizzing me. I flunk already," Deborah declared. "What I want to know is, what did you do that your girlfriend didn't like?"

"You'd have to ask her."

"Where is she now?"

"In New York, studying massage."

"She likes to give massages and you let her go?" Arden asked incredulously.

"I didn't exactly let her go."

"Come on, you can give us one example," Deborah coaxed.

Margaret took a sip of beer. "Well, let's say she wanted to come to this restaurant for a drink. I wouldn't want to go because it's owned by a man, and I only spend money in women-owned establishments. Except for Lucia's Books, of course."

"Was that a dig?" Deborah asked Arden.

"If we ended up here anyway, I would complain all night because the place doesn't have the right atmosphere."

"What's wrong with the atmosphere?" asked Arden. Margaret looked around the room. Almost every table except theirs was occupied by heterosexual couples out on dates. Arden followed her gaze and said, "Oh."

"Then I would point out that this section of the restaurant has waitresses, while the area where people are ordering meals has waiters. So apparently women get the low-tip jobs here."

"I see her point," Deborah said.

"So why aren't you doing any of that now?" Arden asked. Margaret looked down at her drink. "I don't know. Maybe I should be, but I just don't feel like it."

"Don't tell me we're corrupting you."

"Could be." *I'm different, all right*, she thought. She didn't know if it was because of them or if she had happened to stumble upon them after the process had already started. But she was changing, and she was not sure she liked it.

"Deborah, now you have to tell us about your sex life," Arden said.

"There's something else I have to do that's more pressing."
She pushed back her chair. "I'll try to make up some good lies
while I'm in the bathroom."

"Margaret, were you upset when your love affair ended?"
Arden's eyes strayed to the archway through which Joe had
disappeared with his date.

"I was heartbroken. It was my first serious relationship."

"Do you still think about her?" Arden continued.

"Yeah, sometimes. Sometimes I wonder if it was even real."

"What do you mean?" asked Arden. "You wonder whether
she was your 'One True Love?'"

"I guess. I don't really believe in that, especially because the
concept of 'One True Love' always goes hand-in-hand with the
idea that there's one man out there who will make my life
worthwhile, and I know that's not true. But I do believe in
love. And sometimes I wonder whether that's what I felt for
her or if I wanted to be in love, so I made it up."

"Did you love her when you were with her?"

Margaret nodded.

"Did you grieve for her when she left?"

She nodded again.

"Then it was real."

"Well, what about you? Were you devastated when your
romance with Joe ended?"

"Not really . . . I can't remember exactly when things
changed between us. Probably I never really noticed. I just got
used to expecting less than I wanted, and then a little less, and
then a little less. Before I knew it, it was gone entirely, and I
was already used to it. It was sad, but not traumatic."

Arden's casualness shocked Margaret. At twenty-four
Margaret still believed that love and drama were the same
thing.

WILD KARMA

Something strange is happening here, Margaret told herself as she hurried down the slushy sidewalk toward Mama Peaches, the women's vegetarian restaurant where she was to meet Joan. She felt nervous, excited, as if she were on the verge of making a discovery and wasn't sure if it would be a welcome one.

It was probably just a coincidence that Arden, Deborah, and Margaret had ended up at the Tenth Street Cafe last night at the same time as Joe and his date. Her eerie suspicion that they had all been drawn to the restaurant for the specific purpose of playing out that scenario was purely imaginary. And perhaps it wasn't all that odd that Margaret and her childhood friend had found each other again as lesbian feminists at the exact moment in time when the women's movement was about to change the world.

Still, two coincidences in one night seemed to be pushing it. She felt as if a pair of huge hands holding pencils were reaching across the sky over her head, drawing lines that were invisible to her but would nonetheless shape her life. That was the problem, she thought irritably. No matter how hard you tried, you could never discern the pattern of your own future. The only way to see it was to look back, and by then it was too late.

Margaret stood in the doorway of Mama Peaches for a few moments, letting the slush drip off her boots before she crossed the creaky wooden floor. The restaurant was in a large, open rectangular space that might have once been a warehouse. Now the room was painted a soft peach color, ceiling pipes and all. Women's music flowed through mismatched speakers. Colorful posters from the Women's Graphics Collective hung on the walls, and near the entrance stood a small stage for live performances. Only a few tables were filled at this hour, and it was easy to spot Joan leaning against the order window in the back, talking with someone in the kitchen. She was like a beacon, with her red hair and her short stocky body radiating energy.

Joan waved her to a table against the wall. "This is some kind of wild karma, Margaret." She plunked down two fragrant mugs of hot apple cider with a cinnamon stick bobbing in each. "I can't get over running into you like this, can you?"

"No, I can't. I've been thinking about it all day. What do you suppose it means?"

"Oh, no." Joan peered into Margaret's face intently. "You're not one of those 'what does it all mean' dykes, are you? You know, throwing the I Ching, reading the tarot, seeking wisdom from the moon?"

"No. But I think it's pretty damned weird for us to meet again after all these years, don't you?"

"Absolutely. Well, good thing you're punctual. We've got a lot to catch up on, and I have to work later."

"Where do you work?"

"Right here." Joan opened her arms in a grand gesture. "I'm part of the collective. Just joined last week."

"Well, congratulations. What do you do?"

"Oh, everything. Cook, wait tables, buy supplies, line up entertainment, wash dishes. We all rotate jobs. That way we can learn all the aspects of running the restaurant, and no one gets stuck with the shit work."

"Sounds good. Now tell me how you got into this, and start way back, like in seventh grade."

"Geez, I can't remember that far back. I do remember that I missed you like hell when we moved away. Never found another best friend I had so much in common with."

Margaret laughed. "I guess now we know why."

"Really. Anyway, I don't know what to tell you. I was just a regular girl. Got really into the anti-war movement after Kent State and Jackson State, but I got so sick of the sexism that I had to back off after a year or so. I found feminism, fell in love, and came out the next year."

"That's it?"

"Pretty much."

"Is someone charging you by the word?" Margaret demanded. "Come on, let's hear some details. What about this woman? What happened next?"

"Well, you've turned into an impatient bitch."

"Stop trying to change the subject."

"All right, all right. Her name's Suzanne. We met in school in Madison, and we both felt this is it, this is what we were meant to do. After graduation we moved to Seattle. Suzanne got a job at the zoo. A degree in history didn't really do too much for me in the job market, so I worked here and there, just figuring things out and having a good time. After a couple of years Suzanne and I went our separate ways, and I moved to Chicago a few months ago."

"I'm glad you're here, but that's too bad about Suzanne."

Joan shrugged and stirred her drink with the cinnamon stick. "It turned out okay. We're still close; we call each other every couple of weeks. And she's living with a great woman in a house the woman built by herself." She grinned, revealing a slight gap between her front teeth. "You know that song Meg Christian sings about 'Give her your keys, please, because she's a real good woman'? That's kind of how I feel about Suzanne and her lover."

"What do your parents think about all this?"

"Well, they weren't exactly pleased, but they came around. I thought about not telling them, but you know how tight we always were. I pictured a whole lifetime of never being able to tell them who I am, how I live, who I love. Then I bit the bullet and came out to them. It was really hard at first, but now they're..." she paused to choose her words, "comfortable with the idea, and really supportive of me. They used to invite Suzanne to all the family events." She laughed. "It's lucky my sister Barb has gone on a one-woman crusade to populate the earth, or I'd be hearing a lot of wistful comments about grandchildren. As it is I've got two nieces and a nephew. Maggie, what's the matter?"

Margaret shook her head and took a sip of her cooling drink. "Where did you say your parents live now?"

"They moved to Indianapolis. They see your folks sometimes; I'm surprised your parents didn't mention that I was here."

"I'm not sure they know that I live here."

"What do you mean?"

Margaret explained the situation to her. "I guess it's kind of like the cramps," she concluded. "This has been going on for years, so when am I going to get used to it? Sometimes I still can't believe it happened."

"Geez. I'm real sorry to hear it. I always liked your folks, too," she added musingly. "Hey, do you think my parents could talk some sense into yours?"

Margaret remembered her father's face on that distant afternoon and shook her head. "I don't think it would work. When I came out, the topic was, as my father used to say, not open for discussion."

"Were you involved with anyone then?"

"Not seriously. Why?"

"I just thought maybe it would be easier for them to relate to the fact that you're in love with a particular woman than to swallow the idea that their daughter is"—she gave a dramatic shudder—"queer."

She laughed. "I suppose my strategy wasn't too sophisticated."

"I told you all about me, Osborn. What's your story?"

Margaret told her about the newspaper, her book, and her new job.

"I've seen your paper all over the place," Joan said, "and from now on I'll be a loyal reader."

"Aren't you a loyal reader already?"

"Well, I did read it once, but I didn't see your name. And I usually don't have time to read."

"We don't believe in bylines. You just have to guess which articles are mine by their elegant style. And what do you do that keeps you too busy to read?"

"I'm working on the ERA campaign."

"You're kidding."

"Why would you say that?"

"Well, I support the ERA of course, but I always felt it was kind of a straight women's issue, and that we should be working on our own priorities."

"No, you're wrong." Her mobile face took on a serious, dedicated expression. "The ERA is important to all of us, for a lot of reasons. I don't have time to go into them all now, but I can tell I'm going to have to take you under my wing and teach you a few things." Joan glanced at her watch. "Well, I have to get to work. Want to stay for dinner? We're serving a fantastic vegetable quiche. I got blisters cutting up the vegetables."

"Not tonight. I'm having dinner with some friends. But we're going to the coffeehouse later. Maybe you could meet us there."

Joan looked doubtful. "Maybe for the second set, if things slow down here. Saturday is our busiest night."

Margaret spent the evening with her friends Samantha, Donna, Lucy, Kay, and Maureen. They lived in a tall, narrow house that was sandwiched between two apartment buildings. In addition to the five women, the house was tenanted by Kay's children Barry and Jill, a fluctuating population of friends passing through town on their way to and from various women's events, and three identical black cats named Athena, Demeter, and (this one had been named by the children) Jumbo.

These women prepared delicious vegetarian meals, helped with homework, carpooled the kids' basketball teams, established careers, organized boycotts, strategized at political meetings, quit smoking over and over again, supported each other through emotional crises, mourned departed lovers together, volubly approved or disapproved of new ones, and wove tapestries to adorn their friends' walls. They were politically correct in all ways but one, their insistence that Kay's son Barry be raised with the sense that he had an equal place in their women-centered world.

Margaret yearned to be one of them and at the same time recoiled from their relentless togetherness. For in that household overflowing with generosity, support, and involvement, solitude was the one amenity that could not be found.

After dinner, the six women piled into Maureen's van and drove to Mountain Moving Coffeehouse. The chilly church basement was the only place in the city that each week offered women live music, discussions, and the chance to be alone together without fear or pressure.

In the front of the room was a performance area with a rudimentary sound system and an out-of-tune upright piano. In the rear stood long tables covered with political literature. In the center were women—sitting around the candle-lit tables, leaning against the walls, lounging on the cement floor, holding hands, laughing, expanding in the freedom of this strange and luminous underground.

Margaret and her friends sipped herbal tea and talked quietly as they waited for the performance to begin. "I believe my supervisor, Madman O'Malley, may have told his last faggot joke today," Donna announced.

"What makes you think so?" asked Maureen.

"We were all in the lunch room when he came in and told some stupid joke about gay men—something to do with doorknobs, I don't remember what it was—and I confronted him."

"Good for you." Kay gave an emphatic nod that set her gold earrings dancing. Margaret always imagined that Kay had a fire of righteousness burning in her soul. Good deeds fueled the fire and made her blue eyes spark, her light brown hair glow. She was ablaze as she beamed her approval at Donna. "What did you say?"

"I just told him that I didn't find his joke the least bit amusing. And he said, 'What do you care? You're not a faggot.'"

"Did you tell him you were a dyke?" Margaret asked.

"No. I figured our household needed my income more than I needed to make moral points with a fool." Donna was a minor executive in the personnel department of the phone company. Margaret had actually seen hanging in her closet the smart suits and high-heeled shoes she wore to the office, but it was hard to picture them on this woman in her work boots, patched jeans and "No More Fat Oppression" t-shirt.

"You figured right," Samantha said. "What happened next?"

"I said I couldn't find humor in the oppression of minorities, and that if he ever gave a thought to the history of Irish Catholics in this country he'd agree. Well, he turned red up to the top of his bald head, muttered something about not meaning any harm, and took his tray to another table. I don't think the women I was with really gave a damn about the principle, but they sure were relieved he wasn't going to sit with us."

"Speaking of luncheon engagements, guess which dyke-about-town was seen in deep conversation with an unidentified red-head at Mama Peaches this afternoon?" asked Samantha.

"Who?" Lucy played along.

"None other than our little Margaret."

"Are you spying on me now?" Margaret demanded, tremendously flattered. "It's getting so a girl can't even go for a drink at the local lesbo country club without being grilled about it afterwards. Who told you, anyway?"

"Mary Jean."

"I didn't see MJ there."

"Apparently you were too engrossed. Who is this woman? Is romance about to enter your life again? Not that you asked me, but I think it's about time."

"Sorry to disappoint you, Samantha, but it would be like incest. Joan was my best friend when we were little girls. I haven't seen her in ages, but we ran into each other out of the blue last night. It turns out she's a dyke too."

"Kind of a cosmic coincidence," Lucy pointed out.

Kay reached for one of the burnt-tasting carob brownies in the center of the table. "Oh, Lucy, you think everything has some cosmic significance."

"Maybe it does," Maureen said, tossing back her long black hair. "After all, we don't know everything—not even you, my love."

"Would you and Kay please stop making goo-goo eyes at each other?" Donna begged. "You've been together for five years now. It's time to stop acting like newlyweds."

"You're just jealous," Maureen laughed.

"I know." She fingered a cigarette she was not allowed to light in the coffeehouse.

"I think it's wonderful that two women from such different cultures can stay together the way you have." Samantha patted their clasped hands. "Besides, that romantic glow is such a sweet feeling. Remember those days?" she asked Lucy.

"Yep."

Donna groaned. "If we have to hear one more time about how you two fell in love in that damned consciousness raising group in '69 —"

Margaret interrupted her. "Well, I'm impressed that ex-lovers can stay best friends like you and Lucy."

Samantha gave a rueful smile. "Yes, that does seem to be one of my special talents, turning lovers into friends. And what do I have to show for it? Nothing."

"How about the co-op we started together?" Lucy asked indignantly.

"Okay, nothing but a food co-op," she amended cheerfully. "That reminds me, Margaret, we're getting a big shipment of

organic vegetables from California next month. Why don't you
join the co-op? I know you'd enjoy it."

"Samantha, I'm thrilled that you keep pursuing me like
this. But I live alone. Can you imagine how long it would take
me to use up a ten-pound bag of brown rice, not to mention a
fifty-pound sack of organic potatoes?"

Samantha held up both hands. "You're right. I just hate to
see you miss out on a good thing. It makes my old heart happy
to match good people with good food."

"You're so sentimental," Margaret teased her.

Samantha gave one of her knowing smiles. "So are you.
You try to act tough, but inside you're mushier than a
Hallmark card."

Margaret could feel herself blush, and Samantha patted her
arm. "Don't worry. It's very charming."

"Exactly how old is your heart, anyway?"

"Never you mind. A lot older than yours, that's for sure."

Samantha's age was only one of the mysteries that
intrigued Margaret. Her extensive experience in the civil rights
and anti-war movements seemed to place Samantha in her
thirties or forties, but she looked like a twenty-year-old except
for her bushy dark hair streaked with gray. She had been
married for many years but would never reveal the name of her
former husband. Margaret suspected that he must be famous,
because there was no other way anyone would know him and
thus no reason to keep his name a secret. Samantha always
wore home-made overalls in bright colors, equally vivid
t-shirts, and a colorful scarf around her neck or waist. On her
feet were tiny black slippers from the People's Republic of
China. She was hard to miss in a crowd whose predominant
color scheme was denim.

"Well, I think we've found a place for the LCC," Maureen
announced, "but there may be a problem with it."

In Margaret's two years with *Feminist Times* she'd covered
dozens of meetings dealing with the need for a Lesbian
Community Center. The women were looking for a building
that contained a large room for meetings and dances, and
several smaller rooms for discussion groups, child care, a
resource library, and office space. The obstacle, as usual, was
money.

"What kind of problem?" asked Samantha.

"Well, one of those rich dykes that we all swear must exist introduced herself and offered to lease us a building for a really good price. But it's in Evanston."

"Oh, forget it," Donna groaned.

"Why?" Margaret asked. "We've been looking for a building for years, and if this one's affordable, why turn it down? Evanston's not the end of the earth. The el goes right up there."

"We don't want to get involved with a lot of suburbanites," Donna maintained.

"It would be more convenient than the place we're considering in Hyde Park," Samantha replied.

"For us."

"That's my point, Donna. Most of the lesbians we happen to know live on the north side, but that doesn't mean that most of the lesbians in the Chicago area live here. We don't know where they live, so it's kind of silly to try to find a central location. We should take what we can get."

"A lot of the activities would take place at night. I think it might be nice to have the Center in a safe neighborhood," Kay said, perhaps thinking of her midnight commutes to Cook County Hospital, where she worked a rotating shift as a maternity nurse.

"I agree," said Lucy. "The LCC's important. I don't think we can afford to be picky about the location."

"Besides, the deal with the Hyde Park building fell through," Maureen informed them.

"I take it you're on the search committee?" Margaret asked.

"Of course. If you have a name like Maureen Littlebear, everyone wants you on their letterhead." She sighed. "I keep telling people that most of the Native Americans in Chicago live in tenements in Uptown. My life is no more like theirs than that rich Evanston woman's life is like ours."

"It's true you can't speak for them, but maybe you can speak *to* them better than the rest of us," Samantha pointed out. "I mean, if someone has to do outreach to the lesbian community, I'd rather have that Evanston dyke do it than some straight woman."

"You're right. That's why I keep agreeing to be on all these committees."

"I don't know about this new place." Donna shook her head. "Just the thought of going to the suburbs gives me the creeps."

"Just the thought of working for the phone company gives me the creeps," Samantha said, "but if you can stomach that you could probably stand going to Evanston."

Donna laughed. "Well, maybe."

"I used to live in the suburbs when I was married," Kay said. "I met a lot of good women there. You'd be surprised."

The lights flickered, and a woman from the coffeehouse collective stepped up to the microphone to read some announcements. A murmur swept through the audience as the doors to the outside closed.

Like her friends, Margaret lived in a world where her feelings and experiences were never portrayed on television or pictured on billboards or reflected on movie screens or described on the radio. To be a lesbian in such a world was to be starved for the sustenance that comes from music. She thought of these Saturday nights in the coffeehouse as more than entertainment: they were basic life support.

Tonight's performer was a tall, solidly built, black-haired woman named Montana Gold. Margaret wondered whether that was her real name, and if not, why she had chosen such a strange one. Montana strapped on her guitar and stood motionless, surveying the audience with her exotic dark eyes. Margaret would not have been surprised if she opened her set with some bizarre religious chant. Instead, she swung into a funny, spirited version of "California Girls."

Throughout the evening, Montana alternated between songs she had written herself and popular rock numbers performed with a new lesbian twist. She had a rich alto voice and a way of making her acoustic guitar serve as both accompaniment and rhythm section. The audience loved it. They laughed, cheered, hooted, clapped until their hands stung, and wouldn't be satisfied with two sets and two encores.

Finally Montana waved the crowd into an expectant silence. Without haste she slipped her guitar strap over her head, leaned the instrument gently against a chair, and pulled the microphone close. Again she paused until the wait was almost painful. Perhaps she was about to make some devastating announcement. Perhaps she was experiencing the waking nightmare of drawing a blank, unable to think of a single thing to sing or say.

But no, she was simply setting the mood. She tapped her foot in time and slid into a smoky, *a capella* rendition of "I Only Have Eyes for You." As she sang, her head turned slowly, and she fixed one woman after another with a long, caressing gaze.

Her dark eyes rested on Margaret and lit up her space in the world for a few seconds before moving on to the next table. It was a practiced, studied look, Margaret knew, but it warmed her anyway. She could not remember the last time someone had looked at her like that: not necessarily in a sexual way, but as though there was no room in her gaze for anyone else.

Had she ever really been the focus of that kind of intimacy? she suddenly wondered. Yes, she had; it was coming back to her now. Lovers, roommates, best friends—even her mother had sometimes looked at her as if there was no one else on earth to see at that moment.

Now Margaret was unfettered as the wind, and as homeless. There was no single person who could not do without her, she realized, just as there was no single person she could not do without. It was a strange revelation, at once isolating and liberating. Margaret had chosen independence, but in the process she had somehow built a life in which no one worried if she was late, no one reminded her to bring a sweater, no one saved a certain smile that was only for her. She was free, but she was also freezing.

MRS. ROGERS'
NEIGHBORHOOD

"Well, aren't we bright and cheery," Deborah trilled the next morning. She unlocked the door to Lucia's Books and shoved Margaret inside. "Had a late night, did we? And to think, I came here laden with presents."

"I'm just laden," Margaret yawned.

"Well, better get unladen, because you're on your own today, and I want you friendly and alert."

"Don't worry, I'll wake up after I have a cup of coffee," she lied. Margaret trudged to the back of the store and flicked on the lights. She could hear Deborah bustling around behind the sales counter, humming a little tune.

"Oh, Ms. Osborn!" Deborah called. "Please come up here and take a look at this."

"A coffee maker. Great idea!"

"Well, I thought so," she said modestly. "I thought, 'Why should all my loyal employees have to rely on me and my thermos for their daily dose of caffeine?' And I thought, 'Look at all the bucks I've saved George over the years.' So I took some money out of petty cash and bought this little beauty." She petted the machine like a cat.

As Deborah spooned coffee into the filter, Margaret dragged the *Chicago Tribune* out of her backpack and thumped it onto the counter.

"I can tell your training has not been complete," observed Deborah.

Margaret glanced around the store. "Why? What did I do wrong?"

"You brought your own newspaper. Don't you know we carry the Sunday *New York Times?*"

"I know, but I need this paper."

Deborah handed her the coffee pot. "Would you fill this, please? Cold water only."

"Yes, Betty Crocker."

"So tell me. What could you possibly want from a newspaper that you can't get from the *New York Times?*"

"Local rental listings. I have to move soon."

"Why?"

"Oh, the owner's doubling rents in my building. I think he wants to get all of us queers out and rent the place to respectable people. Anyway, I won't be able to afford it anymore."

"Well, when do you have to go?"

"March first."

"But that's not even a month away." Deborah rummaged through her floppy leather bag.

"I know. I've kind of been procrastinating."

"Kind of." She pulled out a wrapped object and tossed it to Margaret. "Here's a bagel to eat with your coffee. And here is your very own key to Lucia's Books." Gravely she pressed it into Margaret's hand. "Today is your first day alone in the store, and the first day of the rest of your life, unless you screw up, in which case I'll have to kill you." Deborah zipped her jacket. "So be good."

"I'll try. Thanks for breakfast."

"Don't mention it. Listen, if you have any questions or problems, call me at home. I'll leave you to your want ads." And she walked out, singing, "'Maybe it's late, but just call me,'" as she strode away.

Margaret felt a strange excitement, a kind of acquisitive lust, as she scanned the want ads. She knew she could not afford it, but the one thing she wanted in life was a bedroom. Never for a moment could she relax in her one-room apartment without feeling the silent pressure from her books, files, and typewriter, reminding her of how much she had to do and how little she had accomplished. But if she had a room with a door, all that would change. And just think what a bedroom would do for her social life, should she ever develop one. So between customers she sipped coffee and circled ads and dreamed about her new life in a new apartment.

Later that afternoon, Margaret was on her hands and knees, re-alphabetizing the Biography section, when a pair of orange work boots presented themselves in her view. She looked up and there stood Charles.

"Hello."

"Hi." Margaret rose, dusting off her pants. "What are you doing here? Don't you get enough of books during the week?"

"I don't think you can ever get enough of books. Do you?"

She looked around the store. "No, I suppose not. Want some coffee?"

"Sure." He followed her behind the counter. "Hey! This coffee maker must be new. I could have used it last month when Ellen was sick and I had to cover for Deborah a couple of nights."

"I keep hearing about Deborah's mysterious daughter, but I've never seen her. What's the deal with her?" Margaret sat on a stool and put her feet up on the counter.

Charles took a sip of his coffee. His mild blue eyes took on a far-away look. "Well, let's see. Deborah and Richard got married while Deborah was still in college. I guess she was around twenty, and he was twenty-two."

"What was he like?"

"He was good looking, intelligent, and one of the most amusing people I've ever met. God, he was entertaining. Richard had just one flaw: you could never believe a word he said."

"What would he lie about?"

"Everything. His past. His career. How much his car cost. What he had for dinner last night. I mean, everyone lies sometimes, right? But he lied when he had nothing to gain from it, almost like he was doing it for the practice."

"Well, how did you and Arden catch on to him?"

"Strictly by accident. He told each of us a different version of a story, and then had a perfectly glib explanation for the contradictions. But that made us re-examine some of the things he had said in the past, and it suddenly dawned on us that the guy simply didn't recognize the difference between reality and fiction."

"So you tried to convince Deborah not to marry him?"

"Of course. But the more we warned her, the more she wanted him. Deborah has a wild streak, you know."

"Come on. Deborah?"

Charles gave Margaret one of his slow smiles. "Oh, yes. You don't see it often, but it's there, believe me."

"So what happened?"

"They got married. Deborah realized he had a little problem but thought love could change him. She moved in with him and finished school. He was working as a salesman for a pharmaceutical company then. A couple of years later, Deborah announced she was pregnant. Richard strutted around like he was the first guy in the world to figure out how to do that."

"Probably a lot of men feel that way when their wives get pregnant."

He shrugged. "A lot of men can get away with doing a lot of things that are repulsive when Richard does them. Anyway, by the time Ellen was born, Deborah was seeing him a little more realistically. She even asked Arden to be her Lamaze coach instead of him."

"Why?"

"Because she couldn't rely on Richard to attend the birth of their own child. And he didn't, either. He was out of town."

"For what?"

"He made up such fantastic stories, no one ever knew. Some of them were true, too. That's what made it hard—you could never be sure. By the time Ellen was two, Deborah didn't care what was true anymore. She kicked him out, and they got a divorce."

"So where is Ellen now?"

Charles took off his glasses and rubbed the bridge of his nose, as if the whole story made him tired. "With Richard. They share custody. She lives one year with him, the next year with Deborah. Richard lives near here, so Ellen goes to the same school and plays with the same friends."

"How old is she?"

"Six."

"How could Deborah let her live every other year with a man like Richard?"

"It's hard to believe, but it seems like something finally clicked when Deborah threw him out. He went into therapy and got a job where his persuasive powers are not his stock in trade." Charles paused thoughtfully. "Richard's really turned his life around. He's certainly become a good father, which shocked the hell out of everyone. But I can't change my mind like that. Someone hurts Deborah or Arden and they're dead meat to me."

She smiled into her cup. There was something sweet about the contrast between Charles' gentle demeanor and his fierce talk. Not until much later did Margaret stop to wonder if his comment had been meant as a warning for her.

"How about Joe or Paul?" she asked.

"Same goes for them," he nodded earnestly. "Dead meat."

"No, I mean do you feel as protective toward them?"

"Not really. We're good friends, but they kind of married into the family. Deborah and Arden and I grew up together."

As Margaret rang up a customer's purchase, she thought about the peculiar family they had created. "So you all went to the same school or something?"

"Yes. As kids, we lived on the same block. We went all through high school together and even went to the same college. Of course, the University of Illinois is a big school. It's not like we were roommates."

"Then how did you all end up living in the same house?"

"Arden and Joe moved in first and lived there for a year or so. When Deborah broke up with Richard, she and Ellen moved into the first floor. A while later, Paul moved in with her and I moved into the upstairs apartment."

"So you didn't plan to live together."

"No. It just happened. But it worked out well, don't you think?"

"Yes. And now you've got another vacancy to fill."

He gave her a quizzical smile. "You're welcome to apply. Deborah said you'd be needing a new place soon."

"News travels fast around here." She picked up a pen and began to doodle complex borders around the want ads she had circled.

"You know what they say about small towns. Why don't you think about it? Arden will be glad to talk to Mrs. Rogers for you. She's our tenants' union representative."

"Thanks, but I don't want to live —" she stopped herself.

"With men," he completed the sentence.

"Right."

"Well, don't men live in your building now?"

"Yes, but not in such close proximity."

"It's not so close. It's just that our building's smaller. You'd have your own apartment." Charles paused and glanced at the browsers, dotting the black floor like exotic mushrooms in their brightly colored down jackets. He lowered his voice. "Besides, you and I could turn the third floor into our own gay ghetto."

"You're gay?"

He nodded. "But I'm not . . . outspoken like you are. Not many people know about me. At least I don't think so. Did you guess?"

"No. But now that you tell me, it seems right. If I had known one of you was gay, you know who I'd have picked?"

"Who?"

"Joe."

He chuckled. "Never let him hear that. He works so hard at being macho."

"I would have thought it came naturally for him."

"I'm not sure it comes naturally for any of us," Charles said thoughtfully.

"Oh, it must. Don't tell me you do it on purpose."

"Well, I don't."

"I didn't mean you. I meant men."

He shrugged. "I can't generalize about men. I'm surprised you can. I got the impression there weren't many in your life."

"There aren't. But the slave always knows more about the master's culture than the master knows about the slave's."

"What a charming way to put it."

"Oh, for christ's sake." Why was it that men could discriminate against women as a class, but women were supposed to consider each of them individually? "Look, don't take it personally, Charles."

"I'm not. I'm looking at it as a metaphor, and I think maybe you're right. But it's still not pleasant to hear."

"The oppression of women is not pretty," she intoned. "Why should we use pleasant phrases to describe it?"

He thought about it. "Damned if I know," he replied with a sudden disarming smile.

She stared down at her paper. What was it with these people, anyway? She barely knew them, and here they were inviting her over for dinner, discussing their private lives with her, suggesting she move in with them. And now she and Charles had had a fight and gotten over it instantly, as people do with their old friends. Maybe they were some kind of cult, and they were wooing a new member.

"Margaret, why don't you stop in after work and look at our apartment? I don't get a finder's fee, you know. But I'd just as soon have someone we like move in, and you might as well have a nice place to live."

"I don't know. Maybe I will."

"Just buzz my apartment. You don't have to be sociable." He drained his coffee and reached for his jacket. "See you later."

Elaine arrived at six to take over, but Margaret delayed leaving, busying herself with unimportant little tasks.

"What are you hanging around for?" Elaine asked as she settled down with the *Times* crossword puzzle.

"I'm just trying to figure out what I want to do now."

"Sounds like you've got some choices. Lucky lady. By the way, do you know what the state tree of Oklahoma is?"

"Why would I know a thing like that?"

"So you could do crossword puzzles."

"Sorry." Margaret slipped into her coat. "Have fun."

"That's the plan." Elaine gave a distracted little wave and bent over her paper again.

What the hell, Margaret thought, I'll go see their apartment just to get them off my back. And tomorrow I'll look at some of the places I found in the newspaper. And then I'll end up in some scummy studio right above the el tracks. What difference does it make?

"Follow me, madame," Charles said as he started up the back stairs. She heard a television droning in Deborah's apartment, then several people talking and laughing as she climbed past Arden's floor. They stopped on a small landing that faced two identical dark wooden doors. "Ladies and gentlemen, behind door number two—" he announced, and swung open the right-hand door.

Margaret was in love.

The apartment was the most adorable thing she had ever seen. It brought tears to her eyes. They entered directly into the living room, which was shaped like an upside down L, with the foot pointing to the right. The main part of the room formed a long rectangle, with two doors placed at even intervals along the left wall, and a single door on the right wall. At the far end, the living room widened into the foot of the L, and two bay windows overlooked the back yard.

She opened the door to the right and stepped into the kitchen. It was so narrow she could stretch out her arms and touch both walls. But somehow the kitchen didn't seem cramped, because everything in it was so small. She walked through the room, trailing her hand over the tiny gas stove, the high porcelain sink, the small white metal cupboard, and the old-fashioned round-topped refrigerator.

Forgetting all about Charles, she crossed the living room and explored the first room on the left. It was small and square, with one window that looked out over the driveway. Like the rest of the apartment, the room had gleaming dark wooden floors and trim, and the walls were painted white but had faded over the years into a cream color. She noticed a couple of lighter squares on the walls where pictures had once hung.

Margaret opened another door and crossed into the bathroom. In it were a toilet, a tall square sink, and a modern shower stall that looked very much out of place. The floor was made of tiny white tiles with a line of black tiles marking a border.

To the right of the sink was yet another door, which opened into a second small bedroom. This room was almost identical to the first: dark wooden floor, creamy walls, one door that led to the bathroom and one that opened into the living room. But there was a difference. Like the living room, this room had a bay window at the far end. And it was the bay window that gave the place such a sense of openness, of possibilities, of home.

The apartment felt as if it had been made for Margaret. It was small, but so was she. There was something endearing about it, with its old-fashioned fixtures, its faded walls, its uneven floors. She no longer cared that it was in the suburbs, that men lived there, that it was owned by a tyrant. That apartment called to her and she wanted it.

"You were right," she told Charles. "It's perfect. How much does she want for it?"

He told her what Cindy had paid. "That's when the apartment was furnished. Since it's empty now, you'd think the rent would go down, unless you knew Mrs. Rogers."

"What about security deposits and all that?"

He shrugged. "She didn't ask me for one, but I don't know how she'll handle it now that she's been burned. You might ask Arden. She seems to have some kind of rapport with Mrs.

Rogers. Of course, Arden has some kind of rapport with everyone."

Margaret glanced at her watch. "I should be getting home. The el doesn't run very often on Sunday night, and I don't want to be stranded." She gazed around the apartment again. What if someone else made a claim on it? The Lill Street crowd was obviously trying to place someone they knew here, and surely she wasn't the only candidate. "Yeah, let's go talk to Arden. Or should we go straight to Mrs. Rogers?"

"That's a fate I'll spare you until the need arises." He led the way downstairs. Margaret barely noticed Joe and their guests as she and Charles followed Arden through the living room and into Arden's bedroom.

It was a curiously dignified room, painted a flat white, with framed posters advertising the Moscow Ballet on the walls. The floor was carpeted in navy blue, and a light blue quilt rested on the double bed. The windows were bordered with print curtains in shades of blue. Along one wall was a dresser, with a small TV on the end facing the bed. On the opposite wall stood a tall bookshelf, filled with hardcovers. Margaret did a double-take as she realized that the books were printed in a foreign language with a strange alphabet.

She took one off the shelf and examined it. "Is this Russian?"

"Yes."

"So when you want to do some light bedtime reading, you can just pick up something in a foreign language?"

"It's amazing what a college education can do for a girl, isn't it?" Arden sat on the bed, and Charles lounged next to her.

"It is," Margaret replied reverently, sliding the book back in place.

"Now, don't act too impressed," Charles admonished her. "We don't want Arden to get a big head."

"What's up with you two?" Arden asked.

"Oh, right." He rolled over on his stomach and leaned his elbows on the bed. "Margaret likes the apartment upstairs. I wanted you to talk to Mrs. Rogers about it."

"Well, there goes the neighborhood," Arden said, but she smiled.

Margaret spent the next two weeks in perpetual motion. She met Mrs. Rogers, covered some stories for the paper, worked nights and weekends in the bookstore, completed a little research for her book. In her spare time she dug through clothes, books, and files, deciding what to discard and what to pack. It wasn't until the week before the move, when she had some friends over for a farewell dinner, that she realized the enormity of what she'd done.

"Next time we see Margaret, she'll probably have a new hairdo and a manicure," Donna teased as she leaned back in her chair for an after-dinner smoke.

"If not a new boyfriend," added Lucy.

"Come on, I just ate." Margaret tried to joke, but she was beginning to feel a little panicky.

"You people are being unfair," Alice spoke up. "I know enough about Margaret to feel that she could move to a condo on Rush Street and still stay true to her ideals."

Kay turned to Laura, Alice's lover. "Very eloquent. Where did you get her?"

"The Salvation Army. But isn't she cute?" Kay and Laura knew each other from the hospital, where Kay worked and Laura had done her training as a nurse-midwife.

"I agree," Joan nodded. "I don't know any of you too well, but I've known Margaret since she was a little girl, and she is a true-blue dyke. A suburban address isn't going to change that."

Samantha looked up from the joint she was rolling. "The only way we'll know for sure is to find out how often we see her after she makes the big move."

"Look at us," Margaret said. "Nine of us are crammed around a six-person table in a one-person studio. Think how much nicer it will be when we can all stretch out in my big new living room and breathe some of that clean suburban air."

"Here. Breathe some of this." Samantha handed her the joint.

Donna reached over and plucked the joint from Margaret's fingers. "Don't waste this good Galena green on Margaret," she chided Samantha. "You know she only holds it for a minute to be polite before passing it on."

"I was testing her friendship," explained Samantha.

Margaret announced, "I'll tell you what the true test of our friendship will be."

"I knew this was coming." Lucy shook her head, making her spiky blond hair wave. "No such thing as a free meal."

"The true test will be when I see how many of my sisters offer to help me move next Monday."

"Count us out," Laura said, putting her arm around Kay's shoulders. "We nurses need our fingers too much to risk them moving furniture."

"I've gotta say it," Joan added. "Only you would move from a fourth floor walk-up to a third floor walk-up. Haven't you ever heard of elevator buildings?"

"At least she's coming down in the world," Alice pointed out.

"Give me a break." Margaret gestured around the small apartment. "Do you see any heavy furniture? Box springs? Stereos? TVs?"

"No," Donna replied. "But I see books. Lots and lots of books."

"Well, you're off the hook anyway because you'll be at work."

"Not that I'm not grateful, but why did you choose Monday as your moving date?"

"Because I'll be working all weekend." Also because she was not quite ready for her old friends to meet her new ones.

"I'll help if Lucy will cover for me at the co-op," Samantha declared.

"Yeah, me too," said Kay.

"I'll be there if I'm not catching babies," Laura said. "I won't know my schedule for a few days, though."

"I'll be working, but Kay can use my van," Maureen offered.

"I guess I could skip *Good Morning America* once," Alice grumbled. "Expect me for a few hours in the morning, but then I've got to get some sleep."

"'Lean on me, I am your sister,'" Joan sang.

"Can I take that as a yes?"

"Did you ever doubt it?"

"Thanks a lot. I really appreciate it." Margaret looked around the crowded table. "You know, with all of you helping, I don't think it'll be too bad."

"The move, maybe. It's what happens afterward that worries me," Donna said.

"Yeah, I know. The suburbs. But I love the apartment, and I hope you're not all going to abandon me just because I don't vote in your district anymore."

"Margaret, don't worry so much," Samantha said soothingly, patting her knee. "It sounds like a beautiful place. We'll probably be jealous."

"Yeah, and if we notice anything weird happening to you, we'll just go out there and drag you back to the north side." Joan looked positively energized by the idea.

Alice drew a headline in the air. "'Dyke Patrol Rescues Woman from Suburban Torture Ring. 'They wouldn't stop feeding me white bread,' sobs victim.'"

Moving day arrived bright, clear, and glittering with cold. Margaret sat up in bed, pulled the blankets to her shoulders, and looked around the room. She was amazed at how quickly it had ceased to be hers. Her books were stacked in neatly tied bundles near the front door, her posters were rolled up and leaning against the wall, her clothes and small belongings were packed into two fat duffle bags. Already the apartment looked like a photograph that she might come across some day and wonder where that room was and what it had meant to her.

A half hour later, the troops arrived. "Well, I see where we start." Joan eyed the piles of books.

Alice squatted and twisted her head sideways, trying to read the titles. "If you've got any of my books here, you can forget about seeing them again after I get my hands on them."

"I'm good about returning books, unlike some people."

Alice looked up sheepishly. "I haven't finished them yet."

"Come on, Alice, I'll race you." Joan had a bundle under each arm, a bundle hanging from each hand, and a devilish look in her auburn eyes.

Alice groaned. "I just got off work." But she grabbed some stacks and followed Joan out the door.

All morning the women worked in relays to transport loads down four flights of stairs. Double-parked, Kay stayed with the van and managed the engineering feat of finding space for all Margaret's possessions: the boards and cinder blocks that comprised her bookcases; a tall garbage can heaped with kitchen equipment; the kitchen table that served as both desk and eating area; six metal folding chairs with the name of a funeral home stenciled on the backs; four large, fat cushions; a small pasteboard dresser; three cardboard file boxes stuffed with papers and office supplies; a radio; an electric typewriter;

and piles of books. Finally, cranky and aching, they drove to the new apartment.

Margaret's anxiety grew as they left the city. She had only been in the apartment twice since she first saw it, once to meet Mrs. Rogers and once to clean it. What if it wasn't as adorable as she remembered? What if these women took one look at the affluent suburban neighborhood and thought she had lost her mind? What if they were right?

Everyone fell silent as they turned onto Lill Street; Kay even turned off the radio. "It's at the end of the street," Margaret instructed her. She had never seen the house in full daylight. Now, as they rolled up the long driveway, she saw it through her friends' eyes: an imposing Victorian structure, white with charcoal gray trim, with porches, bay windows and eaves jutting out like bristling eyebrows.

Joan let out a low whistle.

"I feel like the Beverly Hillbillies," Alice said. Kay gave Margaret a doubtful look. "Are you sure you're up for this? We could always turn around."

"I'm sure it will be lovely," Samantha claimed staunchly. "I lived in a house like this when I was first married."

"You did? Where?" Margaret demanded, ever on the alert for clues about her past.

"Never you mind." Samantha patted Margaret's knee. "Let's get out."

Margaret took out her new keys and fumbled the back door open. "Why don't we take the mattress up first? That'll be the hardest."

"All right," Kay took charge. "Joan and I will carry that. You lead the way."

Margaret grabbed a couple of book bundles and started up the stairs, turning on the dim lights. Behind her she could hear muttered curses as the two women struggled to maneuver the heavy mattress up the narrow, winding stairway.

They leaned the mattress against Charles' door, and Margaret pushed open the door to her apartment.

In the sunlight, it looked even better than she had remembered, the aged wood warm and glowing. They moved the mattress into the bedroom, and she gave everyone a quick tour.

"I especially like the room that's going to be your office," Alice said. "You could get a lot done in a room like that."

"I love the view here in the living room," Joan exclaimed, looking out the windows. "It's so peaceful. And with the sun streaming in, the room looks so cozy and bright."

"Lucky thing," Samantha pointed out, "since there are no light bulbs in the ceiling fixtures."

"But there were. I've been here at night before, and the lights always worked."

"Well, they're gone now." Samantha took a pen and a small pad out of the front pocket of her lavender overalls. "We'll start a list of things you need."

"Aren't you efficient," Joan marvelled.

"When you've moved as many times as I have, you learn what to expect."

"You know what's really amazing about this place?" Alice asked.

"It's just Margaret's size," Kay guessed.

"That's true, but it's not what I was thinking. There are no closets. Apartment as metaphor."

"We'll put that on the list," Samantha said crisply.

"You can't buy a closet, Samantha," Kay laughed.

"That's what you think."

"C'mon, let's bring up some books," Joan suggested.

"All right, but I'm not racing with you anymore," Alice grumbled. "Go pick on someone your own age."

"Sore loser."

"That's for sure," she muttered, massaging her calf muscles.

Finally they carried the last load up the stairs. The five women sprawled on the living room floor like rag dolls, their scarves and coats flung in various corners.

"I can't thank you enough for all your help," Margaret said.

"You got that right," Alice replied in her toughest voice.

Kay rolled onto her stomach and slowly climbed to her knees. "Well, I'd love to stay and visit, but I've got to get going."

"Me too," Samantha said dully. "How?"

Joan gave her a hand and pulled her to her feet. Margaret gathered their coats and walked them to the door. "Thanks again. Now I owe you all a big favor."

"You've done a few for us," Kay said, and gave her a hug.

"Well, when I'm settled I'll invite you over for dinner and tell you all about life in the suburbs."

"That'll be fun." Joan embraced her and followed Kay out the door. "Don't forget!"

Alice added, "We'll be counting on some good stories."

"Call us." Samantha held her tightly for a moment. "By the way, where's your phone?"

"They're connecting it tomorrow."

"Okay. I'll expect to hear from you tomorrow night." Samantha tore the shopping list out of her little pad and handed it to Margaret.

"It's a deal." Margaret stood in the hallway, listening to their clatter recede down the stairs and out the back door. For a moment she held her breath, waiting for a stab of remorse or loneliness. What she felt instead was a spreading sense of lightness, which she finally identified as contentment.

Margaret spent the next couple of hours happily arranging her new home. She made her bed, put some clothes away in the dresser, placed a folding chair near the wall, set the alarm clock on the floor next to the mattress, and the bedroom was completed. The office took even less time. She set the kitchen table and a folding chair facing the bay windows, stacked the file boxes against the wall, placed the typewriter on the table and plugged it in. In the living room, she opened the four remaining folding chairs and made a vague semi-circle out of them, then set the fat colorful cushions here and there on the dark floor.

It took her a bit longer to wash and dry her silverware, dishes, and glasses, and to find places for them in the toy kitchen. She was setting up cinder blocks to build a bookshelf in the living room when she heard a knock on the door. "Come on in," she yelled, and Deborah strode into the room, bringing with her the fresh smell of outdoors.

"Welcome to the neighborhood." Deborah took off her coat and tossed it onto a chair. "Let's see what you've done with the place."

"What are you doing home so early? It's not six, is it?"

"I scheduled an early day for myself. It's only four, but it's already getting dark in here. Why don't we turn on some lights?"

"Because there aren't any." She pointed to the ceiling fixture. "All the light bulbs are gone. I was planning to go out later and get some."

Deborah smacked her forehead with her palm. "I can't stand that woman! Cindy didn't take the light bulbs. Mrs. Rogers must have."

"Why would she do that?"

"You don't suppose she's going to give you sixty cents' worth of used light bulbs for free, do you? I'm surprised she didn't unscrew the knobs from the faucets. Did you check?"

Margaret laughed. "The faucets are fine."

"I'll get you some bulbs from my apartment. Want anything else while I'm down there?"

"No thanks."

When she returned, Margaret walked her around the apartment. "Very nice," Deborah said. "I can see you belong to the minimalist school. What are these?" She nudged the rolled-up posters with her toe.

"Posters."

"What are we waiting for? Let's put them up."

"I haven't decided where I want them to go."

"Don't let me rush you." Deborah pushed up the sleeves of her sweater. "How about these shelves? Want a hand with them?"

"Sure."

"How do you want your books organized?"

"By category. Pretty much the way they're stacked now."

"It's funny how many methods people use." Deborah snipped the twine off a pile of books. "I like to organize them alphabetically by author. Bookstore training, I guess. Paul tries to make sure that books that were written by authors who were friends end up on the same shelf. So the books shouldn't get lonely, he says."

They worked in companionable silence, Deborah humming a funny little tune. Finally Margaret asked, "What are you singing?"

Deborah looked surprised, as if she didn't realize she had been making a sound. "Oh. I was humming the theme song from the kids' TV show, 'Mr. Rogers' Neighborhood.' Do you know it?"

Margaret shook her head.

Deborah sang, "'It's a beautiful day in the neighborhood, a beautiful day for a neighbor, would you be mine?'" She smiled. "Ellen and I used to sing it all the time, before she got too old for it. Seems strange that she's too mature for it, and I'm still singing it."

"I don't think so."

"Are you suggesting I'm immature?"

"No. But I don't think as a mother you'll ever grow out of her childhood, and she will. You'll still cherish it, and she'll have to reject it, at least until she grows up."

"You're pretty wise for one so young."

Margaret shrugged, embarrassed. "I don't know why I said that. You know much more about it than I do."

"Did you drop a couple of kids that I don't know about?" Deborah saw Margaret straining to reach the top shelf, took the book from her hand and easily slid it into place.

"No. I've just been thinking about it lately, how you spend your whole life kind of fighting to loosen your parents' grip. And now that I'm grown up, every now and then I'll hear something pop out of my mouth that's exactly what my mother would say. The weird thing is, I don't really mind."

"Well, you should tell her. I'm sure she'd be very pleased." Deborah set the last few books on the top shelf.

"Maybe." Margaret didn't want to talk about her parents. That seemed to be all she did lately: first with Lillian Green, then Joan. It was a little like coming out as a lesbian. At first she didn't tell anybody, then she went through a phase when she told everybody, and finally she got sick of telling people and let them figure it out for themselves.

"Deborah, you're pretty handy to have around the house. Do you want to do the books in the office now?"

"Only if I get first dibs on borrowing them."

"Fair enough."

They finished a little before six. "Thanks for your help. The books really make it look like home, don't they?"

"Yes, a monk's home. We've got to do something about the walls."

"Like what?"

"Posters, paintings, wall hangings, murals—something to warm the place up a little bit. And paint these funeral chairs. Some nice primary colors should do it."

"Why are you so eager to be my decorator?"

"I just like to do that kind of thing. Humor me." Deborah smoothed down her sleeves. "All the people with real jobs should be home soon. Would you like to come down for dinner? We're having beef stew, thanks to the crockpot—the only useful gift Paul's family has ever given us."

"No thanks. I've got more to do up here."

"Oh, I forgot. I don't suppose you could just pick out the meat?"

Margaret shook her head.

"Well, maybe Arden's having something vegetarian."

"Deborah, just because I live here doesn't mean I'm going to be freeloading off you two all the time."

"Hey, I'm just trying to be neighborly."

"I appreciate it. But you and Arden have a communal style that's a little difficult for mere mortals to get used to."

They walked toward the door. "You're just shy, Margaret. You'll get over it." Deborah tilted her head like a bird and listened to the footsteps climbing the stairs. "In fact, here's your first chance." She threw open the door, and there stood Arden in work clothes and a long gray coat, holding a black wool beret and shaking back her hair. "You're just in time," Deborah told her.

"For what?"

"The tour bus is about to start. If you hurry you can still get a seat."

Arden laughed and gave Margaret a sympathetic look. "Has she been hanging around all day?"

"No, just the last couple of hours. She's been a big help, too."

"I know it may seem that way, but it's only because she's tall. I keep Joe around for the same reason."

"Just keep talking about me like I'm not here," Deborah said. "I don't mind."

"May I come in?" Arden asked with exaggerated politeness.

"Please do." Margaret breathed in her outdoor smell. It struck her suddenly that this freshness was what she could expect every time she went outside, instead of the traffic fumes of her old neighborhood.

"Do you want to do the honors?" Arden asked.

Margaret led her to the office first. She spent a long time studying the books. "You wouldn't be interested, they're all in English," Deborah said, and hurried her through the bathroom and into the bedroom. Once again, she took in the room in a glance, then gave her attention to the books. Finally she turned to Margaret and said, "Where are you going to hang your clothes?"

"I don't know. What did Cindy do with hers?"

"Removed them," Deborah replied.

Arden squinted. "I think she had one of those old-fashioned wooden wardrobes that had drawers on one side and a hanger rod on the other."

"Oh, yeah," Deborah said. "That was pretty nice. Hope it looks good in her new place."

"I imagine she's sold it by now. It wasn't exactly her style."

"No, but at least it matched the other furniture she took. Anyway, it wasn't Margaret's style either."

Margaret was just about to ask what they thought her style was when Arden gave her a little push. "I have an idea. Joe went through a handyman phase. He bought this coat rack at a garage sale, and was going to strip it and refinish it. Unfortunately, he lost interest before he got to the refinishing stage. You're welcome to it if you want. Your clothes would be hanging out in the open, but at least they'd be hanging."

"Don't you ever use it?"

"Sometimes we use it to fight over, but that's about all."

"Sure, I'd like to borrow it."

"Let's go get it," Arden said.

"By the way, I have a lot of garbage. Where do I put it?"

"Garbage is kind of a tricky subject around here, what with Mrs. Rogers' mental illness and all," Deborah said. "Better stick it on my front porch for the night, and then we'll check out the situation in the morning."

"Deborah, don't be so dramatic," Arden laughed.

"Just looking out for the new kid on the block."

Margaret found her way to Deborah's front porch, then stood squinting in the icy wind trying to find an inconspicuous spot to hide the garbage bag. Finally she stuffed it into a corner of the dark porch, and, shivering, made her way back to the stairs.

The door to Arden's apartment was open, and as she climbed toward the second floor she could hear Joe and Paul talking in the kitchen. She had almost reached the landing when she heard Joe mention her name.

"You weren't very happy when Cindy moved in either," Paul replied in his rumbly voice, "but she turned out okay."

"Yeah, she stole everything she could carry."

Paul laughed. "Then you can relax. Everything of value is already gone."

"Are you sure? Where's Deborah?"

"In Margaret's apartment, with Arden."

"My point exactly."

She heard a sound like a glass being clunked roughly onto a table. "Joe, if you lose that woman it's your own damned fault. Now I babied you through the last little episode, but I'm not going to do it again."

Margaret didn't hear what Joe said next, because she turned and flew up the stairs, her face burning. Near the top she stopped to regain her composure. What had she gotten herself into on this strange little planet? What was Joe's problem? And what in the world did Arden see in him?

She clenched her jaw and gripped the banister tightly. This was her home now, and she'd be damned if she'd let some man destroy it. The sound of women's laughter called her to her own apartment, and she climbed the last few stairs and closed the door behind her.

Very few things upset Margaret now in the same breathless, heart-pounding way as that snatch of conversation overheard so long ago. But if something did, Margaret wonders, would she have the determination to march up those stairs anyway? Or would she have to confront Joe and explain to him her point of view? It is not that Margaret has lost courage, only that it is summoned up more self-consciously with the years. She has gained an appreciation of what courage costs.

If Margaret had known then what she knows now, she would not have let Joe's comment concern her. She would not have believed that her world was only as solid as the approval of those around her.

Nevertheless, Margaret is happy that she did not know then what she knows now, that she does not yet know what she will someday learn. The glance that will flare into passion, the love that will burn into ashes, the cough that will turn into cancer— who would want to know these things ahead of time? Even this very instant, as she hangs up the phone after saying to Gwen, "I'm sorry; I don't know if I can move in with you," Margaret is content to let the moment unfold as it will.

This is the mellow lesson of her middle years. For this reason, Margaret would not wish to be in her twenties again, or her thirties. She would not be a day younger. She would not go back to the time on Lill Street, even if she had the power to change the way things turned out.

COMRADES IN ARMS

"What a fine figure of a woman you make, standing there so straight and tall." Deborah stooped to check the binding on Margaret's skis. "Well, maybe not that straight." She stood and looked down at her. "Maybe not that tall, either. Okay, now. Just like we practiced. Ready?"

"Ready." She looked at Deborah, they moved in unison, and Margaret was cross-country skiing for the first time.

"What do you think?" Deborah asked, coasting effortlessly beside her.

"It's okay so far."

"That's what I like about you, Margaret. You're such a sports enthusiast."

"I'm trying." She wished Deborah would stop talking so she could concentrate on coordinating her legs, arms, and lungs.

"I know it feels like work right now, but it's like learning to ride a bike. All of a sudden your body will get it, and it'll be so easy you'll wonder why you waited this long to try."

"Are you working on commission or something?"

She laughed. "Okay, I'll shut up. I'm going to take a little spin. Call me if you need help."

Margaret focused on "left, right, left, right," for a while, but soon grew bored. She studied the clarity of their tracks in the fresh snow, then noticed the fragile blue of the sky. It looked like a dome of ice that might split at any moment to reveal the greasy gray clouds of a city winter hiding behind it. There was something ostentatious about this country quiet, and try though she might she could hear nothing but the steady "shuss shuss" of her skis.

Suddenly she realized she was skiing. She didn't dare glance down to see how her legs had managed this trick, but she could watch the snow-covered trees gliding steadily past. She kept the miracle to herself for several minutes, exhilaration rising like a balloon in her chest. Finally she had to share it.

"Deborah!" She was too far away to hear. Margaret turned her body toward Deborah and somehow the skis followed. "Hey, Deborah!" she yelled again. "Look at me. I'm flying!"

"Bend your knees!" Deborah called back.

An odd response, Margaret thought, but had no time to pursue the idea because the world passed in a blur and she crashed through the soft snow onto the frozen ground beneath. She tried to regain her footing and her dignity before Deborah could see, but it was too late.

"Are you all right?" Deborah asked, and burst out laughing when Margaret nodded.

"I'm glad you're so amused." Margaret kept trying to stand, but it was very difficult because her toes were trapped in the middle of two long planks.

Deborah took her hands and hauled her up. "If you were hurt, I wouldn't laugh. But you have to admit it was a funny sight."

"You didn't tell me we'd be going down hills."

"Margaret, these aren't exactly major slopes. We're on a golf course."

"Well, it felt like a mountain."

"You don't want to quit, do you?"

"Hell, no. I was just getting to like it. Next time we get to one of those hills, I'll watch you and see how you do it."

Deborah pulled off her wool cap and ran a hand through her curly blond hair. "Let's go then." They took off together, Deborah whistling "Ain't No Mountain High Enough" until Margaret threatened her with the pointed end of her pole.

". . . and then Margaret had a terrible accident, but she rose from the ashes like a phoenix," Deborah told Arden later as the three of them climbed the front stairs together. Arden had arrived home from the laundromat just as the other two returned from their wilderness excursion.

"Now I'm getting worried," she replied. "Last Sunday we went sledding in that state park. Today you two went skiing. What will you make us do next week, ice fishing?"

"No, I know!" Margaret took the laundry basket so Arden could open the door to her apartment. "That 'sport' where you zip around on skis and shoot rifles at moving targets. What's that called?"

"Forget it, Osborn. I'd be scared to let you near a gun." Deborah hurried to the kitchen to make the hot chocolate she'd been talking about all the way home, leaving Arden and Margaret in the living room.

Margaret watched Arden carry an armful of clean clothes into her room and another batch into Joe's room. Arden was wearing jeans and an old flannel shirt, her chestnut hair frizzing out slightly with the static electricity generated in the dry house. She looked relaxed and peaceful as she crossed and recrossed the chilly room, putting away towels and tablecloths.

Smoothing a sheet, she stopped in front of Margaret, who was sitting on the floor in front of an overstuffed chair. "Skiing must agree with you. Your cheeks are pink and your eyes look very blue. Do you ever wear your hair loose?" Arden shook out the sheet she was holding and laid it, still warm from the dryer, across Margaret's legs.

Margaret stared up into her greenish brown eyes, trying to figure out what that tender gesture could mean.

"What did I miss?" Deborah demanded.

"I was just telling Margaret how good she looks," Arden answered casually.

"Yeah, everybody looks good after a workout." Deborah set the mugs on the coffee table and flopped onto the couch. Arden sat next to her.

"Whose skis did you use?" Arden asked Margaret.

"Deborah's. And she used Paul's."

"You dummy, that's why she kept falling," Arden turned to Deborah. "Your skis are much too long for her."

"Maybe so," Deborah yawned, "but her salary's much too small for her to rent skis, so we compromised." She scrunched down on the couch and drew her knees up under her chin. "You know, I'll always have a soft spot in my heart for cross country. That's how I first met Paul."

"How?" Margaret asked.

"I was skiing with a few friends in Kettle Moraine. It was real early in the morning and it had just stopped snowing. You know that clean, powdery, fresh snow that hardly even feels cold?"

"Yes."

"At one point I went on ahead of my friends, and I found myself in this breathtaking area. It was a long hallway of evergreen trees with their branches covered in snow. The path stretched like a white carpet through the trees and up a small rise at the end. The trees arched over the path like the ceiling in a cathedral. It was so silent and the snow was so pure it felt like no one else had ever been there before."

"It sounds beautiful," said Margaret.

"It was magnificent. I mean, I was practically praying. I skied down the path and started up the little hill. Then all of a sudden this huge creature appeared at the top of the rise and swooped down on me. I screamed so loud I had a sore throat for days. At first I thought it was a bear, but it turned out to be a man."

"Paul?"

She nodded, smiling. "In those days he had a big Afro and a beard, plus he was wearing these funny ski goggles."

"Well, what happened?"

"When he saw me he screamed too, and then he started laughing really hard and sat down in the snow. I started to laugh too, and the relief made my knees weak so I collapsed next to him. We were just laughing like maniacs. After a couple of minutes he took his goggles off and wiped tears off his face, and I saw his sweet, sweet brown eyes for the first time."

"Now don't get too sappy," Arden warned her. "You were doing just fine."

"He said, 'I don't know who you are, but you scared the shit out of me.' And I said, 'You should talk. I must have a big hole in my jacket, where my heart shot out and flew away.' So we introduced ourselves, and we were just sitting in the snow laughing and talking, waiting for our bodies to get back to normal after our big scare.

"A moment later, a group of people on skis appeared on top of the little hill behind him, blocking out the sun. Then my friends skied up behind me on the trail. And all of a sudden there was this bunch of white people staring at this bunch of black people, and Paul and I didn't feel much like laughing anymore. So we stood up and dusted ourselves off, and our friends skied past each other saying 'Hello' and 'Good morning' in these ultra-polite voices."

"That's a very romantic story, Deborah, but how did you two ever get together? Did you keep going to that forest cathedral at dawn, hoping he would show up?"

"Actually, we met at a party about a month later and got to be friends after that. It was anti-climactic but a lot warmer that way. Besides, I was still married."

Margaret folded the sheet Arden had draped on her and hung it over the arm of the couch. "After you were divorced and started dating Paul, was it difficult? I mean, because he was black?"

"Actually, it was more difficult because I was white. I grew up in a liberal household. Eleanor Roosevelt and Adlai Stevenson were our patron saints. So my parents were a little skittish, but in general they were okay. After all those years of taking me to candle-light demonstrations where everyone sang 'Black and white together,' they could hardly have complained at this point. Besides, they thought Paul was a big improvement over Richard."

"What did Paul's parents think?"

"They were horrified. Of course, once they got to know me all of their fears were instantly put to rest."

"Naturally."

"Really, that's not true," Deborah continued seriously. "They like me now, but it's taken a long time. His parents were very disappointed that he didn't find a black woman, and some of his friends were downright hostile about it. Some of my friends and relatives were too, but I expected that. I was enough of a racist to think the problem would be one-sided."

"We dropped some friends who couldn't accept Paul," Arden said. "They all had good reasons why they were uncomfortable with the relationship, and none of the reasons had anything to do with race. Why, some of them had barely even noticed Paul was black."

"But it is hard to be going against the grain all the time," Deborah pointed out. "Margaret, you must know what I mean."

Margaret nodded. "Yes. But there are ways for people to express their concern that you're going to face hardships, and ways to make it clear that they're trying to force you back into line. And it's easy to tell the difference."

"Is it?" Deborah asked. "I'm not always sure."

"Oh, everything's so unambiguous to you, Margaret," said Arden. "You don't have doubts like the rest of us."

"That's not true," she protested. "I have lots of doubts."

"Well, I've never noticed any."

"Me neither." Deborah stood and stretched. "I think I'm going to take a nap before Paul gets home."

"Margaret, can I assume that you've started to trust us?" Arden asked when they were alone. "I mean, you didn't even ask if we were secretly serving Nestlé cocoa. The first few times Deborah brought you over here you were so careful about everything, like we were trying to poison you with our nasty politics."

"I trust you. I'm not completely comfortable with your politics, but you're probably not completely comfortable with mine either."

"I wouldn't know, since you never talk about your politics."

Margaret stared at her. "What do you mean? I talk about them all the time."

"No you don't. You talk politics—boycott this, support that, write letters about something else—but you never talk about why you feel that way or what it means to you."

Margaret thought about that for a minute, confused and startled. "I guess I always thought of it as a given."

"Well, it's not. I can make assumptions about what drives you, but I don't really know."

"What drives me is knowing that things are wrong," Margaret replied quietly. "I don't mean a few things, like the fact that we don't get paid the same as men or that we don't have any women on the Supreme Court. I mean everything. Our whole culture is built on the subjugation of women. And you and Deborah and I—all women—have been trained not to see the truth, to perpetuate it by pretending that everything's all right."

"Then why aren't you miserable, if all you can see is that women are oppressed and hated and you've been lied to all your life?"

Margaret shook her head. "I'm not explaining this very well. It's true I see the deceit and hostility. But I also see the joy of women working together to change things."

"I don't know. It sounds pretty grim to be always fighting."

"Always surrendering is worse. Besides, we're fighting *for* something, which is more empowering than fighting against something."

"Well, what exactly are you fighting for?"

"Women's freedom." Margaret felt a smile spread across her face as she said the words, because they were so holy to her. "The freedom to walk down the street in safety. The freedom to have children if and when we want to. The freedom to love women if we choose to, and to love men only *because* we choose to and not because we're forced to by repressive laws or cultural propaganda. And there's more, lots more. Things we don't even think about because they're so ingrained."

"I take it you don't think much of my brand of feminism," Arden said with her ironic smile, one eyebrow raised.

Margaret hesitated. "No, not too much. Although maybe I'm mistaken about what your brand is."

"What do you think it is?"

"I think you believe feminism is important, but a lot of other issues are just as important. I don't think you feel in your heart that this is your cause, that it's your life we're fighting for."

"Let's say you're right. Where does a nice suburban girl get started down this long path to enlightenment?"

"I don't know. Is there any aspect that interests you especially?"

"Well, Joe and I belong to NOW and NARAL," she suggested dubiously.

"Do you go to meetings?"

"No, we just send checks. Actually, I send checks and he swears he'll pay me back later."

"Well, that's a place to start. Or you could try to get the company you work for to publish more women's writing. That would be an important contribution that only you can make."

"But I want to get involved in something I can do with you."

Margaret considered her, in her soft red shirt, with her fine hair and frank eyes. Finally she saw a truth that she had been edging toward for weeks, maybe since she had first moved in: Arden was the heart of the house on Lill Street, and in her warmth was where Margaret needed to be. Not constantly, not forever, but for a little while. Long enough to thaw out.

Arden's hand was resting on the back of the couch, and
Margaret touched it very lightly, saying "I'd like that very
much."

*When Margaret thinks of that conversation now, a flush of
embarrassment washes over her. It's not the ideology that makes
her cringe, but the bullying, hectoring way in which she
expressed it.*

*In those days her feminist commitment was like a sleek,
powerful dog who stalked beside her on a leash, barely under
her control. Now the dog lives in her house and sleeps on her
kitchen floor, and Margaret wonders if she has tamed her too
well.*

*How has our language gotten so refined? she asks herself.
When did our demands get so polite? Why did we move from
destroying the patriarchy to deconstructing it? And the biggest
question of all is this: if the world is still as hostile and cruel to
women as she has always believed, how has Margaret gotten so
comfortable in it?*

Later that afternoon, Margaret was working at her desk
when she heard Deborah yell, "Are you busy?"

"I'm in the office. Come on in."

Deborah padded into the room in her thick reindeer knee
socks, turned a metal chair backward and straddled it, her
folded arms resting on the back. "I don't know," she said,
looking slowly around the room. "The place looks better, but
it's not there yet."

Margaret liked the look of the room, spare but
businesslike, with file boxes stacked neatly against the wall and
papers, pens, and typewriter placed precisely on the work
table. "Where do you want it to be?"

"That poster with all the names of lesbian writers on
it—nice, but too monochromatic. And these other posters, the
woman with her fist raised, and the one with the big women's
symbol painted on her typewriter, and those women working
in the fields—I mean, everyone looks so stern. Don't you find it
a little intimidating to have them staring down at you?"

"Not at all. I like images of strong women. They make me
feel hopeful."

"I guess," Deborah said vaguely. "What are you working
on?"

"A chapter about *Feminist Times* for my book. I'm really having a hard time with it."

"Why? That chapter should be the easiest, since you know it so well."

"That's the trouble. I'm being as objective as I can, but I don't think the editing collective uses its power very effectively, and that's what I have to write. Now I'm afraid people who read the book won't have a good opinion of the newspaper."

"Don't worry. No one's going to cancel their subscription because you've revealed the inner workings of the paper. Besides, maybe the editing collective will read it and clean up their act."

"I doubt it."

Deborah rested her head on her arms. "Well, I can tell you're not going to be any fun."

"What's the matter?" Margaret turned off the typewriter.

"I'm bored. Paul dragged home some big electronic gizmo, and he's got it spread out all over the living room so he can work on it this weekend. Never fall in love with an engineer."

"What's everyone else doing?"

"Charles is at work, and it's that time of the month for Arden and Joe."

"What do you mean?"

"Once a month they have a battle over the bills. You know, she calls him a spendthrift and he calls her a shrew. That kind of thing."

"I wouldn't think they'd have any money troubles."

"Well, Arden doesn't make that much."

"I know, but I thought Joe made a ton."

"He does. But he spends two tons."

"On what?"

Deborah ticked the items off her fingers. "Clothes, liquor, restaurants, books, records, stereo equipment, plane tickets, movies, plays, and whatever else strikes his fancy while he happens to have his credit cards handy. Which is all the time, except when he's in the shower."

"Poor Arden."

"Stupid Arden. I keep telling her he'll never learn unless she stops babying him. She closed their joint savings account after he emptied it out a few times, but whenever he gets a nasty letter from Mr. Mastercharge, she still lends him enough to bail him out."

"Why?"

Deborah shrugged. "She thinks he has some kind of disease, like alcoholism, only with money instead of liquor."

"Galloping consumption."

"That's a terrible pun. Arden will love it."

"Do you share everything with Arden?"

"If you're asking me whether I can keep a secret, the answer is yes—if you force me to. Why? Do you have some?"

"Some secrets? I guess everyone has at least one."

"Oh, good. I love a challenge."

"Mine aren't very interesting. What about you?"

Deborah thought for a moment. "I don't really have any secrets. I must be a very dull person."

"Oh, I think you're okay."

"Yeah, I do too," she replied casually.

Margaret stared at her. In one off-hand statement, Deborah had identified a quality that Margaret admired in her but had never been able to define. Deborah really *did* think she was okay. She must not have her own version of the carping, cramping commentary that ran ceaselessly in Margaret's head, urging her to do better, to be better, to remember that whatever she did could never be enough. Margaret had always assumed this was universal background noise, these cheerleaders from hell. Now she wondered if she was the only one who heard them.

Deborah stood and reached for the ceiling, then stretched and placed her palms flat on the hardwood floor. "Are you coming down later?"

"For what?"

"We're all having a drink together at Arden's."

"No, thanks. I've got some plans tonight."

She straightened up. "Margaret, you haven't joined in any of our little co-ed get-togethers. Face it—you live here now and so do Paul and Joe."

"So does Mrs. Rogers, but I don't notice you hanging around with her."

"Good point, but you're still wrong."

"Deborah, it's nothing personal against them, it's just that I don't have any interest in spending time with men."

"What about Charles? You have coffee with him all the time."

"He's an exception. Besides, he makes a mean mocha java."

"It's terrible the way you queers stick together." Deborah slid her chair under the table. "Well, if you'd rather sit alone in your apartment and stare at those mean-looking women, go ahead. But if I can get up at dawn to take you skiing, the least you can do is come downstairs and have a drink with me and my loved ones."

"Okay, all right, you win."

Deborah beamed. "I had a feeling guilt would work with you. See you later."

Margaret hesitated in the doorway of Arden's living room. The Lill Street group looked like a commercial for a way of life she had never chosen. Arden lounged at one end of the couch, Paul sat next to her, and Deborah leaned against him. Joe slouched in the easy chair, looking big and handsome in his heathery blue sport coat. The snapping fire cast a shifting coppery light, and Marvin Gaye's "What's Going On?" rolled like good times from speakers tucked in all four corners of the large room. Margaret sat on the floor next to the glass coffee table, wondering how she had gotten so miscast.

"We saw more of you before you moved in," Paul said in his rumbly voice. "I was beginning to believe you were a myth."

"You wouldn't think so if you had to hear that typewriter all the time," Charles claimed as he entered the room with six icy beer bottles tucked between his arms and chest, and a large bowl of potato chips in his hands. "Hurry, I'm freezing." He set the bowl on the coffee table and bent over so they could slide the bottles out of his grip. "One of the librarians brought this beer back from her vacation in Colorado."

Margaret was dismayed to see that not only were they were drinking Coors®, but they considered it a special treat. Didn't they know any better? She resisted the urge to lecture them and quietly ignored the bottle Deborah handed her. Charles took a seat on the floor.

"Paul, why don't some of you electronic whiz kids invent a silent typewriter?" asked Arden.

"I've heard rumors that one of the big companies is doing some R and D on that. But as far as I'm concerned, it's a waste of time to put more energy into a technology that's almost obsolete. Everyone knows that typewriters are going the way of the dinosaurs."

"That big company must not think so, if they're trying to redesign their typewriters," Charles pointed out, rubbing the condensation into his gray sweater.

"I'm sure somebody was redesigning the buggy just as Model T's were rolling off the assembly line," Paul laughed.

"Yeah, and look what that brought us." Joe leaned his elbows on his knees. "Air pollution. Abandonment of the inner cities. Dependence on the oil companies."

"Howard Johnson's," Deborah added.

"Like it or not, the microchip is going to change the way we live, and soon. Personal computers will be accepted into our daily lives just like calculators were. It's not a political statement, it's a fact." Paul leaned back smugly and clasped his hands behind his head.

"But there's always been a connection between technology and social policy," Margaret pointed out. "Look at how the introduction of typewriters changed clerical work from a good entry-level job for men to a dead end for women."

"Right," Joe said. "Personal computers sound good, and I'm sure I'll be among the first to run out and buy one," he added with a self-deprecating laugh, "but I have a lot of questions to be answered before I'll welcome them with open arms. Remember the book *1984*? That's only eight years away."

Paul raised both hands in a gesture of innocence. "All I do is make sure the damn things work. Don't look to me for answers."

"Well, when computers do run our lives, we'll be glad we know Paul," Arden said.

"Not until then?" he asked her.

"No, I'm afraid not."

Joe stood and straightened the crease on his pants with smart little slaps. "I'll be right back," he said, and sailed out the front door.

Deborah sent Arden a questioning look.

"Who knows?" she replied.

"So what are you up to tonight?" Deborah asked Charles.

"I'm going out on a date," he answered shyly, looking at the floor.

"Good for you. Who is he, someone new?"

"Of course he's new," Arden blurted. "When was the last time Charles had a date? Tell us all about him."

"His name is David, and I met him at the library."

"Well, give us the details." Deborah stretched her legs across Paul's and Arden's laps.

"He's thirty-three years old, he's a psychologist, and he's really cute. Every Saturday he comes to the library and takes out an armload of books. Lately I've been reading the books he returns so we'd have a lot to talk about if we ever met."

"Did you finally manage to run into him?" Margaret asked.

"Oh, no. I saw him talking to one of the other librarians, and I asked her to introduce us."

"I had no idea you were so proper."

He gave her a slow smile. "I'm an old-fashioned kind of guy. People don't think we exist any more, but we do."

"So what happened?" Arden asked.

"We started talking about books, and one thing led to another, and he asked me to go to the theater tonight. He has season tickets."

"But Charles, I thought you had symphony tickets tonight."

"I do. I was hoping two of you might want to go instead."

"Sold!" Deborah sang out. "I'd love a nice romantic evening with my boyfriend here." She threw her arm around Paul's shoulders. "Unless you'd rather be communing with that machine downstairs," she added sweetly.

He grinned. "No way."

Arden looked at Margaret. "Well, Joe's got plans later, he told me. Seems like everyone's spoken for tonight except you and me."

"Actually, I am busy tonight, but you can come along."

"Have you ever heard such a warm invitation?" Deborah demanded.

"It's just that I don't expect it to be a fun evening. I'll be freezing my buns and breaking the law at the same time."

"Sounds intriguing." Joe strode into the apartment and set a paper bag on the coffee table in front of Margaret. "What exactly will you be doing?"

"What's in the bag?" Arden asked.

"It's for Margaret. Open it up."

She reached into the bag and pulled out a six-pack of Budweiser®. "Hey, thanks," she said, surprised and touched.

"We had more beer," Charles pointed out.

"You don't think Margaret would do anything to enrich the Coors family, do you? What a bunch of fair-weather liberals." Joe gave her one of his blazing grins. "So what crime are you committing tonight?"

"Nothing major. I'm helping a friend deface public property by putting up posters advertising an ERA march."

"Downtown?"

She nodded.

"Hope you put some up near the bank. It'll be a nice change to see a poster that isn't written in Farsi."

"I'll come with you," Arden announced.

Deborah nudged her with her foot. "Arden, maybe this is Margaret's perverted idea of a date," she stage-whispered.

"It's not a date," she laughed. "You're invited."

Joe turned to Arden with an odd smile. "Hope you have a good lawyer."

When it was time to leave, Arden insisted on driving.

"But we won't need a car," Margaret argued. "We're going to spend eight dollars on parking alone."

"I'm not taking the el home late at night. Get in."

"This is like taking a cab to the revolution," Margaret muttered.

"Better than coming home in an ambulance. So who's this friend we're going to meet?"

"Her name is Joan. We were best friends when we were little kids. I never saw her again until we ran into each other at that Tess Gallagher reading. She's really into the ERA campaign."

"Does that mean you're not?" Arden glanced at her.

"I haven't thought about it much, if you want to know the truth."

"I always want to know the truth," Arden replied seriously. "Why haven't you thought about it?"

Margaret watched the traffic whizzing past, in the opposite direction. In front of them lay a fluid carpet of red tail-lights. "I think of feminism as a way of life rather than a way of getting certain legislation passed. When I do focus on specific issues, I usually choose ones that don't have as much popular support as the ERA."

"You mean lesbian issues."

"Mainly."

"What about the rest of us?"

"I know a lot of lesbians who work hard for abortion rights, birth control, an end to sterilization abuse—issues that

generally don't affect us. I've never known any straight
feminists who gave more than lip service to lesbian rights."

Arden was silent for a moment, maneuvering past a stalled
truck. "Don't get mad, but why should they? If there are all
those issues that affect straight women, and other issues like
the ERA and job discrimination that affect all women, why
should the majority fight for things that only pertain to a
minority? That seems like a luxury that maybe we can't afford
right now."

"But don't you see that no woman is free unless lesbians
are free?"

"Well, philosophically—"

"No, not philosophically. Literally. If lesbians can be
evicted from their homes, and lose their children, and forfeit
not only their jobs but the right to practice their professions,
don't you see that the only way for any woman to be safe from
that is to attach herself to a man? And don't you think that's a
form of enslavement? Don't you think that's part of the plan?"

"I'm not sure it's a plan exactly."

"Suppose you were going out with Joe tonight. Would you
be afraid to take the el with him?"

"It's just a fact that you're safer with a man than you are
with a woman. It doesn't matter if you're straight or gay."

"Right. Because you're every man's prey unless you're one
man's property."

"No, because men can fight back better."

"Either way, a woman can't feel safe on the streets of her
own city unless she's with a man."

"What does that prove?"

"That the only way women can be safe—from assault or
discrimination—is to relate to men. I don't think that's a
coincidence, do you?"

"But what's that got to do with lesbian rights?"

"I think lesbians are oppressed not because we're
'homosexual,' but because we flaunt the basic rule of
patriarchy. We don't need men. That makes us dangerous. And
that's why we have to be slapped down, before other women
realize that they don't need men either."

Arden pulled into a parking garage. They drove slowly past
dark rows of empty cars and backed into a spot. Far away they
could hear the staccato click of a woman's high-heeled shoes as
she hurried toward the elevator. "What about looking to men
for other things," Arden argued, "like love and intimacy and

support?" Her voice sounded hopeless, as if she knew the answer but must ask anyway.

"Is that what you've found?"

Arden studied her face, sighed, dropped the car keys into her purse. "I guess that's why my mother's books are so popular."

Joan was conspicuous in the Saturday night crowd, carrying a bucket of paste and a roll of posters. Two large sponges stuck out of her jacket pockets. Enthusiasm sparked from her in all directions like her wild red hair. She led them down the block, chatting easily with Arden.

Margaret trudged grimly behind them. Why couldn't she take things lightly like Joan or Alice? Why did she have to lecture all the time? Arden would never want to be with her if she couldn't manage to perk up and be more fun.

Joan selected a spot and handed Margaret the bucket. "You're the look-out. Arden and I can spread paste on these babies and slap them up."

"What am I looking out for? There are a million people on the street."

"The only ones to worry about are cops," Joan said. "I don't think we'd end up in jail if we got caught. Probably just pay a fine."

"Didn't you find out what the penalties were before you agreed to do it?" Margaret asked.

"What for? It had to be done."

"Oh. Right." Margaret stepped back and admired the poster, which advertised a national march to be held in the state capital in a few months. "I suppose you're going to this march."

"Of course. I'm one of the organizers," Joan said proudly. "How about you?"

"We're going," Arden replied.

For two hours they worked together, sometimes centering a single poster on a lamp pole, sometimes gluing a dozen right next to each other on a wall. They had just finished a block and were about to turn the corner and start on the next one when a man's voice boomed out, "Hold it right there, girls."

In unison they swivelled around. Several yards behind them stood a Chicago police officer, hands on his hips, his uniform proudly proclaiming 'We Serve and Protect.' "What do you girls think you're doing?" he demanded.

"We're putting up posters," Joan answered.

"You don't say," he replied sarcastically.

Arden strode toward him. Margaret called after her, but Arden waved her away and began to speak to the cop in a strange language.

A smile broke across his face as he answered in the same language, and his hands strayed from his gunbelt and hung casually at his sides. They chatted for a long time, and he even laughed once or twice, while Joan and Margaret stared.

His hands moved to his back pocket. "Uh oh, here come the cuffs," Joan hissed, but instead he brought out his wallet and handed Arden a bill. Then he said something that made her laugh, and with a cheery wave, he turned and sauntered away.

Margaret grabbed her arm. "What happened?"

"Nothing. I spoke to him in Polish and explained what we were doing, and he let us go." She handed Joan a five-dollar bill.

"What's this?" She stared at it as if she had never seen one before.

"I asked him for a donation," Arden replied breezily. "He has five daughters."

"How did you know he was Polish?" Margaret demanded.

"He had an accent. Didn't you hear it?"

"You are a bold woman," Joan said with a wide-eyed look of admiration. Margaret was surprised to feel a twinge of jealousy.

"I figured it couldn't hurt to approach him in his native language. But we can't put up any more posters on his beat. He said he'd have to take us in next time."

"We're through for the night anyway," Joan declared. "Come on, let's go to His 'n Hers to celebrate."

"We can put this junk in my car," Arden said. As they headed for the garage, Margaret realized she was still gripping Arden's arm, but she didn't let go.

Joan made the first toast. "To sisterhood." She gave Arden a deep gaze with her Irish setter eyes. "Glad to have you on our side."

Arden clinked glasses and turned to Margaret, one eyebrow raised. "I wouldn't dream of being anywhere else."

OUR DAILY BREAD

Like most WASPs of her generation, Margaret grew up eating a smooth, spongy, snow-white substance she called "bread." It was not until she was in her twenties that she tasted a homemade loaf, fresh from the oven, warm and springy to the touch, the heady aroma only a pale preparation for the rich blend of flavors that burst forth from her first bite. And suddenly she realized: this must be the real thing. This, and not the air-whipped, plastic-wrapped concoction she had always known, must be what the poets refer to when they write about bread.

She had the same experience, tremendously amplified, when she first loved a woman. The revelation exploded in her consciousness: so *this* is love. Suddenly all the romantic books and plays and movies and songs made perfect sense. They were dazzling commercials, but for the wrong product. She remembered her fumbling adolescent attempts to fit into the heterosexual world, and she grieved for her straight friends, condemned to dine on white bread while the banquet awaited just next door.

So it was with mixed feelings that she received the news that Deborah and Paul were getting married.

"But why?" she asked when Deborah came up to tell her.

Deborah sat in the middle of the oval rag rug, her legs stretched out flat against the floor, her head easily dipping to her knees as she performed stretching exercises. "Because we love each other. Why else?"

"I thought maybe you needed a blender or something."

"Remind me to share my good news with you more often."

"I'm sorry." Margaret looked at the floor, wishing she too could hide her face in her knees. "I am happy for you, Deborah. I like Paul, and I think he treats you with respect."

"But?"

"It's just that I want the best for you."

"He's smart, he's funny, he's affectionate, he's good-looking—how much better could he get?"

Margaret took a deep breath. "Deborah, I'm going to say it now and then I won't mention it again. I worry for you. I think in the long run we're all happier when we stick to our own kind."

Deborah sat up abruptly. "Are you referring to the fact that he's black?"

"Oh, for christ's sake, who cares about that?" She waved the question away. "He's male, Deborah. He's not like us. They live in a different world. They speak a different language. How are you ever going to overcome that?"

Deborah responded with a hoot of laughter. "Margaret Osborn, conscience of the world, telling me to stick to my own kind. I should have known you meant women."

"Yes, you should have."

Deborah drew her knees up to her chest and wrapped her arms around them. "I don't mean to get schmaltzy, Margaret, but I want you to understand that he is my kind. He's more my kind than anyone I've ever known. Paul is like . . . like a gift-wrapped box that only I can open. Everybody else sees that he's sweet and gentle, but I'm the only one who gets to see the incredible things that are inside him."

Margaret studied her for a few moments, thinking of the Deborah she knew: funny, warm, generous, independent, but lost to her now, bonded socially and emotionally and soon legally to a man. "I guess that's a pretty good recommendation for Paul," she said finally. "But when the revolution comes, don't forget which side you're on."

"Well, I know better than to ask you to be in the wedding, but I hope you'll come. It'll be in Arden's apartment, on Saturday, May 15th at seven o'clock. Paul and I have already bought Ellen a tiny tuxedo that we saw in the window of a second-hand store. In fact, I think that may be why we're getting married, to give us an excuse to dress her in the little tux. All modesty aside, I'm sure you can imagine how adorable she'll look."

"She'll be pretty cute."

"And next year she'll be living with me, so you'll really get to know her."

"If she's like a little Deborah, that'll be fun."

"Well, she's not. She's like a little Ellen. But it'll still be fun."

As the wedding date approached, Margaret noticed a special spirit in the house, a kind of silent humming. She had her own quiet cause for celebration. She had finished six of the twelve planned chapters for her book and was ready to get outside opinions on her work for the first time. Arden and Deborah had both agreed to read the manuscript, as had Alice and Samantha.

One night Margaret came home from the bookstore and stopped in Arden's apartment on her way upstairs. She found Deborah's curly blond hair and Arden's smooth chestnut hair practically touching as they bent over a clipboard.

"I was wondering when you were going to get here," Arden said. Was it Margaret's imagination, or did Arden seem particularly eager to see her these days? She could not deny the fact that she was thinking about Arden more and more often, and that she felt as though a cloud had passed over the sun whenever Arden left the room.

Of course Margaret recognized these feelings. She had experienced them before for other women, even some as inaccessible as Arden. But she was puzzled by Arden's feelings for her. Sometimes it seemed Arden included Margaret in her general warmth; other times Margaret caught a flash of something special between them. Sometimes she thought she had nothing more than a minor crush on Arden; other times she feared she was in deep trouble.

"We're very depressed because everyone's accepted their invitations to the wedding," Deborah informed her.

"Why should that depress you?" She sat next to Arden and tried to ignore the glow that spread through her body as a result.

"Paul and I wanted our wedding to be a small, intimate affair. Just a few friends and relatives and lots of champagne. But now that everyone's coming, I'm afraid it's going to turn into a big deal."

"Deborah, there are only thirty names on the list," Arden reminded her.

"I know," she said fretfully. "I just worry. We're going to have his parents and my parents, and his two sisters, and my brother, and some of his college friends, and some of my college friends —"

"That's us, you jerk," Arden interrupted her.

Deborah gave her a blank, dazed look, then blinked and laughed at herself. "I don't know what's wrong with me. I'm acting like a bride in one of those wedding magazines."

"How would you know that?" Margaret demanded. "Have you been reading them secretly?"

"I haven't sunk that low. Not yet, anyway."

"Don't your parents get along with his?"

"They're great pals. My parents are so excited to be the first liberals on the block to have black *machetunim*."

"What's that?"

"It's a Yiddish word for the relationship between two sets of parents whose kids are married. The Sterns and the Atwoods, together at last."

"So what is it that worries you about the wedding?" Arden pressed.

"I don't know. I just have this feeling that something might go wrong."

Arden patted her leg. "Don't worry, everything's covered. We've got lists of our lists. All the tasks are delegated. I'm making quiches and the dips for the vegetables. Joe is taking care of the drinks and snacks. Charles is baking the desserts. The wedding couple doesn't have to cook. All they have to do is to keep the guests occupied."

"What's my job?" Margaret asked.

"You're making little hot dogs in blankets."

"That's a joke, right?"

"How about cutting up vegetables and making a fruit salad?"

"Much better."

"Who did you find to perform the ceremony?" Margaret asked Deborah.

"A radical rabbi my mother knows from her Ban the Bomb days. But he's speaking at a benefit the same night, so he has to leave by eight-thirty."

"Unless he's really long-winded, that shouldn't be a problem. The wedding's scheduled for seven," Arden pointed out.

"I know."

"Well, the flowers have been ordered, your mom's wedding dress is being altered, and we all know what we have to do. I guess we can relax for the next few days."

"I think it's nice that you're wearing your mother's dress. What did you wear to your first wedding?"

Arden and Deborah laughed. "Don't ask," said Deborah. "It was some floor-length thing made of Indian cotton, with little round mirrors sewn in here and there. I wanted a dress that I could wear forever, instead of a traditional wedding gown. Little did I know the dress I chose would be out of date in a week."

"It was a very meaningful experience," Arden said solemnly. "She had flowers in her hair. We burned incense. Richard wore a Nehru jacket."

"Oh, Arden, he did not."

"We did burn incense, though."

"Thanks for reminding me. I had almost managed to repress that."

"So what does your ex think about all this?" Margaret asked.

Deborah sighed. "He's dead set against it. He doesn't want Ellen to become 'culturally confused,' as he puts it."

"What does that mean?"

"It means he doesn't want her to start thinking she's black, now that I'm marrying a black man."

"That makes no sense at all."

Deborah shrugged.

"Maybe Richard's afraid that Ellen will love Paul more than she loves him," Arden suggested.

"But that doesn't make sense either," Margaret objected. "Deborah's been living with Paul all this time. It's not like Ellen's going to meet him for the first time at the wedding."

"I know this will come as a shock to you, Margaret, but people's behavior doesn't always make sense," Arden told her.

"I've reassured him over and over again that my marriage won't change our custody agreement," Deborah went on. "As long as Ellen's happy, we'll keep things the way they are. I'm sorry he's upset, I really am. But I can't arrange the rest of my life so he's comfortable with it. I did enough of that when we were married." She looked up at Arden. "You know Richard. What do you think?"

"I agree with you. He's working hard to change his ways, and I give him credit for that. He should work hard; he's got a lot to atone for. But remember how he always had to dramatize his life in some way."

"Right. He was the only salesperson in the world who never made a regular sales call. When he went on the road, he always claimed he was making a speech to a major trade convention, or having lunch with the president of some multi-national corporation."

"Exactly. Maybe he's still dramatizing his connection to you."

"I hope not. That's pretty pathetic."

"He did pine for you a long time after the divorce."

"Yeah, more than he did before the divorce."

"I don't think any experience is real to Richard until he turns it into a story he can tell his friends. And think what a good story this is. His former wife—the only woman he's ever really loved—has spurned his heartfelt attempts to reconcile. Now she's not only marrying another man, but she's dragging his beloved daughter into the certain hell of a mixed marriage. Naturally he'll do whatever is in his power to save his girls from this tragic fate."

"That's pretty good," Deborah admitted. "We're just lucky there's nothing he can do to save us." She gave a rueful laugh. "Richard can be so convincing when he wants to be. The silver screen lost a major talent when he joined the business world."

"Isn't that the truth." Arden tossed her pencil onto the coffee table. "So Margaret, are you bringing a date to this momentous event?" she asked in a tone that might have been just a touch too casual.

"No."

"Are you kidding?" Deborah demanded. "Her friends would be horrified. And our friends would be scared of her friends, just like we used to be scared of Margaret."

"Get a grip on yourself, Deborah. I don't believe you were ever afraid of anyone, much less me."

"It's true," Arden said. "We thought you were one tough dyke."

"Well, I am. So be sure to save a few dances for me. We are having dancing, aren't we?"

"Paul is downstairs right now, recording all our favorite dance music onto cassettes for the party," Deborah said. "By the way, Arden, he wants to bring our stereo up here and take yours downstairs."

"Isn't our stereo good enough for him?"

"Nope. Ours isn't either, but he thinks it's better than yours."

"Well, if he'll take charge of the whole operation, it's okay with me."

Suddenly Deborah shoved the clipboard away. "I'm sick of thinking about this wedding. Let's talk about something else."

"I have another subject," Margaret said shyly. "It's time for you to critique my book."

"I'm ready, but remember we're not real critics."

"You don't even think we're real feminists," Arden added.

"I've got a real editor and a real feminist lined up to read it. But I want to hear your reactions to it too."

"Where's the manuscript?" Deborah asked.

"I'll leave a copy outside your door in the morning on my way downtown. You can read it at work if it's slow."

"What are you up to tomorrow?" Arden asked.

"I have my usual busy social schedule. Breakfast with Alice at seven, a few charming hours with the editing collective, a late afternoon lunch with Joan, and then back at Lucia's Books by six for the evening shift."

"Where you'll be too worn out to work, after all your socializing," Deborah complained.

"Hey, you want me to be popular, don't you?"

"Not too popular," Arden replied.

Margaret had barely swallowed her last bite of avocado and alfalfa sprout sandwich at Mama Peaches when Joan snatched their plates away, whipped a damp rag across the table, and spread piles of papers and envelopes across the surface.

"You don't mind, do you?" she asked. "I thought we could do something with our hands while we talked. Like knitting, only more politically correct."

"What is all this?"

"It's a mass mailing about the march. This is the last one, thank the goddesses. I'm so sick of paper cuts." She took a short stack of form letters, folded the entire pile in thirds, and with machine-like swiftness slid each letter into an envelope.

"No one can say you're not prepared to bleed for the cause." Margaret tried to match her speed, but found it was harder than it looked.

"No, not like that." Joan reached across the table. "If you fold them like this, so the salutation is the first thing they see when they open the envelope, they're more likely to read it."

"I had no idea it was such a complicated process."

"The politics of paper-folding. We spend a lot of time discussing it. Of course, we spend a lot of time doing it, too."

"Aren't there machines to do this kind of thing?"

"Sure. The anti's have them."

"I should have guessed." As they talked, Margaret found herself developing a comfortable rhythm: fold, stuff, stack, fold, stuff, stack. It was satisfying, in a mindless sort of way, to see the batches of completed envelopes filling the table. She only hoped Joan wasn't going to ask her to lick them.

"So how many *Feminist Times* reporters will be covering the march?" Joan asked.

"Well, none, actually."

"What do you mean?"

"We discussed it this morning at the editorial meeting. The editing collective feels that the march will be covered by the straight press, and that we should spend our limited resources on issues that our readers won't see elsewhere."

"That's the biggest line of bullshit I ever heard." Joan shoved a letter into an envelope with such vehemence that it skittered off the table. "You people need to climb out of your hole and look around. And if the editorial collective is too stupid to see what's really happening, you should apply your talents somewhere else, Margaret."

"What do you think we'd see if we climbed out?"

"That this is no time for personal solutions. This is a time for political action. I know the idea of lobbying legislators is gross. It pisses me off that we have to ask them for our rights. But if we want this amendment passed, they're the only ones who have the power to do it, so we have to convince them in their own terms."

"Do you really think things will change if the ERA is passed?"

"Yes, I do. Short of a revolution, the ERA is the only way to force the men in power to treat women equally whether they want to or not."

"I don't know. It makes sense when you talk about it, but I can't get fired up to all this talk about vote counts and three-fifths majorities."

"Well, you should, because it's your life they're voting on."

"And then there are the people who seem to represent the issue. You know, those NOW types in their little bow ties and their shiny leather pumps. How can you stand working with them?"

Joan laughed. "Margaret, you wouldn't believe how many fantastic women I've met in this campaign. And a lot of them are dykes. It's like paradise, working on a feminist issue with all these intense, committed women. You probably feel the same about the newspaper."

Margaret grimaced as she thought about her battles with the editing collective. "What's so important about having *Feminist Times* cover the march? It seems like you'd get much more mileage out of the boys' press."

"You know how they cover women's events. Equal time for the thousands who attend the march and for the six who show up to protest it." She piled Margaret's finished envelopes into a box and handed her another stack.

"Yeah, but we're a monthly. The article wouldn't be out until July at the earliest."

"So? You think the fight will be over by then?"

"I guess not."

Joan mesmerized Margaret with one of her fervent, saintly stares. "This is what's happening now, in our time. Think of the feminists in the first wave, Margaret. Most of them are dead. Most of their writings are lost. How do we even know they existed? Because they left us the nineteenth amendment. Thanks to them, we have the right to march into that booth and vote these pigs out of office."

"And vote our own pigs in," she joked.

Joan ignored her. "It's great to have our moon rituals and our menstrual sponges and our women-only spaces. But this is a movement, and movements should move. If your paper doesn't think the ERA is important, you're failing your readers. Anyway, you're going, aren't you? Arden said you were."

"We'll be there."

"Then bring your notebook. Just write the story like it was an assignment, and maybe they'll run it anyway."

"Do you know how much work it is to write a story that no one's going to publish?" Margaret asked incredulously.

"Do you know how much trouble it is to organize a march that no one's going to cover?" Joan mimicked.

"Okay," she laughed, "I'll write the story. Maybe it'll develop into a good chapter for my book."

"Oh no. You're not writing about the power structure of this campaign. There are some things that only insiders should know."

"Bad things?"

"I'm not going to tell you. If you want the inside story, you can get involved."

"I never knew you were so devious, Joan."

"A person can change a lot in twelve years."

As Deborah and Paul's wedding date loomed, the housemates cleaned all three floors as if preparing for a military inspection. "It's Paul's mother," Deborah explained as she and Margaret washed out her fireplace. "Everything in her house is spotless all the time. I don't want her to think we're slobs."

"Don't ever tell Deborah that I told you this," Paul grunted as he climbed the rickety wooden ladder, "but her parents had a maid when she was growing up. A black maid. So everything in her house was always whiter than white, pardon the expression." Margaret handed him a bucket of eye-stinging ammonia mixed with hot water, and steadied the ladder as he washed the window.

"You know, Deborah and I could both be making a lot more money if we wanted, but we made some other choices about what was important to us. I don't want her parents to look around and worry that we made the wrong decision." He handed Margaret the bucket and climbed down.

"Joe is one of those guys who notices clutter but not dirt," Arden said as they stood at her kitchen sink washing and drying her best dishes. "As long as everything's tidy, he never thinks of cleaning. Charles, on the other hand, is fastidious. He likes everything to look just right. When he bakes one of his elaborate desserts, he wants it served on the finest china. Of course, we don't have the finest china, but we can shine up what we've got." She held up a large, white oval tray she had just finished drying. "This ought to look good filled with pastries."

"Arden is kind of a perfectionist," Charles informed Margaret as they stood side by side dusting the dark wooden doors that led to their apartments. "Haven't you ever noticed that about her?"

"I'm not sure what you mean."

"Well, like when she serves food. Not only is her cooking wonderful, but her presentation is superb. She always arranges the table so it looks like a picture in a magazine."

"Yes, I guess I have noticed that. I like it."

"You like pretty much everything about her, don't you?" he said with one of his slow smiles.

"What do you think, doctor? You've known her all her life. Is my case hopeless?"

He poured a little Brasso® on his rag and bent to polish the door knob. "Let me put it this way. I don't believe the issue has come up before, but I'm not sure it would be entirely unwelcome."

"Gee, thanks. That's a lot of help."

Charles straightened up and slid his glasses back in place with one finger. "Sorry. That's the best I can do. Next move is yours." He handed her the can of Brasso.

On the day of the wedding, Margaret worked in the bookstore from ten to two. She could imagine all the frenzied cleaning, cooking, and checking of details that must be taking place while she contentedly inventoried paperbacks.

For Margaret, the wedding itself was fraught with ambivalence. Of course she was happy for Deborah and Paul. On the other hand, she felt that Deborah had officially declared her allegiance to the other side in a battle she refused to acknowledge, although it was raging all around her. And Margaret hated all the pageantry of heterosexual ritual. She knew that as weddings go, this one was very simple: a brief ceremony in a friend's home performed by a rabbi who had a more pressing engagement later that evening. Still, the trappings were there, although they had been refined to mere hints.

Arden phoned as Margaret was preparing to turn the shop over to Elaine. "Can you take my car and pick up the champagne? There's a place downtown that's having a good sale."

"Can I use someone else's car? I don't know how to drive a stick shift."

"Oh, shit. Paul's picking up his parents at the airport, Deborah's running some errands in Joe's car, and Charles has a stick shift too." She sighed. "I guess I'll have to send Joe. God knows what he'll come home with."

"Write him a list."

Arden gave a resigned laugh. "A lot of good that'll do. Well, get home as soon as you can. You've got a lot of vegetables waiting for you."

After she had cleaned and sliced acres of carrots, celery, cauliflower, and broccoli, Margaret tried to arrange the vegetables artistically, the way Arden would. Next she went to work cutting up fresh fruit and mixing it in the large glass bowl Deborah's mother had provided.

She was sprinkling lemon juice over the fruit when she heard heavy footsteps approaching. "Margaret?" Joe called from the open front door.

"I'm in the kitchen. Come on in."

He squeezed into the doorway, arms wrapped protectively around a grocery bag. They laughed as they realized there was no space for both of them in the tiny room. "Are those ready to go?" He nodded toward the bowls.

"As soon as I cover them."

"Good, I'll take them downstairs. Can you fit four bottles of wine in your refrigerator?"

"Sure. But I thought all the liquor for the party was staying in your apartment."

"This is special. Careful, it's heavy." He handed her the bag.

"What is it?"

"It's Dom Perignon, the Rolls Royce of champagne. There was a fantastic sale on it, so I thought I'd buy some as a surprise. After all the guests have gone and we can relax, we'll open the good stuff. I got it for only seventy dollars a bottle."

"Seventy dollars a bottle! Can you really tell the difference?"

"You bet. Now don't tell Arden. She loves surprises." He grabbed the bowls. "See you later."

As evening fell, everyone gathered in Arden's living room, now alien in its elegance. All vestiges of daily life had been erased. No longer could one find a phone message stuck to the mirror, a roll of stamps on the shelf, a book left face-down on the couch. Even the records and tapes stood upright in their racks. The wooden floor gleamed, the tables were fragrant with furniture polish. Small bowls of pastel mints dotted the room. In the spotless brick fireplace, a tall vase of white gladiolus fanned out like a demure flame.

The residents of the house had been transformed too, clustered together in their finest clothes. Deborah looked beautiful in a floor-length gown the color of aged ivory. Her blond curly hair was brushed back from her face and held in place by a mother-of-pearl comb on either side of her head.

Next to her stood Paul, proud and jittery in a black tuxedo with a jaunty peacock-blue cummerbund and bow tie. "I wish we could sit down and have a drink or something," he said, "but I know the minute we do the doorbell will ring. Or I'll spill on my shirt. Or both."

"Where is Richard?" Deborah asked for the second time. "He promised to drop Ellen off at six-thirty."

"When have you ever known Richard to be on time?" Arden replied reasonably. "Relax."

The buzzer sounded, and they all jumped. "That's probably him now," Charles reassured her as Joe went to answer the door. But it was Mr. and Mrs. Stern with the rabbi in tow.

By the time all the greetings and introductions had been completed, more guests had appeared, and the round of kisses and exclamations started all over again. Finally it was seven-fifteen, and the rabbi was glancing at his watch, and Ellen still had not arrived.

"I'll call him," Charles murmured into Deborah's ear as she introduced her brother to Paul's sisters. A few moments later he returned and said quietly, "No answer. He must be on the way."

The room felt stuffy despite the fresh spring air. The guests seemed intent on shouting over one another. Laughter clattered like falling silverware. As the minutes ticked on, Deborah, Arden, and Charles kept exchanging glances like small electrical shocks. Finally Margaret saw Deborah hurry into Arden's room and close the door.

Soon Deborah came striding out of the bedroom. She spoke in a clipped whisper. "Arden, I just talked to the bastard. He decided not to let Ellen come to the wedding. I'm going to get her."

"I'll go. You should stay here."

"No, I have to handle this myself. You know how he can be."

"Well, at least take someone with you for moral support."

"And give Richard an audience? No thanks. I'd rather go alone." She beckoned to her brother. "Alan, go talk to the rabbi and keep him cool. I know he has to leave soon. This will only take a few minutes. And Alan, don't let Mom and Dad worry."

"Like I could stop them," he muttered, and sauntered over to the rabbi. Deborah spoke briefly to Paul and then slipped out the door. The news of her absence spread quickly, and Paul turned up the classical music to hide the edge of panic that was creeping into the party babble.

The minutes dragged to eight o'clock and then eight-fifteen. The rabbi was in deep conversation with the groom and both sets of parents, the bride was nowhere to be found, and it was no longer possible to hide the fact that something serious had gone wrong.

When the phone rang, it sliced through the brittle party talk. The crowd fell silent as Arden hurried to her bedroom to answer it, and then the chatter resumed even more loudly as everyone pretended that they had not been trying to hear Arden's conversation.

A few moments later, she stuck her head out of the bedroom and beckoned to Joe, Charles, and Margaret. "Excuse me, Paul?" Arden called sweetly. "Could you come here for a moment?" He hurried over. "Don't worry, folks," she said brightly to the crowd that now stood silent, staring at her. "We just have a little problem. Nothing serious. You'll be throwing rice before you know it."

They retreated to her bedroom. Arden closed the door and leaned against it. "Richard won't let Ellen go to the wedding, and Deborah won't leave without her."

"Damn him!" Paul socked his fist into his hand. "That man is too stubborn to live."

"I agree, but maybe Deborah's being a little stubborn too," Joe suggested cautiously. "Couldn't she come home now, and fight about Ellen later?"

Paul eyed him coldly. "I think Deborah has a right to have her own daughter attend her wedding."

"Does she, Joe?" Charles asked. "I mean, legally?" he added quickly.

Joe hesitated, wiping his hand across his mouth. "I don't know much about this area of law, but I think if it's not her weekend to have custody, she can't compel him to let Ellen attend."

"You guys are missing the point," Arden said impatiently. "The rabbi has to leave in fifteen minutes. After that it won't matter if Ellen's here or not."

"Couldn't Mrs. Stern convince him to stay just a few minutes more?" Charles suggested.

Paul shook his head. "He's told me a hundred times he's got to leave at eight-thirty."

"Paul, don't your parents know any ministers?" Margaret asked.

He tugged on his mustache. "None that would run over here at the last minute to marry me to a white Jew."

"A judge!" Arden exclaimed, turning to Joe.

He held up his hands. "It's Saturday night. It would take me hours to find one, even if I could convince one to come out here."

"I've got it." Charles snapped his fingers. "Why don't we take the rabbi over to Richard's house and do it there?"

"That's out," Paul snapped.

"Well, I'm going over to Richard's," Arden declared, pulling a sweater out of her closet.

"To convince Deborah to come back?" Margaret asked.

"That would be pointless. I'm going to try to persuade Richard to let Ellen go."

"Not that it will make any difference," Paul said miserably. "The rabbi will be long gone."

Margaret turned uncertainly to Paul. "I may—*may*—be able to find a minister who would come over here and marry you tonight."

His face lit up. "Then get going!"

"But it's a long shot."

"Try it!"

"Here, take this." Arden tossed her a jacket. "You can use Joe's car."

"Keys are on my dresser," he said.

"Should I go with you?" Charles offered.

Arden interrupted, "No, I need your help with Richard. Paul and Joe, you guys will have try to keep things under control here."

Margaret raced to the north side where the Metropolitan Community Church, the city's gay church, would just be concluding services. She had interviewed one of the ministers for *Feminist Times* and had spent some time with her at the coffeehouse and other women's events. If Margaret could find her, maybe Emma would agree to perform this ceremony.

She was a little embarrassed to be enmeshed in such an alien rite, but if this wedding was so important to Deborah,

she would do what she could to help. And her own pride was
involved too. Tonight she had seen how smoothly Arden took
control of the situation, just as she had taken control of the
situation with the Polish policeman. She had also seen exactly
how the Lill Street crowd functioned as a group and how
superfluous she was to those dynamics. It would not do any
harm to whatever was blossoming between Arden and
Margaret if she could demonstrate her own ability to handle a
crisis.

She rushed into the MCC building as the churchgoers
streamed out. Emma was standing near the door, talking to a
few stragglers, her round face relaxed and smiling. Margaret
took her arm and pulled her aside. "Emma, I don't have time
to explain now, but could you come with me tonight and
perform kind of an emergency wedding?"

"Why, Margaret, have you gotten some woman in trouble?"
She had to laugh. "No, but a friend of mine is in trouble."

Emma listened to Margaret's tale, leaning her big,
comfortable body against the wall as if she was in for a long
night. "Are you sure they'd want a minister to pinch hit?
Jewish folks usually don't go in for that."

"Only the bride is Jewish. The groom is—I don't know
what he is, but he's not Jewish. So I figured if you were
available, you might marry them."

Emma thought about it for a moment, and a smile broke
across her face and lifted her sandy eyebrows. "Well, it's
certainly the most interesting offer I've had today. I'll get my
coat."

"Thanks, Emma."

"Since when did you become so intrigued with the fortunes
of straight folks?" Emma asked as they drove back to Lill
Street. "Last time we talked you were spouting a pretty
separatist line. In fact, you were furious at the last 'Take Back
the Night' march because men were involved."

"I still don't think men have any place at 'Take Back the
Night' events," she replied. "But I guess I've gotten a little more
lenient on other issues. I'm not necessarily proud of it."

Emma gave Margaret a speculative look. "Is it possible that
one of these days I'll hear a sickeningly contrite apology for
some of the cutting things you've said in print about my
attempts at community outreach?"

Margaret grinned. "It's possible. But either way, thanks a
lot for coming tonight."

"Hey, I want to see how it all turns out. This is better than the soaps."

All conversation ceased when the two women stepped into the crowded living room. Margaret could feel Emma behind her, a solid, comforting presence, but she couldn't think of a single thing to say. Finally Arden moved toward her and broke the spell. "Everyone," Margaret announced, "this is Reverend Emma Taylor."

"All right!" Paul yelled from across the room. The silence split into a dozen noisy conversations. Someone popped open a champagne bottle, Charles slipped another tape into the cassette deck, Deborah took Emma into a corner to meet the wedding party, and Margaret sank into a chair.

"Here's to you," Arden said, handing Margaret a glass and taking a sip from her own. "Not only is she politically correct, but she's so resourceful." She perched on the arm of Margaret's chair.

"Well, thanks, but you're the resourceful one. How did you pry Ellen away from Richard?"

"We reminisced about a few of the things he did to Deborah while they were married. The man's had a guilty conscience for so long he forgets to pay attention to it. I just reminded him."

"And it worked?"

Arden waved a hand toward Ellen, with her dark eyes and glossy dark hair, leaning against her mother, smiling and proud in her little tuxedo. "It worked. And a lucky thing, too, because I think Deborah was about to punch him out."

Margaret pictured Deborah, with her sweet smile and her strong arms, pushing up the sleeve of her wedding gown to sock her ex-husband.

"It is a funny thought, isn't it," Arden said as if she could read Margaret's mind. "Maybe I should have stayed out of it."

"No, you did the right thing," Margaret looked up at her, "as usual. But do you think he'll come here later and try to disrupt things?"

Charles sauntered over and draped his arm casually across Arden's shoulders. "He can try," he chortled. "While Arden was inside with Richard, I was in the garage removing his distributor cap. God, crime is fun! If I didn't have such a pacific nature, I could really get into this."

"Charles, I had no idea you knew how to do things like that. I'm so impressed."

"Hey, I'm a man. We're born knowing our way around an engine. Didn't you know that?"

"I forgot for a minute."

"Oh, you girls are so forgetful. No wonder you can't get any good jobs."

Arden gave him a little peck on the cheek. "Just don't *you* forget that you have to go back there tonight and put that thing back in, Tarzan."

"Okay, folks, we're ready," Emma called out. The guests shuffled to their places. Emma opened her prayer book and gave everyone a big grin, as if they were all in on a good joke.

Margaret was never able to remember the rest of that night, only the outline and a few of the details: Deborah and Paul hugging each of the guests; the raucous party, with windows and floorboards vibrating to the Motown music; Deborah in the center of the room dancing wildly with Paul's mother while his father and Mrs. Stern two-stepped sedately beside them; the furious look Arden shot Joe when he broke open the Dom Perignon; the glass of champagne Margaret shared with Arden, too dazed by her closeness to remember that it cost seventy dollars a bottle; Charles giving her a big wink as he sailed past with Emma; Joe cutting in as Margaret and Arden danced to "You Keep Me Hanging On"; the guests trickling away, leaving the apartment a shambles of empty glasses and filled ashtrays.

Arden and Margaret drove Emma home. "I know it's none of my business," Emma began, scooting forward and leaning her arms congenially on the back of their seats, "but since I was involved in this fascinating escapade anyway, how in the world did you get Deborah's ex to let the little girl go? Either you've got a touch of the blarney stone in you—which wouldn't surprise me a bit—or you've got something on him."

Arden hesitated for a moment. "Well, you know Ellen is the most important thing in Richard's life. So I took him into another room and told him about the night she was born."

"But why would that have any effect on Richard now, after all these years?" Margaret demanded.

"Because I reminded him of where he was that night while I was with Deborah."

"Where was he?" Emma asked.

"In New Orleans. With another woman."

"Okay, the guy is slime," Margaret said. "But why would that make him change his mind tonight?"

"Don't you understand? I reminded him of one of his worst sins just as he was about to commit another one."

As the three of them talked, Arden kept glancing at Margaret. She had an odd expression, as if she were about to laugh or cry and couldn't decide which. Finally she took her right hand off the steering wheel and slipped it into Margaret's.

Margaret's heart leaped and she squeezed Arden's hand, meeting her ironic smile.

"So how long have you two been together?" Emma asked in her hearty, friendly, tactless way.

"Not long," Arden answered easily. "In fact, you might say this was our first date."

It was very late when they dropped Emma off and turned back toward Lill Street. Traffic was light and the only sound was the rattling of the old Honda.

"This is not going to be easy," Arden said quietly.

"What?"

"You and me."

"How do you know? Maybe it will be."

"There are a lot of things you don't know about me."

Margaret glanced at Arden but could barely see her strong profile in the dark car. "Then we'll learn about each other. That's the fun of it."

"I don't think I'm a lesbian. I don't know if I want to be. But I do feel something for you, I think."

Margaret laughed and took her hand. "What an impassioned declaration. As you told Emma, this is just our first date. Let's take it slowly and let it unfold, like a good novel."

"I hope we read the same language."

"Maybe we'll invent a new one."

"You're so optimistic, I can hardly stand it."

"If you knew what I know, you'd be optimistic too."

"What do you know?"

Margaret wanted to tell her about the banquet, about the whole tender, tempestuous, emotional, contentious, fulfilling world waiting behind the door marked 'Women Only.' But instead she smiled and said, "Wait and see."

THE FIRST NIGHT

Late on a Thursday night, a few days after Deborah's wedding, Margaret watched her clothes tumble in the laundromat's dryer and told herself to stop brooding about Arden.

The fact that she hadn't been alone with her for one minute since the wedding didn't necessarily mean anything. Margaret had made her offer, sort of, and Arden could take it or leave it. All that rapture and passion and talking in the dark that Margaret had envisioned with her—who needed it? She had her politics to keep her warm.

Thus fortified, she leaned back and opened the latest issue of *off our backs*. The rumble of the machines and the gentle vibration of her plastic chair made her feel as if she were on a train, rolling comfortably to nowhere in particular.

The laundromat was empty except for one other person, a young woman with curly light brown hair and mischievous blue eyes. After several minutes she approached Margaret. "Would you help me fold these sheets?"

"Sure." Margaret took one end of a warm sheet and folded it with her. The woman pulled another sheet out of the dryer, and they repeated the ritual, moving closer with each pleat.

"Now would you like to help me mess them up?" she offered, looking into Margaret's eyes with the same playful expression.

"Uh, no thanks," she stammered, shoving the sheet into her hands and stepping back hastily.

"Don't tell me you don't swing."

"Swing? No. No, I don't."

She shrugged, laying the sheets in her basket. "Oh well.
Maybe next time."

Margaret considered trying to explain to her that sex
between women was an important event, a political act, almost
a sacred experience—certainly not a frolic to be discussed over
hot sheets in an empty laundromat. But by the time she got her
thoughts together, the woman was gone.

She hardly had time to settle back with her newspaper
when the door behind her opened again. Margaret groaned
inwardly, wondering who had arrived to interrupt her solitude
now.

"I thought I'd find you here," a familiar voice said. She
whirled around, and there stood Arden, jingling her keys and
leaning against the large front window of the laundromat, a
manila envelope tucked under her arm. She was wearing faded
jeans and a baggy red sweatshirt. Margaret thought she had
never seen anyone look so good.

"What are you doing here?"

"I came to talk to you. Also, I didn't want you walking
home alone at this hour."

"Well, thanks, but I've always walked home."

"Not since you've been mine."

Margaret gaped up at her. "Am I yours?"

"I don't know. That's what I wanted to talk to you about."

God, she was bold. Margaret stared at her, speechless with
admiration.

Arden pulled a scratched plastic chair over and sat facing
Margaret, clutching her envelope. She waited.

Finally Margaret blurted, "Arden, I've hardly seen you
since the night—since the wedding. I thought I'd scared you
off. Then I thought, no, maybe she just needs some time to
think things through. Then I thought—never mind what I
thought. Where have you been?"

"I've been hiding in my apartment, doing all of the above.
Being scared, and being excited, and thinking it over. And I've
been reading this." She patted the envelope.

"What is it?"

"Your manuscript."

Margaret caught her breath. "Well, what did you think?"

"I loved it. I thought it was very, very you—serious and
thoughtful, but with a dry little joke popping up every now
and then. And I learned a lot too, about the women's groups in

town, and about the effort that goes into trying to make sure the right decisions get made for the right reasons." She sighed.

"Uh oh. Sounds like you're getting scared again."

"A little bit," Arden admitted, looking at the grimy linoleum floor.

"But why? What is there about my book that scares you?"

"I don't know. I guess it gave me some insight into the way you think, and I'm not sure I want to analyze everything the way you do. I'm not sure I have it in me."

"Why should you? I'm not trying to mold you into my own likeness."

Arden gave Margaret one of her wry smiles. "Well, I'm someone who doesn't get involved with women, so you're going to have to do some molding somewhere if this is going to work."

"That's where you're wrong. You've always been involved with women. You're much closer to Deborah than to Joe, for example."

"Now I am. It wasn't always like that."

"Maybe not. But anyway, I'm not going to mold you or push you into anything. I just want us to get to know each other, and if that leads to . . . well, we'll see where it leads."

"Leads us to the bedroom, you were going to say."

Margaret laughed and hitched her chair closer. "Look, Arden, I feel something for you. Let's call it X."

"How very romantic."

"And you, I hope, feel something for me. Let's call it Y."

"Why can't it be X, like your feeling?"

"Maybe it is. I don't know yet. All I'm saying is, let's take it slowly, whatever it is."

Arden sat back abruptly and looked away.

"What's wrong?"

She shook her head.

"What is it?"

She clasped her hands in her lap and stared down at them. "I feel really stupid."

"Why?"

"I think I might have made a terrible mistake."

Margaret gripped her arm. "Arden, what are you talking about?" Here we are, she thought, two women who work with words every day of our lives, and now when it's important we can't communicate.

Arden looked up at Margaret, then let her gaze slide away toward the line of empty dryers, their glass doors hanging open like the shutters of abandoned houses. "I've been experiencing something that I never felt for a woman before."

"You mean like . . ." This is no time for cowardice, Margaret told herself, and forced the words out. "Sort of like beginning to fall in love, in a way."

Arden nodded and turned toward her again. "And I thought that's what you were feeling too. But now that I hear you say we should take things slowly and see where we end up, I realize that's probably not what you were talking about at all. And I just assumed that's what was happening because you're a lesbian."

"No, you're wrong. I mean you're right. I mean—I don't know what I mean.

"I *am* falling in love with you, Arden, or whatever phrase you want to use. I'm very attracted to you. If my sheets were dry, I'd invite you up to my place right now," she joked feebly. "But I think we should be careful. This is new for you, so I want you to be sure of what you feel. And I don't want to get my heart broken."

"Neither do I."

"I would never break your heart."

"I've heard that before."

"I know this isn't your first experience with romance, Arden, but I promise you it's going to be different."

"I believe you."

"But you're still scared."

"Does it show?" Arden put her hands up to her cheeks to feel her expression, or perhaps to hide it.

"Arden, I want you to know that we don't have to be lovers. I hope we will be, but if things don't work out that way, I could settle for friendship with you and still feel pretty lucky."

"For a tough dyke, you can be very sweet."

"For a straight woman, you can be very tough."

"You know, Margaret, I'm not as brave as you think I am. In some ways I'm very timid. And I haven't always had the best luck in affairs of the heart."

"Neither have I," replied Margaret. "But that was the past. This is the future."

"And this is a present." Arden closed her eyes and leaned toward her.

As if in slow motion, Margaret watched Arden's eyelashes sweep down and lie fluttering on her skin. She realized how long they were and wondered why she had never noticed before. She thought that only a straight woman would choose a lighted window in a public place as the scene of their first kiss. All this passed through her mind in a split second. After that Margaret was only aware of Arden: her clean, powdery smell; her thick, soft hair; the sweet indentation on the back of her neck; her passions, her dreams, her mysteries, everything, everything about her that Margaret was longing to explore.

The heavy manuscript slid off Arden's lap and hit the floor with a smack. They leapt apart.

"Did I pass?" asked Arden.

"Flying colors." Margaret was surprised her voice sounded so natural.

"Yeah, so did you."

"Were you scared?"

"A little bit. It was easy, though."

"That's how it's always going to be with us," Margaret said earnestly.

"Sometimes you sound so young. Come on, I'll take you home." Arden picked up the envelope. Margaret stumbled to the door behind her. "Margaret, aren't you forgetting something?"

"What?"

"Your laundry."

"Oh. Right."

They parted outside Arden's door. Mechanically, Margaret climbed the creaky stairs to her own apartment, lost in that particular fog of new romance.

Margaret remembers that night very clearly: the way a dreamy light burnished all the homely objects in her apartment, and even her primly folded sheets and towels seemed to emanate a kind of magic as she tucked them into her cardboard dresser.

She feels no such magic now. Instead the afternoon light reveals piles of Margaret's faded sweaters, her unpublished articles, her unanswered mail: all the evidence of Margaret's shortcomings and fallibility that Gwen must not yet have seen, or she would not want Margaret so much. To stop herself from dumping out the moving cartons and stuffing everything back in her drawers, Margaret replays in her head the sound of Gwen's

warm, humorous voice when she said— seriously for once—
"Margaret, it's time for us to move in or move on. I'm getting too
old to date."

The relationship she has built with Gwen is not the teetering,
newborn thing Margaret knew that night on Lill Street. It is sturdy,
mature, based on compatibility and compromise. Why, then, is
she so scared? What is the difference between that day and this
one?

She was young then, and the idea of growing to love
someone did not carry with it the baggage of fatigue and defeat
that one accumulates with experience. Margaret had not yet
learned to ask herself whether she had the strength to embark on
that journey one more time.

"I heard an interesting tale from Emma last week," said
Samantha. She and her housemates had just finished their first
dinner in Margaret's new apartment. Samantha leaned back in
her folding chair and placed her tiny feet in Lucy's lap. From
her hot pink ballet slippers to her baby blue overalls and bright
yellow t-shirt, she looked like a spring garden. Only the
laughing look in Samantha's brown eyes warned Margaret she
was in for trouble.

"I didn't know you knew Emma," Margaret replied,
pushing away her empty plate.

"Oh yes. For many years."

"She belongs to our co-op," Lucy added.

"Why, Samantha, whatever did you hear?" asked Maureen
with exaggerated innocence.

"I'm glad you asked that, Mo. It seems that our little
Margaret has been instrumental in helping a neighbor of hers
get yoked to a man. It seems furthermore that while she was
doing this, Margaret was busy making eyes at a sister of the
straight persuasion who, oddly enough, was making eyes back
at her."

"And I thought ministers were supposed to keep everything
confidential," Margaret muttered, reaching over to refill Kay's
wine glass.

"That's only if you confide in them," Kay replied. "You
didn't confide in her, did you?"

"Not exactly."

"I knew this would happen," Donna said, pulling the bowl of pasta primavera toward her and picking out the remaining pea pods. "First you move to the suburbs. Then you fall in love with a straight woman."

"I am not in love," Margaret maintained indignantly. "At least, not yet."

"Oh, puh-leese," Samantha groaned. "You're shining so bright you're practically radioactive. Where are my shades?" She patted the many pockets of her overalls.

"Maybe in those packages you brought," Margaret suggested coyly. "What's in there, anyway?"

"Never you mind. You'll see soon enough."

"Is she attracted to you?" Maureen asked with her quiet intensity. "I mean to you, and not to whatever it is she thinks you represent."

"I think so, but how can you be sure about that?"

"Oh, you can be sure," she replied, trading smiles with her lover Kay.

"Straight women sometimes have secret motives," Lucy offered uncomfortably. She ran a hand through her do-it-yourself haircut, leaving blond hair spiking in all directions. "I mean, I'm sure you've thought about this, and I don't want to upset you, but you know how sometimes they want to have affairs with us just as an adventure."

"Or an experiment," Kay added.

"Or to polish up their feminist credentials," Maureen said.

"Or to make sure they'll have a good time in bed for once," Donna yawned.

"I know about all that," Margaret exclaimed, rising to clear the table. Kay stood too but Margaret waved her back to her seat. "I just think Arden is different."

"Well, I trust your judgment." Samantha handed over her empty plate. "Let's not forget, we were all straight once. I was older than Arden—and married—when I met my first woman lover. Where would I be now if she hadn't taken a chance on me?"

"President of the Junior League," Lucy suggested.

"Or the DAR," Maureen said.

"Ever since I made the mistake of confessing that my family came over on the Mayflower, you can't stop reminding me that your family was here first," Samantha complained good-naturedly. "And look what we have to thank you for."

She reached across the table and shook Donna's pack of cigarettes.

"More than we have to thank you for," Maureen replied without a smile.

"True enough."

Kay stacked her plate on top of Maureen's and handed them to Margaret. "How are her politics?" she asked.

"Kind of liberal."

"That figures," Donna said sourly.

"But why should we all have to be the same?" Margaret demanded from the kitchen. She plunked the dishes in the sink and bustled back into the room. "What's wrong with relating to people whose ideas are different from ours? Maybe she'll change, just like we changed. Maybe I'll learn something from her. Maybe ten years from now we'll look back at the things we believe today and wonder how we could have been so wrong-headed."

"Look out! She's armed and dangerous." Samantha touched Margaret's shoulder and blew on her fingers as if she'd been burned.

"I have just one question," Lucy said soberly. "Does she have the glow?"

"What glow?" Donna asked. She plucked one last mushroom before Margaret grabbed the bowl away.

"You know, the Lesbian Feminist Glow. Margaret, wasn't it your friend Alice who invented that term?"

"Yeah, and she's the walking personification of it, too," Kay answered promptly.

"What's that supposed to mean?" Maureen demanded.

Kay laughed, a dimple popping into one cheek like an exclamation point. "Don't you worry your pretty little head about it," she cooed, putting her arm around Maureen's shoulders.

"If you two wouldn't mind interrupting your perpetual honeymoon for a few moments," Donna said mildly, "I'd like to hear about this glow. What is it? Do I have it?"

"Sure." Margaret sat down and slid an ashtray to Donna. "We all do. It's that special air of confidence or strength that lesbian feminists have. Sometimes you can see it in women's faces, or in the way they walk."

"So does Arden have the glow or doesn't she?" Lucy repeated.

She hesitated. "No, but she has other things. She has warmth. She has presence. She has—oh, I don't know, some kind of complexity or something."

"Very eloquent," Lucy observed.

"Yes, even Emma was impressed with her—what was it—" Samantha squinted, "self-assurance, I think she said."

"That's it. She's an adult," Margaret exclaimed. "I never realized it until just now, but I think that's what first attracted me to her."

"Well, those of us in the gray-haired crowd enjoy hearing that from you youngsters." Samantha gave her bushy hair a coquettish pat.

"But she's still straight," Donna said firmly and lit a cigarette. "Drop her and find yourself a nice dyke. There are plenty of us out there."

"Always room for one more," Samantha added sweetly.

"So when do we get to meet this wonder woman?" Kay asked.

"Soon."

"Tonight?"

"Not that soon."

"Chickenshit," Donna snorted.

"I know. I wanted to tell you about her before I subjected her to your scrutiny."

"Well, I guess we have no choice then," Samantha sighed.

"About what?" Margaret asked.

"If you won't talk about your new girlfriend any more, we'll just have to open the presents."

Amidst a general clamor of assent, Samantha pounced on the large brown shopping bag and dragged it to the table. "Let's see. What have we here?" she asked avidly. "First of all, dessert." She handed a foil-wrapped package to Donna. "Second, drugs." She tossed a couple of joints onto the table.

"Always a welcome addition," Lucy said drily.

"Third, a gift from all of us." Samantha pulled out a bulky sack and placed it in Margaret's lap.

Margaret peered into the sack and unfolded a beautiful tapestry of the night sky, presided over by a sanguine moon goddess. "This is gorgeous," she breathed, studying its shades of lavender, pink, purple and silver. "Thank you. I love it." She ran her fingers lightly over the threads of varied textures.

"Now don't wear it out," Lucy chided. "Let's hang it."

"In the office," Margaret suggested. "That's where I spend the most time."

Kay and Samantha exchanged glances. It was clear they had already chosen a spot for their work. "We think the living room needs a little adornment," Samantha said diplomatically. "How about right over here?" She stood against the wall and spread her arms in the blank spot between the bedroom and office doors.

"Perfect," Margaret acquiesced, and went to find a hammer.

"We've been working on this wall-hanging since you first mentioned you needed a new apartment," Kay told her later. She took a delicate puff of the joint and handed it to Maureen.

"I think our next project should be to paint these folding chairs," Samantha mused. "What colors do you like?"

"You're acting like my neighbor Deborah. Why does everyone want to decorate my apartment for me?"

"Because it's fun," Lucy replied. "Besides, you don't care about these things."

"Should I?"

"No," answered Maureen. "Yes," Donna asserted at the same time.

"What difference does it make?" Kay asked. "If you don't mind letting your friends treat your apartment like a doll house, might as well humor them."

"But if you do mind, speak up," Maureen admonished firmly.

Margaret smiled at her across the table. She loved to look at Maureen, with her stern beauty. Her features were so clear-cut: black eyes, sharp nose, cheekbones like two shelves, a straight curtain of blue-black hair on either side of her face. And her vision was equally clear-cut. She seemed unacquainted with the doubts, uncertainties, and vacillations that nipped at Margaret's heels more and more frequently as she tried to follow the one true path.

"Hey, I almost forgot," Samantha exclaimed, biting into a second piece of carrot cake. "There's one more package in that bag for you, Margaret."

Lucy reached into the bag and handed her a box. Inside Margaret found her manuscript, peppered with comments marked in red felt-tip pen in Samantha's tidy private-school printing. "Oh, Samantha, thank you." She riffled through the pages. "Your opinion means a lot to me. I can tell you really put some time into this."

"You should have seen her," Kay said. "Every night for a week she sat with Barry and Jill at the dining room table and they did their homework together. I wish we had a camera."

"It was pretty adorable," Lucy agreed.

"I thought you did a really good job," Samantha said. "There were some places where I disagreed with your analysis, but I marked them for you. I can't wait till you finish the book."

"How come there was no chapter about Women of All Red Nations?" Maureen asked.

"I couldn't get an interview with them," Margaret admitted.

"Well, why didn't you call me? We should be represented in your book. I'll take care of it on Monday."

"Yeah, and how about a chapter on our food co-op?" Lucy demanded.

Margaret laughed. "I didn't think that would be exactly fair reporting, since I know you so well."

"You had a chapter about *Feminist Times*, though."

"And you should see how they came off," Samantha told Lucy. "Mei Ling is going to shit. If that's how Margaret writes about her friends, let's hope she leaves us out of it."

"So what happens next with the book?" Kay asked.

"Now I make revisions and send the first half to my publisher, and then I finish the second half of the book."

"I have a great idea!" Samantha exclaimed. "When it's published we can rent Mama Peaches and have a big party. You know, invite all the people whose groups are mentioned in the book and all our friends."

"Yeah, and Margaret can sit on a throne and sign autographs," Donna added.

"Hate to spoil the party, but I've got to get going," Kay yawned. "My shift starts at seven tomorrow morning. Cook County Hospital at dawn—what a glorious sight."

"Is it less depressing at midnight?" Maureen asked.

"I wish. Margaret, do you want help with the dishes?"

"No thanks. Listen, everybody, thank you so much for the tapestry. I love it, and now I'll always think of you when I see it."

They gathered at the front door, where each woman gave Margaret a hug and her benediction.

"Good luck with your new romance," offered Kay.

"Make sure she treats you right," asserted Maureen.

"Don't worry so much about our opinions," murmured Samantha. "Do what makes you happy."

"It's your life," agreed Lucy.

"Don't fuck it up," said Donna, and closed the door behind her.

The phone rang just as Margaret finished the dishes. She ran to the office to answer, drying her hands on her jeans.

"Hi, it's Alice. Did I wake you?"

"Not a chance. What's happening down at the news factory?"

"Not much." Margaret could hear a keyboard clicking, and pictured Alice perched on her office chair in front of the computer, her dark eyes intent on the screen, her trim fingers darting over the keys. "I'm working on a sports story. I'm going to title it 'Boys Play Games.' My next piece is an international relations story. I'm going to call that one 'Boys Play Games.'"

Margaret leaned against the wall and slid down to the floor. "Sounds fair to me. So what's up?"

"I read your manuscript. It works, but I had problems with the first and third chapters," she said, clicking away. "I thought maybe you could get together with Laura and me this weekend and talk about it."

"I'd love to discuss it with you, but this weekend is kind of booked up. How about breakfast on Tuesday, the usual place?"

"Okay. You're such a traditionalist. And what are you going to be so occupied with this weekend, if I dare ask?"

Margaret could feel herself blushing. "I'll be working at the bookstore most of the time. And to tell you the truth, things are kind of moving along with Arden, and I wanted to spend some time with her."

Alice stopped typing. "Well, *mazel tov*. I hope you're happy. You don't sound like it."

"Samantha and the others were just here for dinner, giving me dire warnings about consorting with straight women."

"Oh, don't worry about them. They're just mothering you. I think it's great you're getting involved with someone. It's about time."

"You think so?"

"Absolutely. Don't agonize over it. Just have fun. Look, I've got to go now."

"Okay. Thanks for calling, and thanks for not saying 'I told you so' about Arden."

"Would I do a thing like that?"

"I thought you might."

"Well, keep me posted."

Staring into her mirror the next morning, Margaret wondered whether she needed a new look. Not that there was much she could do about her face, she thought, dispassionately inventorying her features: blue eyes tempered with a dash of gray, a small forehead that didn't wrinkle even when she raised her eyebrows, a thoroughly unremarkable mouth and chin. It was an okay face, but one on which nothing had been written, as if it had passed through twenty-four years of life without learning a thing. She thought enviously of the deep smile lines that bracketed Arden's mouth, the strong vertical wrinkle between Alice's brows, the fine cross-hatched web that feathered out from Samantha's eyes.

Of course, one thing could easily be altered. Margaret swivelled to study her hair reaching halfway down her back. It tied her to the earth. Every morning, no matter what was happening in the world, she had to wash, brush, and braid her hair. Even on the bad days, the days when she wasn't sure she really existed at all, it reminded her: here was her brush, here was her braid, here was the little elastic band that held it all together.

But perhaps it was time for a change. Maybe she was ready for one of those short, spunky cuts that had first appeared in the lesbian community and now popped up on the covers of magazines. 'Dyke chic,' Alice had named it. Margaret wondered if Arden would like her with short hair, told herself firmly that it shouldn't matter, admitted with a sigh that it did, and ran to answer the phone.

"I know you're up, I heard your shower running," said Arden. "Come on down. I've been waiting for hours."

"How could you be waiting for hours? It's only nine o'clock."

"Well, it seemed like hours."

"I'll be there in a few minutes."

"Okay. I'll be on the porch."

Margaret hurried through Arden's empty apartment. Furtively, she glanced at the open doorway to Joe's room, noting the tall heavy furniture, the coat and tie slung over a chair, the dark tousled sheets.

Arden jumped as the screen door slammed. "Well, hello." She was sitting in a canvas director's chair, her sneakered feet propped on the porch railing, her smile eclipsing the sun.

"Hi." Suddenly shy, Margaret sat down and gazed at the trees with their new light green leaves.

"Here's your coffee." Arden handed her a mug from the small table between their chairs.

"Thanks. So what's on your agenda for today?" Margaret asked.

"Not a thing. I'm all yours."

Margaret grinned. "That has a nice ring to it."

"Glad you like it."

"So where is everyone?"

Arden looked up sharply. "If you mean Joe, he's playing racquetball. Joe and I have an understanding, you know. You don't have to worry about him."

"You have an understanding about other men. This might be different."

"I don't see why."

"Arden, can I ask you something?"

"Sure."

Margaret hesitated, admiring Arden's clear, candid eyes, so unlike her own cautious, wintery look. "In the time that you've lived with Joe, have you ever gotten involved with anyone else? A man, maybe?"

She laughed. "Up until now it would have to be a man. I've never actually had a relationship with anyone else, although I did have a brief fling with someone. I guess you'd call it a fling. Why?"

"Well, I overheard Joe and Paul talking once about some incident where Joe was afraid he was going to lose you."

"That was the incident, all right. Joe had a fit. But this was before we'd actually discussed the terms of our little understanding. In fact, that was *why* we discussed them. It was a long time ago, Margaret. I've left the porch light on many nights since then."

"Were you lonely?"

"At first. Now when I'm lonely it's not for him."

Margaret twisted in her seat and gripped Arden's leg. Even through the denim she could feel the soft curve behind her knee. "Arden, you don't have to be alone any more." Suddenly she noticed what she was doing and returned her hand primly to her lap. "I mean, unless you want to." Here was the problem with straight women, she thought. You never knew what the rules were, what they were concerned about, how much they worried about the neighbors.

"Sometimes I don't understand you, Margaret. You say these sweet things and the next second you take them back."

"I'm sorry. I get nervous. I don't know what you want."

"*I* don't know what I want. I was hoping you'd lead the way."

"Follow me." She took Arden's cup and set it on the table. "Let's take a walk."

Matching strides, they strolled down the wide sidewalks, their feet scuffing in seed pods that drifted from the trees like tiny helicopter rotors. Margaret savored the neighborhood like a guilty secret. She never tired of studying the fine old homes, picturing the lives they sheltered, the cozy corners built just for reading, the banisters worn smooth by a hundred hands. Did women own many of these places? Margaret guessed not. The large houses with their trim lawns bespoke "daddy": kind, steady, consistent daddies, so much more giving and forgiving than her own. Besides, what woman had the money?

"I love this time of year, don't you?" Arden asked. "It always makes me feel so hopeful. Hard to believe the same climate that produced winter can create this."

"The weather in Chicago is like an abusive husband. One day it's vicious and brutal; the next day all smiles and tenderness, swearing it'll never happen again."

"Do you think of everything in terms of women's issues?"

"I guess it gets pretty boring, but that's how my mind works. I can't help it."

"Well, it's okay with me, but you must think I'm very backwards."

"I think you're perfect."

"Oh, don't say that. I can't take the pressure. Besides, you don't know me very well."

"No, but I'd like to. I want to know everything about you," Margaret declared fervently. "Or at least, everything you want to tell me."

"There you go again. Give and take, give and take."

"Sorry."

Arden squeezed her arm. "I'm joking, Margaret. What do you want to know?"

"How did you decide to become a translator?"

"Whew, that's pretty personal. Let me see if I can delve into my psyche and find an answer."

Margaret nudged her sharply with her hip.

"Well, it was kind of an accident. We had to take a language in high school, so I chose Russian because my best friend was taking it. And I discovered that I had a talent for languages. It was a complete surprise to me and everyone else. Especially Mrs. Orr, my Russian teacher."

"Why was she so surprised?"

"Because I almost flunked out of her course. After the first few months I was so bored I could hardly force myself to go to class. Sometimes I didn't. Everyone else was struggling with 'Katya is picking mushrooms in the mountains,' and I'd be hiding out in the library, poring over the advanced lessons with the help of my handy Russian/English dictionary."

"So what happened?"

"Mrs. Orr called me in for a conference to drop the axe. The way she put it was, 'Don't plan on buying any bikinis this year, because you'll be spending the summer in school if you don't shape up.'" Arden mimicked her bullying tone.

"Well, what did you say?"

"For a minute I didn't say anything. In those days we didn't talk back to teachers, at least I didn't. Anyway, I finally told her that I loved Russian but couldn't stand the class. She didn't believe me. I had to show her my dictionary so she could see how well used it was. Well, she got this crazy light in her eyes and started running around the classroom, grabbing textbooks and firing questions at me. When I answered them tears started running down her face, and she kept saying 'Thank God, thank God.'"

"So you felt vindicated."

Arden stared at her. "Are you kidding? I felt scared to death. I thought she had gone over the edge."

"What happened next?"

"I got to drop the course and she set up a special tutoring program for me. This was practically unheard of at the time, but fortunately her husband was the principal, so it all worked out."

"And then everyone realized what a brilliant scholar you were."

"Not quite. I was never a particularly good student in anything else. It was only that one thing that I happened to be good at. So I worked hard and did well in languages because it was fun. But really it was just a fluke."

"Don't be so modest."

"But it's true. Take writing, for example. I know you work hard; I can hear your typewriter. But if you didn't have the talent, you couldn't be a good writer no matter how hard you worked."

"So you think talent is innate."

"Yes. Don't you? I mean, you could probably destroy it through negligence, but I don't think you can create it through diligence."

"I guess that's true. What kind of things do you translate?"

"All kinds of things. Poetry, fiction, nonfiction. A lot of it is *samizdat*."

"What's that?"

"Margaret, I'm surprised at you. It's underground literature, smuggled out of the writer's country, usually at risk to their lives."

"I never heard that term before. What's the most difficult kind of work to translate?"

"Poetry, by far."

"Why?"

"Because when you translate you have to find exactly the right words, with the right nuance, and try to keep the structure and rhythm of the language intact. For example, you can't trade 'morning' for 'dawn.' It's hard enough with prose, but with a poem, you can destroy the whole piece with one clunky word.

"I've read sentences that float like a feather in Serbo-Croatian and come out sounding like falling bricks in English. My job is to turn them into feathers again while staying true to the original text. And that's not even considering the problem of rhyme." She glanced at Margaret with an embarrassed smile. "I'm boring you. You can tell me to shut up when I babble like this. Everyone else does."

"No, I'm impressed." Her heart raced. Ability was irresistible to her, an aphrodisiac. She would always suffer from it, this intoxication with talent. How could she not want Arden, when Arden could turn bricks into feathers?

She tried to sound casual. "What are you working on now?"

"I'm just finishing up a Russian novel about the Kerensky era. It's called '*Lozhnia Vesná*,' *The False Spring*."

"What does that mean?"

"You know, a false spring, like we had last year. When it gets warm for a few days, and buds start peeking out, and then winter comes back and kills everything."

"Can I read it?"

"Sure. I'll bring it home next week."

They cut across a small park and claimed a bench. In the distance a group of girls played frisbee, while two gray squirrels chased each other up and down a nearby tree. Margaret looked at Arden in her faded jeans and her blue v-necked sweater, with her soft hazel eyes and her chestnut hair shining in the sunlight. She reached for her hand.

"Do you realize," Arden said, "that this is the first time you've made a move toward me?"

"I didn't realize you were keeping score."

"Well, I am, and it seems like I always have to make the first move. I was beginning to think this whole lesbian business was just something you read about in books."

"What you do read about in books," Margaret replied seriously, "is lesbians recruiting straight women and jumping their bones. That's not the way it works in real life, and I never want you to feel that way about us."

"Margaret," she said with her teasing smile, "you are the soul of forbearance. I'll tell you the minute I feel you're rushing me. In the meantime, rush me a little."

"You're on." Margaret tried to drag her gaze away, but her eyes were locked into Arden's. She wondered if her face had the same melting look as Arden's did. She felt herself drawing closer. In a moment the frisbee players would have something new to talk about.

It was Arden who pulled back suddenly, with a flustered glance around the park. "Maybe we should get some lunch. I'm starving."

They ended up at a restaurant that sported a few tiny metal tables on the sidewalk. The fringed umbrellas looked festive, but hid the sun and hissed frantically whenever the wind blew. They sat across from one another, knees almost touching, staring dubiously at limp salads residing under matching blankets of day-glo orange.

"I'm sorry, I can't," Margaret said, pushing her bowl away.

Arden held her plastic fork like a surgical instrument and delicately removed the top layer of her salad. She ate a few bites and gave up. "I guess it's still a little early in the season to be dining *al fresco*," she admitted, smoothing down the sleeves of her sweater.

"I love it when you're bilingual."

"Then we're in luck."

They crossed the park again on their way home. "We're going to do something new and different today," Arden announced.

"What did you have in mind?"

"I'm going to teach you to drive my car."

"What for?"

"So you can chauffeur me around."

"That's what I was afraid of," said Margaret.

"Just kidding. I think you should know how, that's all. What if you wanted to go somewhere at night?"

"I'd take the el like I always do."

"I thought we settled that in the laundromat."

They turned down Lill Street and walked past the house. Sounds of a children's record followed them from Deborah's open front door. Arden backed the red Honda down the long driveway and drove to a quiet dead-end street, demonstrating how to shift the gears. Then she parked and they traded places. She was unperturbed by all Margaret's jolting starts and shuddering stalls, only wincing occasionally when she ground the gears.

"This is different from the trauma I went through with my father when I was sixteen," Margaret said, pulling smoothly to a stop and then lurching into first gear again.

"It's much easier than teaching someone to drive for the first time. Besides, there was probably a lot more going on with your father. You know, his little girl growing up and all that."

"I guess so."

"My mother taught me how to drive, and she wept the entire time. I don't know if she was crying for my lost childhood or out of sympathy for everyone else on the road."

"Well, you're pretty patient."

"You know, you don't have to keep your hand on the stick shift all the time," Arden pointed out.

"Where am I supposed to keep it?"

"Right here." She offered her own.

So they rolled down the broad suburban streets, past the joggers and bicyclers and lawn-trimmers. Whenever Margaret shifted gears, Arden's hand remained open, vulnerable, waiting for hers to return. It was a small thing, but Margaret thought it very brave.

The afternoon was almost over when Arden finally pronounced her a fit driver. "Thanks for the lesson," Margaret murmured. "Maybe I can think of something to teach you one of these days."

"I'll just bet you can."

Deborah and Ellen sat on their front porch swing, Deborah's curly blond hair and Ellen's glossy black hair bent over a scrap book. They raised their heads simultaneously when Arden and Margaret clambered up the steps.

"When I saw who was driving, I racked my brains trying to remember if Arden had ever left any funeral instructions," Deborah said.

"No need. Margaret is a good driver."

"Well, that's a relief," she replied, flashing Arden a curious look.

"We're telling stories," Ellen informed them.

"What kind of stories?" Arden pulled a chair over and rested her feet on the wooden swing, rocking it gently.

"Picture stories." Ellen picked up the scrap book and showed them the magazine photos glued to the pages. "Mom says reading is important but thinking is important too."

Deborah gave an embarrassed shrug.

"So what do you do, look at the pictures and think about them?" Margaret asked. She sat on the sturdy porch railing, swinging her legs.

"And we make up stories about them," Ellen replied impatiently, thumping the book onto Deborah's lap.

"It's a trick I learned from a famous author," Deborah confided.

"Who?"

"Why, Sallie McCarthy. I knew her before she became an important member of the literary canon."

"When I was little, my mother got bored reading me children's books, so she'd make up stories," Arden explained. "Sometimes we'd cut out pictures from *Life* or *Look*, and she'd tell me stories about them."

"Did you get to make up the stories too, like Ellen does?"

"Sure. But my mother's were better. She was a really good storyteller."

"That she was," Deborah agreed. "All the kids in the neighborhood would hang out at Arden's house, and Sallie would tell these tales that were so spellbinding we'd forget to eat our milk and cookies."

"What did you do with them, Mom?" Ellen asked.

"With what?"

"The milk and cookies."

"I don't remember. I think a couple of times we spilled them on the rug and Arden's mom got mad and made us all go home."

"You spilled stuff?"

"Yep. Just like you."

"Was all this before or after she became a famous author?" Margaret asked.

Arden laughed, a fall of descending notes. "Way before. She didn't even publish her first book until I was a junior in high school."

"Oh, so you didn't grow up—"

"—disgustingly rich?" Deborah finished the sentence for her.

"Nope. I grew up disgustingly middle class, just like Deborah and Charles and everyone else we knew. In fact, Mom and I were on the poor side, because we had to live on a woman's salary. Back then Deborah was the most exotic person I'd ever met, because she was a Jew."

"I'm a Jew," Ellen announced proudly.

"Wait a minute, Helene Borowitz lived on our block too, remember?"

"Oh yeah, that's right. I wonder whatever happened to her?"

"I'm a Jew," Ellen repeated.

"Very pleased to make your acquaintance." Arden soberly shook her hand, and Ellen giggled.

"So how'd she start writing?" Margaret pressed.

"Oh, she always wrote. She just never submitted anything. At night she'd come home from her secretarial job and scribble all these fantasies onto yellow legal pads."

"What made her decide to publish?"

"Just get to the part about the Queen of Fun," Deborah ordered. "The rest is boring."

"Well, something happened to her when I was about sixteen. I've never known what it was. I think she had her first orgasm or something."

"What's that?" Ellen demanded.

"I'll tell you later, honey," Deborah said. "Thanks a lot, Arden," she added under her breath.

"Anyway, she suddenly began to believe in fun. She started doing all sorts of crazy things. She typed up one of her trashy novels and submitted it to a publisher, just for fun. And when her books became popular and money started rolling in, she became the Queen of Fun. It was her religion."

"Does she call herself that?"

"Oh, no. That's just a name Deborah and I came up with."

"Sallie's always preaching the gospel of fun," Deborah explained. "In her books, on talk shows, even at the dinner table. She's constantly on Arden's back to lighten up. Drop that dreary job. Step out with someone new."

Arden and Margaret exchanged glances. "Was your father still alive at this point?"

"No, he died when I was five."

"That's right. You told me once but I forgot."

"Honey, run inside and get the mail," Deborah said. "It's on the little bench in the hallway." Ellen jumped off the swing and ran into the house, slamming the screen door. "That reminded me, you got a post card from the Queen today," Deborah informed Arden.

"Where's it from this time?"

"Paris."

"Isn't it nice that Deborah lives on the ground floor, since she gets such pleasure from examining everyone's mail?"

"And Margaret, you got a letter from Lillian Green."

"Big deal."

Ellen returned and dropped the mail into Deborah's lap. "Paul wants to play 'Chutes and Ladders' with me now. I'll be back later." She raced into the house.

"What do you mean, big deal?" Deborah demanded, handing the post card to Arden.

"I also got letters from Jane Fonda and Gloria Steinem this month, both of them asking for money."

"Yeah, but this one's hand-written." She tossed her the letter.

"Let's see." Arden studied the white envelope with its slanted blue printing.

"Read it out loud," Deborah demanded. "Unless it's private, of course," she added salaciously.

"'Dear Margaret,'" she read, hearing the warm, confident voice of Lillian Green. "'Thanks for sending me the wonderful article you wrote. I'm sorry your paper decided not to run the piece, but these things happen, sometimes for no apparent reason.

"'I imagine by now you have heard about Women's Words.'" Her voice faltered.

"What's that?" asked Deborah.

"My publisher." Dread raced through her system like adrenalin. "Arden, you read this."

"'If not, let me be the bearer of bad news. They are closing down for financial reasons, and will be unable to publish any of the books under contract to them. I had an inkling of this when we met in Chicago, but was not at liberty to tell you. The editors will soon be asking writers to return their advances, if possible, to help pay some of the debts the press has incurred." Arden paused and looked at Margaret.

"'This would be a wonderful gesture for women who can afford gestures. But I feel strongly that working writers like you are entitled to keep the money you accepted in good faith to create a product that you have no doubt produced in good faith. Of course, each writer must make this decision herself.

"'I have often thought of our conversation and the confidence you shared with me. You reminded me of the day-to-day life of a young activist, something that's easy to forget when one's time is taken up with speaking, fundraising and deal-making. Good luck, and keep on fighting. I know you will find another publisher. Yours in sisterhood, Lillian.'"

No one spoke. Margaret thought of the women she had written about, their struggles and heroism that would never be recorded, the days of interviewing and observing, the nights of instant coffee and lengthy revisions. Then she hung her head and stared at the scarred, dusty floor.

"I'm so sorry." Arden folded the letter and laid it gently on Margaret's lap. "It was nice of her to write. You must have made a big impression on her."

"It was nice of her," Deborah agreed, "but I still think she could have found a way to warn you when you first met her."

Margaret sighed. "She did. She told me to be sure to keep in touch with my publishers, but I didn't do it. I figured I had the contract, I was moving along right on schedule, so why write them just to say hello? It's my own damned fault."

"It's not your fault they went out of business," Arden declared fiercely. "If you had known back then that they were in trouble, maybe you wouldn't have written as much as you did. But you wanted to write it, and now you have half a manuscript to show some other publisher."

"It's a good book," Deborah added loyally. "We like it."

"Tell the truth," Margaret said. "If you didn't know me, is it the kind of book you'd pick up off the shelf and say, 'Hmm, this looks interesting'? Would you order it for the bookstore?"

"I would definitely carry it in Lucia's Books. To be honest, maybe I wouldn't pick it up for myself, but then I'm probably not the reader you had in mind."

"No, probably not."

"What I want to know is, what's this confidence she refers to?" Arden asked.

"Yeah. Does Lillian Green know something about you that we don't?"

"Yes."

"Well, what is it?"

"It's not important."

"She must think it is," Arden pointed out. "Anyway, I know what it's about. It's about your family."

Margaret stared at her. "How did you know that?"

"Because you hardly ever mention them. It's pretty odd for someone your age never to talk about her parents unless there's some deep dark secret there."

"Good work, Sherlock." Deborah dragged Arden's chair closer to the swing. She looked at Margaret and patted the seat beside her. "Now sit over here and tell us all about it."

She told them in all the detail she could remember: the sunny graduation day, her father's clenched jaw, her mother's shaky handwriting on the check, the gravel that sprayed in her face as their car sped away. "I never saw them again. Joan's parents get together with them sometimes, and my sister Jane sees them. Otherwise, I wouldn't know if they were dead or alive."

"Have you ever tried to reach them?" Arden asked.

"I wrote them a few times, but they sent the letters back unopened. Once I tried to call, but when my father answered I couldn't speak, so I hung up. Then they moved, and I asked Jane not to tell me where they went."

"I hope they're alive," Deborah said slowly, "so I can kill them."

The sun slipped behind the trees as if it had heard enough. "It's almost funny, this news about my publisher going under." Margaret shook her head. "Accomplishment is the only thing that impresses my parents. When my book was published, I was going to send them a copy to prove that I still existed and that I had achieved something on my own."

"What a couple of schmucks," Deborah growled. "It's a wonder you turned out so well."

"Thanks."

"No, I mean it."

"She's right," Arden said. "You should be proud of yourself, that you took a blow like that and didn't let it screw you up or make you bitter."

"But I *am* bitter!" she cried out, embarrassed by the way her voice cracked. "I am bitter," she repeated quietly, "and to this day I can't believe it really happened."

That night Margaret moved through the bookstore like an automaton, ringing up sales, locating titles, straightening shelves. Her work would never be found in these stacks now, and for the first time it felt as if all the books were merely products to be bought and sold, like shoes or can openers. She realized it was not her book she was mourning, but the hope it had offered, her last chance to reach out to her parents and be received.

Love was like literacy in her family: a given, something to be enjoyed but not extolled. It had never occurred to Margaret that their love might be conditional, or that it could be unrelated to the person she was or might become. What was it they had loved, since it was not Margaret? Was it a daughter figure, a sister shape, some attenuated icon of a family that bore no resemblance to their own? She would never know.

Margaret did not bother to turn on the lights when she got home. She threw herself face down on the bed and cried until her ribs ached. She hated herself for caring, for losing control, for the harsh ragged sobs that wrenched themselves from her throat despite her efforts to contain them. How could she still let her parents get to her like this? Damn them!

After a long time she exhausted herself and lay with her face pressed into the soaking pillow, each breath raking her raw throat. She had never felt so empty. The apartment was dark, the world was dark, and she was not even sure she was conscious until she heard footsteps in her room, breathed in Arden's sweet smell, felt her sit gently on the bed.

"I heard you crying," she said softly.

"I'm sorry. I tried to be quiet."

"You try too hard. Sit up now."

Margaret hoisted herself up on one elbow. Arden handed her a tissue and turned the pillow to the dry side. "Okay. You can lie down again."

Carefully Arden rolled the elastic band from the end of her braid and separated the strands. She stroked her back in slow circles. "Relax, Margaret," she said in the same quiet voice. "You don't have to be strong every second."

Margaret wanted to laugh at the idea of her being strong, but as if to prove the point, she felt too weary. She listened to the soft rustle of Arden's hands on her shirt. "Arden."

"Hmm?"

"I can't remember what my mother looks like."

"What do you mean?"

"When I try to picture her, all I can see is a photograph I have, and not her real face."

"You'll see her again."

"How do you know?"

"Because you're a prize, and she'll come back to claim you."

Margaret thought about that for a moment, then realized she was drifting off. "I'm sorry, I'm falling asleep."

"I want you to."

"Good." A minute or two later Margaret felt herself jerk the way people do when they drop into sleep. Arden must have felt it too, because she started to get up. Margaret caught her hand. "Stay," she murmured into the pillow.

Arden hesitated, then lowered herself onto the bed. Margaret turned onto her side and curved her body into Arden's. She drew Arden's arm across her waist.

And that's how they spent their first night together, with the past washed clean of despair and the air around them filled with promise.

DREAD AND ROSES

"Well, Margaret, it's time," Arden announced the next morning. She stood in the hallway and smiled with one eyebrow raised.

Margaret pulled her into the apartment. "Where did you go? You were gone when I woke up."

"I got up early and went home. How are you doing?"

"Fine, thanks to Dr. McCarthy. But what did you mean when you said it was time?"

"Time to face the music. Deborah is downstairs, brewing some fiendish coffee and demanding to know what's going on with you and me."

"Oh."

"Don't you want her to know?"

"I don't mind. It's just that I wanted us to enjoy it a little while first."

"Anyway, I didn't tell her. Joe did."

"Joe!"

"When he came home to an empty house last night, he figured out where I was. Evidently he barged into Deborah's apartment at a most inopportune moment to tell them the good news. He's been on a rampage all morning."

"Oh, no. Arden, I really didn't want to cause you any trouble."

"You're not causing the trouble. Don't worry, I can handle Joe. This could be a good experience for him. He might learn some things he needs to know. Margaret, have you told any of your friends about us?"

"Yes. The ones who don't live here."

"Good. Then I know it's not some crazy delusion I have that you're too polite to bring to my attention."

Margaret took her hand. "For such an attractive, desirable woman, you don't have much self-confidence."

"Well, it's been a while," she murmured vaguely. Margaret didn't know if she meant it had been a while since she had felt attractive, or since she had left Deborah alone downstairs. "Let's go, if you're ready."

"Wait a minute." Margaret pulled her close, and Arden's arms moved around her as if she had practiced a thousand times. It can't be a coincidence, Margaret thought, that women's bodies fit together so perfectly. Arden's lips were exactly the right height to reach hers without effort, her shoulders and waist were exactly the correct size to fit into Margaret's arms. Margaret was wondering if she should point this out, when Arden made a small sound in her throat that told Margaret she had already noticed.

That tiny sound pierced Margaret with a searing tenderness for her. If Arden wanted to know how it felt to be desired, to be cherished, Margaret could show her. Whatever wounds she had received, from Joe or anyone else, Margaret would pour her love over them like a balm and heal them.

That's how young she was.

Deborah sat on the floor of her large breezy living room, behind a low wooden coffeetable with a mosaic tile top. Her long legs were folded under the coffee table and her strong arms were folded across her chest. She looked as if she were about to begin meditating.

Adding to this air of Eastern ritual was the table setting. Deborah had filled three white demitasse cups with black, muddy-looking coffee. Each cup rested on a dainty saucer with a tiny spoon next to it. In the center of the table sat a white ceramic sugar and cream set. A metal espresso pot perched on Deborah's right, issuing occasional bursts of aromatic steam.

Arden and Margaret sat across from Deborah, who pushed a cup toward each of them. "I know you're wondering where I got all this stuff," she told Margaret. "Don't forget, I was married. Twice." Deborah twisted her cup in its saucer. "Look, you two don't have to explain what's going on. I already figured it out from the way you stumble around in that corny afterglow all the time."

"Actually, it's a pre-glow," Arden corrected her.

"Well, whatever. All I want to know is, why didn't you talk to me about it?"

"We didn't know ourselves," Margaret replied.

Arden stirred cream into her tiny cup. She kept pouring and pouring, but the coffee never changed color. "I'm sorry if you felt left out, Deborah, but we're not keeping anything from you. We're kind of playing it by ear."

"I don't mind telling you two, I find this all very confusing."

"Imagine how I feel," Arden said.

Deborah picked up a spoon and began scooping sugar from the bowl and pouring it back, like a giant child playing in a tiny sand box. "Of course I want you both to be happy. I'm just not sure I want you to be happy together."

"Why not?" asked Margaret.

"Oh, I don't know. A lot of reasons. And don't think I'm being homophobic, because I'm not." She looked up from the sugar bowl. "Arden is a very complicated person. You're an intense person. You can be kind of fierce."

"Fierce? Me?" Margaret glanced at Arden, who simply raised her eyebrows.

"What are you getting at?" Arden asked gently.

"I just don't want you to disappoint each other."

"Well, I don't want that either," Arden replied, "but I'm willing to risk it."

"But it will be hard. Harder than you know, Arden."

"A lot of people thought you and Paul had chosen a difficult path, if you recall."

"I do recall. And they were right. I'm not sorry we fell in love, or even got married, although I do have a ton of thank-you notes to write. But they were still right."

"It's worth it, though, isn't it?" Margaret asked.

"Yes. But that's not my point. Margaret, you know what I mean. It's rough. I know you can take it because of your convictions. But Arden's not like that."

"So you're saying we should forget the whole idea because Arden's not really a lesbian."

"I don't know. I guess so."

"Hey, give me a chance," Arden said. "We haven't even been to bed yet."

Deborah bent her head and buried her hands in her curly blond hair. "I'm not sure what my problem is with this thing. Arden, you know I've been hoping for a long time that you'd find someone who appreciated you. But now, I don't know, I feel so scared for the two of you. Or something."

"Deborah, I think you're just feeling protective." Arden pulled Deborah's hands away from her face. "But you don't have to worry. Margaret and I are both adults. If it doesn't work out, it doesn't work out, and everything will go back to normal."

"That's just it!" Deborah smacked the table, scattering sugar across the mosaic top. "There won't be a 'normal' anymore. Everything in the house has been so nice and cozy and balanced since Margaret moved in. Now it's all going to change. It's changed already. You don't think Joe is going to take this lying down, do you? No pun intended."

"Why not?" Arden asked coolly. "He expected me to take all the lying down he's done with other women over the years. Besides, Joe has forfeited his right to comment on my private life."

"Of course he has, but he wouldn't let a little thing like that stop him."

"I thought you liked Joe," Margaret said.

"I do. He's always been great with me. It's the way he's treated Arden that I can't forgive."

Arden tossed her spoon onto the table with a ringing sound. "I keep trying to explain to people, Joe is my problem. I'll take care of him. You don't have to."

"Arden, he's my husband's best friend. He's my best friend's husband, more or less. How do you think I can discount him?"

"I don't get it." Margaret held up her hands. "Deborah, are you worried about Joe's welfare, or that everyone's going to try to take sides, or is it something else?"

"I don't know! If I knew, I wouldn't be so upset."

"Deborah, what can we do for you," Arden asked, "short of calling the whole thing off?"

"Just don't shut me out."

"I promise."

"And Margaret, try to be patient with Joe."

"What do you mean? I never see the guy."

Deborah drained her cup. "You will."

"I feel like I've been hungry for years, and now you're feeding me," Arden murmured to Margaret late that night. They were sitting on the rug in Margaret's living room, leaning against the wall. A heavy peacefulness settled over the house; they could feel the others sleeping. The room was dark but the moon was bright, frosting Arden's hair and casting silvery shadows through the curtainless windows. "Only you're feeding me a little bit at a time, like you're supposed to do with someone who's starving."

"What am I feeding you?"

"Oh, you know. Affection. Attention. Passion," she added shyly.

"Sounds like a balanced diet."

"Do you know what I mean about starving?"

"I'm not sure."

"Well, it's like . . . going through a dry season. A long one, when you don't get any emotional nourishment, and everything inside you starts to get dry and desiccated too."

"I don't see you that way at all."

"Maybe it doesn't show, but that's the way I feel sometimes."

"How do you suppose that happened? You've got a million friends; people drop in to see you all the time. And you've got Deborah."

"That's true, and I love Deborah. But even she can't give me what I'm hungry for."

"You mean sex?"

"No, although that's way up there on the list. I meant tenderness." Arden was quiet for a few moments, leaning against Margaret and staring at the tapestry hanging on the opposite wall, barely visible in the soft darkness. "I suppose you could say, to stretch a metaphor, that Joe is the desert I've been lost and starving in all these years. And that makes you the oasis. Unless you're a mirage."

"This is no mirage." Margaret wrapped her arms around Arden and rested her cheek against her hair. Everything about Arden delighted Margaret: her sharp-edged sense of humor, her quiet intelligence, her don't-give-a-damn boldness, her hidden vulnerability that sometimes shone in her eyes and touched Margaret every time it appeared.

She loved her. She loved the very idea of her. With perfect honesty and without any self-consciousness Margaret could say to herself: Literature, Music, Arden. Sisterhood, Liberty,

Arden. "Sometimes I can't believe it's happening either," Margaret agreed. "I mean you and me. How did I get so lucky?"

"You're just a lucky kind of gal, I guess," Arden replied drowsily. She closed her eyes. "I like it like this, taking everything slowly. It's kind of old-fashioned, but it feels romantic and exciting."

"Yes, you look very excited."

"Now I'm asleep. When I'm awake I'm excited."

"Why don't you sleep here?"

"It's tempting, but I think I'll go downstairs. I have to get to work early tomorrow. And the next time I spend the night with you, I don't want us to sleep at all."

They said goodnight. Margaret had floated into the bathroom to unbraid her hair when she heard a soft tap on the front door. Arden's changed her mind, she thought, and threw the door open.

It was Joe. He stood there in his spotless white drawstring pants and a vivid blue t-shirt, with his curly black hair still damp from the comb, looking for all the world as if he were going courting and should have a bunch of flowers in his hand instead of a bottle of Budweiser.

Margaret stared at him with her mouth open, wondering if this was a dream, and if so, how long it would take before her alarm clock terminated it.

"Hi," he said with a charming, sheepish smile. "Hope I didn't wake you. I couldn't sleep."

"I'm not asleep either."

"I see that. Can I come in?"

"Um, yeah." She stepped out of the doorway to let him pass.

"This is new," he said, nodding his head toward the wall hanging. "Got any other new things?" Joe examined the apartment, covering the entire place with a few giant strides. He stuck his head into the office and bedroom before she had time to respond. Only later did she realize that he was probably checking to see if her bed looked as if Arden had recently vacated it. He relaxed noticeably after his little inspection tour, so the sight of the neatly made bed must have reassured him. "Want a sip?" he said affably, proffering Margaret the bottle.

"No, thanks. Joe, what are you doing here? It's two o'clock in the morning."

He turned one of the metal folding chairs around and straddled it, crossing his arms on the back. "I know," he said matter-of-factly. "I couldn't sleep. I keep drinking and drinking, and I can't get drunk and I can't get to sleep." He looked reproachfully at the bottle. "That ever happen to you?"

"Not really. Look, is there something you wanted to talk about?"

"That's what I'm here for." He nodded sagely. "Let's talk."

"About what?"

"C'mon, Margaret, don't play games. About you and Arden and me." Sitting hunched over the small metal chair, he stared at her with a challenge in his bleary blue eyes.

"Joe, I don't think you and I have anything to discuss. Your issues are between you and Arden, and my issues are between Arden and me. I don't see that you and I have any issues at all."

"Well, you're wrong. I'm an attorney. Don't try to tell me what the issues are."

"Okay, if you want to talk about it, we will. But not tonight. Let's plan a time when the three of us can get together."

"Why make things difficult? This is between you and me."

"No. We're not going to argue about Arden like two dogs fighting over a piece of meat. If we're going to discuss this at all, it's got to be the three of us."

"Fine. I'm not the inflexible asshole you think I am. We'll do it at your convenience. When's your next night off?"

"Tomorrow," she admitted unwillingly.

"Tomorrow night, then. We'll meet in neutral territory. The Tenth Street Cafe, seven o'clock, in the upstairs bar." He stood and swayed.

"That restaurant is a hetero meat market, Joe. It's hardly neutral territory."

"I know." He looked down at his hands. "But Margaret, she's choosing you," he said quietly. "Give me something, even if it's only the atmosphere."

Margaret was so taken aback by his candor that she agreed. She leaned over the banister and watched him make his unsteady way down the narrow steps.

"Be there or be square," Joe called cheerily over his shoulder, then locked the door to his apartment with an emphatic click that resounded throughout the silent house.

What is *with* this guy, Margaret asked herself. Her living room felt claustrophobic, as if he had taken all the air with him. She opened a window and began to pace across the rug.

Something was bizarre about their conversation, aside from the fact that it had taken place. One minute Joe was charming, the next he was pensive. One minute he was friendly, the next he was threatening. Of course, maybe that was because he was drunk. You'd think on his salary he could afford to get drunk on something better than beer, but that was beside the point.

His entire, aggrieved, "you stole my girl" attitude was completely off-key. Arden was not his girl, and Margaret certainly hadn't stolen her. How many times had Arden told Margaret that her relationship with Joe was over? How many evenings had the six of them been together, when Joe abruptly stood, wished them all a good night, and drove off to meet his date?

Margaret understood his feelings. If she were in his position, she'd be reeling with jealousy. But she'd never let herself be in his position. She'd never let Arden sit alone and unappreciated while she pursued other women. She'd never greet descriptions of Arden's day with, "You think that's bad? Let me tell you what happened to me."

It seemed to Margaret that the key was not what Joe thought or what she thought, but what Arden thought, which was that she wanted to be with Margaret. All Arden had to do was tell him that. Margaret didn't see how she fit into the equation. Granted, she had always suspected there might be some minor unpleasantness to deal with until Joe fully understood the situation. But she had never envisioned a shoot-out at the Tenth Street Corral.

This summit meeting would just turn a private event into a public debate. Why hadn't she said no? Maybe Arden would have the sense to refuse. Yet she knew Arden would agree to meet with him too. It seemed to be a habit with her housemates, this turning of personal occasions into collective experiences, and Margaret was falling right into it. It was as if Lill Street was its own little planet, making erratic orbits around an unnamed moon, and she too was trapped in the strange gravity it created.

Early the next morning, Margaret clattered breathlessly down the stairs into the basement office of *Feminist Times*. She was late for a planning session with the editing collective.

"Oh good, you're here," Mei Ling said amiably, and dragged one of the heavy wooden library chairs up to the table. She waited with her hands calmly folded atop a pile of papers as Margaret pulled a notebook out of her backpack and got organized. Margaret glanced surreptitiously around the table. Janet, Letitia, and Mercedes also sat immobile, studies in patience, each one behind a businesslike pile of note pads and files that contrasted oddly with their faded jeans and exhortatory t-shirts.

"Sorry to keep everyone waiting."

"No problem," Janet replied pleasantly. "We have a few assignments to go over with you, and we wanted to get your input before we put them on the calendar."

"Great. Like what?" This *is* news, Margaret thought as they soberly discussed how her talents could best be put to use for the next issue.

"So we're agreed that Margaret's going to cover the founding of the new battered women's shelter, and the latest attempts to cut off abortion funding to Cook County Hospital," Mei Ling concluded.

"And I may be able to find some women to take over the column on vegetarian cooking and herbal remedies," she added, wondering if Samantha and Lucy could possibly fit it into their schedule.

"Good. And by the way, this is for you." Mei Ling handed her a check for $25.

"What's this for?"

"It's to pay your way to Springfield for the ERA rally this weekend."

"But I thought we weren't going to cover it."

"We changed our minds," Mercedes said. "I'm going too, to take pictures."

"I've even been thinking of going myself," Letitia admitted. "Of course, I'd probably be the only black woman there. And all that stuff about everybody wearing white really turns me off."

"That's what my friend Maureen Littlebear says. She won't go either."

"Well, Littlebear and I have something in common. Maybe you can guess what it is."

"Letitia, a good friend of mine is one of the organizers. She says they ask people to wear white because that's what the suffragists wore, not to make a statement that white is good."

Letitia put her elbows on the table and leaned toward Margaret confidentially. "This friend of yours. What color is she?"

"The same color you'll be wearing on Saturday."

"That's what I thought. Well, look for me anyway. I shouldn't be too hard to spot."

After the meeting Margaret tugged Letitia into one of the tiny, windowless workrooms and closed the door. "What's going on here?"

"What do you mean?" Letitia replied, looking around the room.

"Not in here. Out there. Everyone is being so . . . nice to me."

Letitia laughed and started to rewrap the elastic band around one of her many short braids. "No wonder you're upset."

"No, really. I want to know."

She stopped fiddling with her hair. "Well, we heard about your publisher going belly up. And the collective got together and talked about all the good work you've been doing for us, and we thought maybe we've been a little rough on you, making you prove yourself, you know."

"You mean you've been on my case so much because you wanted me to prove myself?"

Letitia glanced at the door. "Yeah, pretty much."

"I don't get it. What changed your mind? And what's it got to do with my book?"

"Look, Margaret, this is probably going to piss you off, but I'll tell you anyway. Some of us on the editing collective had the feeling that you were kind of using *Feminist Times* as a stepping stone."

"Who?"

"Our votes are secret— "

"—and we don't mix personalities with politics," Margaret recited with her. "I've heard that before. But what kind of stepping stone could this newspaper be, considering how many hours I put in and how little I get paid?"

"Suppose you weren't really interested in the paper. Suppose you were really after fame and fortune. So you get this book contract, and then you use the paper to get access to these women's groups that you're trying to write about. I know it's not true, but it makes sense, doesn't it?"

"No. It's the stupidest thing I've ever heard. Anyone could get access to those groups. They're not secret. Besides, feminist writers don't get rich and famous."

"Some of them do. Look at Lillian Green."

"She may be famous, but she's not rich."

"How do you know? She show you her bank book?"

"Okay, I don't know, but I don't think she is. Anyway, that's not the point. I can't believe you'd think that about me."

"Baby, I told you you'd be mad. We were dead wrong, no doubt about it. Your book's gone and you're still here. But now we're trying to make it up to you. And in the fall we'll have the funding to open up another full-time position, if you're interested. Then you'll be eligible to join the editorial collective when it changes members next January."

"I don't think I want to be on the collective, Letitia. I remember you before you joined it. You were fun to be with. You trusted people. You could think for yourself."

She sighed and threw her arm around Margaret's shoulders, big sister style. "It's true, something weird does happen to you when you're on the collective. Maybe you're right to stay out of it. "

"You know what I think, Letitia? I think you hate success. Not just you, our whole crowd. Anything that even hints at achievement or acceptability is immediately suspect."

As Margaret was giving this tirade, Letitia withdrew her arm and stood facing Margaret directly. The expression on her face was one Margaret had observed on people who were walking into a strong wind.

"You talk about Lillian Green," Margaret continued heatedly. "Everyone acts like she's sold out because she's famous. No one remembers that she only became famous because she dared to say radical things out loud.

"Or take the ERA women. We all look down our noses at them. I know the ERA is about as mainstream as you can get and still be a feminist, but shit, those women are accomplishing something. And half my friends won't even go to the rally for one highly principled reason or another. We're just too cool to care."

They were both silent for a moment. "You finished?" Letitia asked finally, with the beginnings of a smile. Margaret nodded. "Feel better, kid?"

"Yeah," she replied, smiling herself. Margaret felt as if she had shed a backpack full of books. Who cares what the collective thought? She had never needed their approval anyway. Wanted it desperately, perhaps, but not needed it.

"Can we please get out of this cage, then? I hate enclosed places." She flung the door open and Margaret could see she was sweating.

"Why didn't you tell me?" Margaret felt a guilty solicitude for her.

"And listen to you rant and rave about how I'm avoiding the issues? No way. I'd rather suffer."

"Well, I'm sorry I made you suffer."

Letitia took a deep breath and reached for the sky, as if they were in the great outdoors instead of a basement. She turned to Margaret with a grin. "Then we're even. You want to be friends again?"

"Sounds like a good idea."

As Margaret turned the corner onto Lill Street, she was delighted to see Deborah rocking slowly in her front porch swing, her head tilted over a book. "Hey, what are you doing here?"

Deborah waved her over. "The question is, what are you doing here? Shouldn't you be at the gym?"

"What for?" She plunked her heavy backpack on the floor.

"To practice your thrusts and parries. Fencing techniques," she explained in answer to Margaret's baffled look.

"Oh, then I guess you've heard. Did Joe tell you?"

"No, Arden called me at work. She said Joe brought her breakfast in bed this morning and made her promise to meet with you two tonight. I'll tell you one thing, though."

"What?"

"I'd like to be a fly on the wall at that restaurant."

"Why? You know you'll hear every detail. Probably three different versions of it."

"It is true that my services as a confidante are indispensable around here," she agreed modestly. "By the way, a delivery came for you. It's on the little bench inside."

Margaret stood motionless in the hallway and gazed at her delivery. Red roses. Arden was so thoughtful it made her knees weak. She must have known how much Margaret was dreading this meeting tonight, and sent the flowers to remind her of what it was they were struggling for. Margaret was lucky to be having a romance with someone who really knew how to be romantic.

"Well, bring them out here," Deborah yelled. "A dozen roses. She must have spent some bucks on you. Aren't you going to read the message?"

Margaret plucked the small envelope from the holder. She read the card, read it again, threw her head back and laughed.

"Let's see." Deborah read the card aloud. "'May the best man win. Love, Joe.'" She shook her head. "Gotta hand it to him. He's threatened, but he's trying. Probably trying to upset you, but at least he's being creative about it. Margaret, stop laughing. You're beginning to sound hysterical."

"But this is so typical. Doesn't the whole idea of this summit meeting strike you as bizarre?"

Deborah hesitated. "I guess it's odd, but then, so is the situation. It can't do any harm for the three of you to talk it over."

"I must be missing something here, because I can't think of a thing I want to say to Joe on the subject."

"Well, maybe he has some things to say to you."

"Even if he does, I'm not sure I want to hear them. I mean, Joe and Arden may have some issues to resolve. Arden and I may have some issues to resolve. But Joe and I can't have anything to resolve, because we have nothing in common."

Deborah stared into the distance as if she had something delicate to say and didn't want to embarrass Margaret by watching her face as she said it. "I'd guess you and Joe have more in common than just about anyone you'll ever know. You live in the same house. You have the same friends. And now you love the same woman."

Margaret was stunned. It was true. "But Deborah," she whined, "you can't equate the way he feels about her with the way I feel."

"I can't judge that. All I know is that in his own way, Joe loves her very much. It just so happens that his own way of loving is not real efficient."

"What do you mean?"

"He doesn't know how to make her happy. And if he can't keep her happy, he deserves to lose her."

Margaret hunched against the window on the el, although she had the seat to herself in the practically empty car. She studied the stiff, guarded expressions of homebound commuters packed into trains that hurtled by on the opposite track. Emotions flashed past her like the faces of people in those speeding trains. She felt anxious, excited, resentful, protective, curious. Mainly she felt nostalgic for the fifty other things she would rather be doing that evening. But she climbed resolutely to the second floor of the Tenth Street Cafe, her footsteps making no sound and leaving no trace on the thickly carpeted stairs.

Arden and Joe sat at a round table in front of a tall arched window. The sun was setting, and the window reflected a pinkish glow. Arden was wearing a dark red dress and a white linen jacket. Joe had removed his suit coat and was wearing a white shirt and red tie. They were facing each other and talking intently. In the soft backlight of the window, they looked like the handsome couple in a movie, like the handsome couple on a billboard, like the handsome, young, white couples everywhere whose images sold rum and perfume and stereo equipment.

For a moment, Margaret faltered. She felt as if the entire wealth and weight of heterosexual culture was gathered at that small table, arrayed against her. Then Arden's face lit up as she caught sight of her, and Margaret moved toward them again.

Joe actually stood as Margaret reached the table, a courtesy she had never seen him perform before and found rather incongruous now. "Hope you don't mind that we got started without you."

Arden pushed a glass of wine toward her. "We both arrived a little early. Here, I ordered this for you. We're drinking gin."

Margaret glanced at her watch. It was one minute past seven. "Well, at least we beat the rush hour." Empty round tables of various sizes dotted the hardwood floor, each with a healthy green plant hanging above it. The Eagles crooned "New Kid in Town" from speakers hidden in the foliage.

"It's a Tuesday night and pretty early yet," Joe said. "This place really picks up after eight."

"Thanks for the flowers, Joe. No one's ever sent me roses before."

Arden turned to him so abruptly her chair squeaked on the wooden floor. "You sent her roses? Why?"

He shrugged, embarrassed. "Just a gesture."

"A gesture of hostility. I told you, Joe, I'm not putting up with that tonight. Or any night."

He bowed his head. "You won't have to. Look, I'm not here to fight. I'm here to work things out. Margaret, Arden has warned me that she'd walk out if I tried to turn this into a debate. So I want you to know I'm going to be on my best behavior tonight, and I hope you won't take it the wrong way if I have to bring up some uncomfortable subjects just to clear the air."

"Thanks for the warning, but I'm sure we can all handle this like adults."

"Love your confidence," Arden muttered, poking her ice cubes with a little plastic sword.

"This may sound a bit out of line, but I know you'll understand why I have to ask." He gave Margaret a warm smile that evoked an answering one from her. "Do you get a special thrill out of seducing straight women? Or do you have something personal against me?"

Margaret felt the color drain out of her face along with the smile.

Her parents had taught her that good manners consisted of always knowing the proper thing to say. No one who was familiar with the rudiments of courteous behavior needed to be at a loss for words. But she could not recall ever learning the polite protocol for this situation. Joe was watching her, his handsome face composed in lines of genial interest.

"Stop it, Joe," Arden cut in wearily. "We've gone over this a dozen times. When are you going to accept the fact that my relationship with Margaret has nothing to do with you?"

"When someone moves into my house and takes over the woman I love, I find it very difficult not to take it personally." He gave his tie a sharp, angry tug that pulled the knot away from his collar and left it askew.

"Joe, the first time I was in this restaurant was last winter," Margaret said heatedly. "I was here with Arden and Deborah, and you were here with some other woman. So don't try to tell me that I destroyed your happy marriage."

"Look, I don't deny that we've had our problems. But I never felt that I was really losing her before now."

"Don't you hear what you're saying?" Arden looked pale and miserable. "It was all right when you had someone else, but now that I do, you can't handle it."

"Not just someone else," he retorted. "Another woman. If it was a guy, I could accept it. But you're right, I can't handle this. I don't understand it. I mean, this is the seventies. I know lots of gay people, and I'm all for gay rights, so Margaret, please spare us your soapbox. But Arden, you've never been attracted to a woman before. Have you?"

She hesitated. "I'm not sure. Maybe I was but I didn't recognize it. Anyway, I am now, so what difference does it make?"

"It makes a lot of difference. Is that really how you want to live? Hiding in closets? Guarding your pronouns at the office to make sure no one figures out who you spent your weekend with?"

"Margaret doesn't live like that," Arden objected indignantly.

"Margaret has nothing left to lose!"

Stricken, Arden glanced at Margaret. Clearly it had just occurred to her for the first time that perhaps Margaret would not want Joe to know about her family's rejection.

The waitress hurried over, as if summoned by their charged silence. After an awkward pause, they ordered another round. The waitress strode away, and Joe continued in a more subdued tone. "I'm sorry, but I need to know what's going on here. Is this some kind of an experiment, Arden? Or is it your way of getting back at me?"

"Oh, for christ's sake," Arden exclaimed, and rested her forehead on her fist. "I didn't get involved with Margaret to spite you. I did it because of the way she makes me feel. Look, this is confusing for me too. I don't know what's going to happen. I only know that this isn't about you, Joe. It's about Margaret and me."

Margaret patted her hand under the table. Arden caught hers and gripped it tightly for a second.

"I don't believe that," he said quietly. "I know something else is happening here, maybe something you're not even aware of. But it can't be as simple as girl meets girl. Not for you, Arden."

"Why not?"

"Because you're not like that."

"Apparently I am. Joe, I know what you're going through. When you first started seeing other women, I had a hard time understanding that you weren't trying to send me a message, that it really was strictly between you and your friend. Now you're going to have to learn the same thing. Maybe it'll be easier for you because you've had lots of practice as a teacher."

He shook his head with a self-deprecating laugh. "I feel like the guy in the old joke. You know, 'My mind is made up, so don't confuse me with the facts.' Everything you're saying *sounds* right, but it doesn't *feel* right."

"Men always seem to think that everything a woman does has to refer to them in some way," Margaret pointed out. "You think that Arden got involved with me to punish you, and that I got involved with Arden to express hostility toward you. And no matter what we say, you can't believe that our feelings about you or about men in general have nothing to do with it."

"That's a very interesting theory, Margaret, and I'm sure it has a lot of validity," Joe began, his effort to behave shining all over him like sweat. "But I honestly don't think I'm reacting this way because I'm a man. I think it's because I'm the man in Arden's life."

"Why would you say something like that, Joe?" Arden demanded. "You're not the man in my life. Just because I haven't gotten a replacement doesn't mean you still have the job."

"You're right," he replied humbly. Margaret watched him gulp some gin, and it occurred to her that he must have been up there drinking even before Arden arrived. "Margaret, I want to tell you a little something." Joe gave her a lopsided smile.

"Go ahead."

"I don't think you and Arden are going to make it. I know her pretty well, and I can tell you she's not a real lesbian. Wanna know why?"

Margaret didn't respond but he continued anyway. "Because she doesn't hate men. I can vouch for that personally."

"She doesn't have to hate men. All she has to do is love women."

"It sounds like you rehearsed that answer. Have you been through this conversation with other people?"

"Well, your arguments aren't terribly original."

"Oh, so you *admit* you've poached on other men's lives before." He thumped the table with a beefy index finger.

Blood pounded in her ears, and she could feel fury turning her face to stone. She leaned forward and glared into his intense blue eyes. "First of all, I resent your referring to Arden like she's some livestock that you own. Second, you keep

acting like we're involved in a triangle. There's no triangle.
There's only Arden and me, and we're only here tonight
because, like all women, we're willing to go out of our way to
make you feel better. Which is a hell of a lot more than you've
ever done for her."

"You two are making me feel like a rug in some Middle
Eastern bazaar," Arden said. "This is exactly what I wanted to
avoid. If we can't discuss this calmly, I'm leaving. In fact, I
think we should all leave."

"Arden, please stay." Joe held both hands up. "I'm sorry. I
got carried away. I'll be good now, as soon as we can get
another drink. I promise."

"Joe, we just got our drinks a few minutes ago."

"Well, mine's gone. I need another."

"Here." She slid her glass to him. "It's not working
anyway."

"I apologize," he said to Margaret with appealing gravity.
"I realize it's my problem, and you don't have to care, but this
is very painful for me. I know I have some shortcomings, and
maybe I don't treat Arden the way I should. But you have to
admit, there are some things I can give her that you can't."

"As a matter of fact, I think the opposite is true," she
replied coldly.

"But what about marriage? Children. A home. Security.
Safety, even. I mean, what could you do if someone tried to
mug Arden? I could beat the shit out of him."

"Oh, Joe," Arden said sadly. She looked across the room at
the boisterous couples who were starting to fill other tables.
"Joe, listen. There was a time when you could offer me those
things, but that was years ago. I don't want them from you
anymore, even if you could give them. All I want now is a
chance to be with Margaret."

"But you're making a mistake. She can't possibly love you
the way I do," Joe declared plaintively, uncannily echoing the
argument Margaret had given Deborah earlier.

"You and I have been friends for a long time, Joe, longer
than we were lovers. I've been alone for years, and now I've
found someone new. Can't you be happy for me, like a friend?"

Joe looked into her eyes. His gaze slid down her face to the
table top. "I don't know. I'll try." He stared at his clenched
hands. "I know it sounds selfish, Arden, but Jesus, I always
thought you'd be there—"

"—if all else failed?" she interrupted, smiling at him with one eyebrow raised.

"Yeah. That's as good a way to describe it as any." He gave a short, harsh laugh. "Well, I guess I really blew it this time."

"I think you had some help. It just seems to be in your nature that you always want what you can't have."

He flashed her a devilish smile. "Yes, but I always manage to get it, don't I?"

"Not this time," she said gently.

Joe raised his head like a giraffe and drained his glass. "Well, come on, ladies. If you're good I'll let you take me home."

"Where did you leave your car?" Arden asked.

"I don't know. I'll buy a new one tomorrow." He slung an arm around each of them, and they staggered across the floor, trying to steer him in a straight line. "See all these other guys?" he demanded, pointing with both hands.

"What about them?" Margaret asked.

"They're jealous. They think I have two women. They don't know I'm the only man here without a date."

They leaned Joe against the Honda like a sack of groceries while Arden unlocked the door. "Put your head down," she ordered, and they wrestled him into the back. She handed Margaret the keys and collapsed into the passenger seat.

"This must have been a hard night for you," Margaret said quietly as she pulled away from the curb.

Arden nodded. "I feel pretty empty." She smiled at Margaret. "Also very full."

Later, the two women dumped Joe onto his bed, and Arden removed his shoes, belt, and tie.

"Are you afraid he's going to hang himself?" Margaret asked. "That's what they do to prisoners."

"No. I just don't want him to be uncomfortable. He's going to feel bad enough tomorrow." She shut the door to his room firmly, as if closing the cover of a book she had finished and would not read again.

"Are you tired, Arden?"

"Not really. Just kind of drained."

"I know something that's guaranteed to put the roses back in your cheeks."

"And what might that be?"

"Come with me." Margaret took her hand and led her to the stairway.

"Are you planning to get me into your apartment and take advantage of me?"

"That's exactly what I have in mind. I'm not rushing you, am I?"

"No, Margaret," she said with an amused weariness, "rushing me is hardly the way I'd describe it."

Arden sat cross-legged on the bed and watched Margaret pull down the squeaky, yellowed shades and light three lavender candles. "*Nakonyets*," she said softly.

"What does that mean?" asked Margaret as she blew out the match.

"At last."

AN ARMY OF LOVERS

"You know what's so terrible about this?" Arden fluffed her pillow and settled into it, hands clasped behind her head. Above them they heard Mrs. Rogers' clock strike three, faint as a memory.

"I like that," Margaret replied. "We've been lovers for less than a week, and already you've got a list of grievances."

"No, really. Do you want to hear what I think, or are you only interested in my body?"

"Of course I want to know what you think. I want to know everything about you."

"I hope you never do."

"Why?"

"Because then you'll get bored and move on."

"Do I seem like that kind of person?"

Arden hesitated. "I don't know. Ask me again in a few years."

Margaret brushed the hair back from Arden's forehead. "Well, tell me what's so terrible. Then we can discuss my shortcomings."

"It's terrible to think how close we came to disaster."

"What do you mean?"

"Well, I might have been too scared to let myself feel this way about you. And you might have been too politically correct to get involved with a straight woman. We might have missed everything." Arden spread her arms in an encompassing gesture.

"But we didn't."

"I think it would be awful to feel the way I feel now and not be able to share it with you. Margaret, think of all the women who feel this way about another woman and can't tell them. Or worse yet, who may never know it's possible to feel like this."

"I know. That's why it's important to create a climate where women are free to make this choice if they want to."

"It's nice to hear you pontificate again. I've kind of missed it these past few days."

"That's because I don't have room to think about anything but you anymore."

"Why, Margaret," she mimicked, "am I rushing you?"

"I'm not sure what you're doing, but whatever it is, don't change a thing."

Arden turned on her side and rested her head on Margaret's shoulder. "Do you want to hear something else sad?"

"I don't think so. Do I?"

"We have to get up in a couple of hours to catch that damn bus."

"That's your own fault, Arden. You told Joan weeks ago we'd go to Springfield with her for the rally."

"I suppose you were going to sit this one out."

"I could have come up with some excuse."

"I can just see you, calling in sick to the revolution."

"Do you want to go to sleep?" Arden didn't respond. Margaret kissed the top of her head. "Anyone home?"

"I was just thinking."

"About what?"

"It's embarrassing."

"Tell me. It's dark. I won't be able to see you blush."

"About the way you cry out my name when we make love."

"You're right, that is embarrassing."

"But I like it. I've been with other people who yell 'Oh God!' or 'Oh fuck!'—"

"'Oh fuck'?" Margaret interrupted. "That's romantic."

"But you—at the one moment in your life when I know you're not editing yourself—you call out my name. It makes me melt. It makes me feel like you're really making love with me, and nobody else will do. Sometimes I come when you're not even touching me, just because of the way you say my name."

"I know."

"You do?"

"Yes. I love it when you do that."

"See, that's what I mean," Arden continued. "You know what I'm feeling. You're really with me. I never feel that you're, you know, just waiting your turn."

"I never feel that with you, either. That's one of the benefits of loving women." Margaret wanted to kick herself. Here was Arden, candid, courageous, outspoken. And here was Margaret, barely able to mumble another platitude.

Why could she never speak her heart? Why did every deeply-felt emotion come out sounding stilted and overly polite, like an entry from a foreign phrasebook?

Arden had noticed, too, or she wouldn't have made that remark about Margaret editing herself. Maybe she didn't mind it now, in the first flush of new love, but she would. Like everyone else, Arden would grow tired of her reticence, her cowardice, the dry husk around her heart.

Downtown Chicago looked unreal, like an amateurish movie set, as Margaret and Arden joined the crowd clustered under a street lamp. Joan stood on the steps of the chartered bus, counting heads and checking items off a clipboard. The engine idled loudly in the strange silence of empty buildings and deserted streets.

Arden mingled with the others, but Margaret hung back and studied the group in their white clothes with their colorful buttons and banners, as they laughed and talked, shared cups of coffee, dug through tote bags for articles to read aloud. Something was discordant about the scene. Underneath the festival air, she realized, these women fairly glittered with anger. She caught sudden glints of it in their eyes, in a voice raised too loudly, a clenched fist.

Margaret knew none of these women, yet she knew them all. They had colored within the lines; they had kept their knees together; they had put their husbands through school; they had opened the switchboard at eight; they had raised their daughters to be polite; they had trained younger men to take their jobs; they had said no to professors and flunked because of it; they had needed their fathers to co-sign loans; they had loved women and told no one; they had waited for child support checks that never came; they had voted for men who betrayed them in office; they had lived on promises.

Margaret felt the hair on her arms stand up as she recognized the power and peril of the women gathered here. This ERA battle, which she had scorned for so long, was nothing less than an elemental struggle between good and evil, with all the power amassed behind evil, and only rage and righteousness to fuel their side. Joan, she saw now, was a freedom fighter, and she herself was a buffoon, waiting for a more dramatic issue to come along before she dirtied her hands. And as if to underscore the narrowness of her vision, Margaret immediately began to worry: not about how she could throw her energy into the fight, but about how many column inches the editing collective was likely to allot for this story.

"I'm having a great time," Arden announced, coming up behind her. She added in her new, intimate voice, "In fact, I've been having a lot of fun these days. I only wish I'd met you a few years ago, when I didn't mind staying up all night."

"Maybe you can sleep on the bus. It's a five-hour drive."

"Don't you think we'll be singing 'A Hundred Bottles of Beer on the Wall' or something?"

"I don't know. Some of the people brought pillows."

"Wish I'd thought of that. Hey! Here comes St. Joan." Arden waved as Joan bustled her way toward them, her thick hair flying out behind her as if in a force field of its own.

"Boy, am I glad to see you! I know a million people who are going to this demo, and would you believe it, none of them got assigned to my bus." She stared at them. "You two look the way I feel. What's wrong with you?" Suddenly she blushed to the roots of her red hair. "Oh, I get it. I must be slow today." Joan threw her arms around their shoulders. "Welcome to the family, Arden."

"Oh, um, thanks," Arden replied, pleased and startled.

"Well." Joan straightened her purple sash. "Guess we're about ready to roll. Got your notebook?" she asked Margaret.

"Right here."

"Good. You know where the press tent is?"

"Joan, don't worry. I've got it covered."

"Just checking. Well, see you on the bus. We got a woman driver—pretty cool, huh?"

As the passengers crowded into their seats, Joan pulled a green "ERA Yes" button out of her pocket and offered it to the driver, a trim black woman with steel-gray hair.

She shook her head. "We're not supposed to."

"Come on," Joan cajoled. "If you were driving us to a Cubs game, you'd wear a ball cap, wouldn't you?"

"No way. I'm a White Sox fan."

"Oh yeah? Me too. Well, are you with us on the ERA?"

She hesitated, took the button, pinned it on her narrow black tie.

"All right!" Joan slapped her on the shoulder. The bus lurched into motion. "See? We're going to win this thing," she exclaimed, dropping into her seat. "Everyone's for it. Everyone but those idiots in Springfield."

"Aren't they the only ones who count?" Arden asked.

"In a way. But the constituents are going to yell so loudly that they won't be able to ignore us this time. I mean, we're celebrating our country's bicentennial. It's time to get women into the Constitution."

"I believe you."

"So who's speaking at the rally?" Margaret flipped to a new page in her reporter's pad.

Joan mentioned a few people. "You'll get a full list in your press kit. And of course the keynote speaker is Lillian Green."

"Lillian Green—how'd you get her?"

"She's an old friend of Ellie Smeal's. Besides, Illinois is a pivotal state. Why shouldn't we get the big names?"

"Margaret and Lillian are like that," Arden confided, crossing two fingers.

"Oh, yeah, you interviewed her. Maybe you'll get a chance to talk to her again today."

"If she will. The editing collective scrapped my first story."

"Another example of power corrupting, even collective power."

"But don't you want power?" Arden pressed. "I mean, isn't that what this movement is about?"

"We want to be *em*powered," Joan replied soberly. "It's different. And we're sick of men having power over us."

"How about women?"

"As long as they're feminists." She yawned. "Arden, I'm too wasted to talk theory. I've been getting four or five hours of sleep a night for two weeks now. Last night we never left the ERA office at all."

"What have you been doing?"

She rubbed her eyes. "Sending out mailings, working on phone banks, lining up speakers, chartering buses, stuffing press kits. Plus we all have to make a living in the daytime."

"But what do you do in the middle of the night?" Margaret asked.

"Meetings." Joan laughed. "Lots and lots of meetings. They start at midnight, to give us plenty of time to finish our other work first."

"Well, I admire you," Arden declared. "I don't know what keeps you going. I wouldn't be able to do it."

Joan studied her for a long moment. "Oh, yes," she said firmly. "You would."

The loud chatter dwindled to a few murmured conversations as they sped away from the sleeping city. Arden's head nodded to her chest, snapped up, drooped onto Margaret's shoulder. Only the driver remained totally alert, humming to herself as she steered them through the flat Midwestern farmland, with its black, black soil and enormous sky. Fog skulked along the ground like a bad conscience, clinging to tree trunks. Margaret felt her eyelids drift down and did not resist. The bus rolled on through the misty morning, carrying its cargo of hope and fury.

"Isn't this fantastic?" Arden exclaimed. They stood on the curb, part of a cheering, clapping crowd that watched the marchers troop past, waiting for their turn to join. "For the first time, I really feel that sisterhood you're always talking about."

"It's great." An endless column of women passed them, interspersed with some men. They carried stenciled "ERA Yes" placards or satiny banners in the suffrage colors of purple, gold and white that proclaimed each group's affiliation: Lawyers for ERA, Quad Cities NOW, Sangamon State University, Older Women's League, United Steel Workers. Margaret's favorites were the rainbow-hued banners that proclaimed "Failure is Impossible," and "Women of Color for ERA: We Shall Overcome."

Margaret had been in dozens of demonstrations in Chicago, but this event felt different, with the white Capitol building, seat of so many doomed decisions, waiting for them at the end of the march. She had no idea how anyone managed to count a crowd like this, and suspected no one really did.

The anger she had sensed on the bus dissipated in the warm sun. This was a carnival, with women in their picnic whites shouting rhythmic chants and stamping their feet, while marshals in purple sashes pranced alongside like feminist majorettes, waving bullhorns instead of batons. Margaret felt her spirits rise like the escaped helium balloons that dotted the sky with green and white. She had marched for many causes, but none that had seemed so *possible.*

"These rallies look so joyless on TV," Arden observed, "but in person they're just the opposite."

"Yeah, I was thinking that too."

"I want to march, but I can't decide which contingent to join. Look, there's Joe's bank!" She pointed to a group of women carrying a large banner printed with the bank's slogan, "Continental Bank: We'll Find A Way."

"I see. Where's Joe?" Margaret asked acidly. Arden didn't respond. "There's the group I'm going to march with, just turning the corner now." Far away they could see a multi-colored sign identifying 'Lesbians for ERA.' "I think Samantha and Kay are with them. Want to come?"

"Not just yet. Can you give me some time?"

"Well, sure, but what for?"

"Margaret, one week after you first slept with a woman, would you have wanted to march under a lesbian banner in front of thousands of people and TV cameras?"

"I don't know. I think so."

Arden laughed. "My little revolutionary. Now, don't get all insecure. I don't have any doubts about you and me. It's just going to take a while to get used to . . . a new definition of myself."

"Okay. I was hoping to show you off, but I'll wait. Maybe you'd be more comfortable marching with them." She pointed to a handful of women carrying a placard that read 'Stepford Wives for ERA.'

"Thanks for making this so easy."

"Arden, you know I'm joking. Take all the time you want. Why don't we split up and meet at, say, three o'clock."

"Sounds good. Where?"

Margaret pulled a diagram out of her press kit. "There's a media platform in front of the stage at the rally site. I'll look for you here, at the lower right-hand corner."

"Okay. Wait for me if I'm late."

"I will."

"And don't run off with someone who's more 'out.'"

She grinned. "I won't. Anything else?"

"That's all I can think of."

"All right. Well, out of the revolution and into the mainstream." Margaret pushed her way into the line of marchers.

"So where is she?" Donna demanded later, between shouts of "Hey hey, ho ho, the patriarchy's got to go."

"Who?"

"Your new babe."

"She's around," Margaret evaded. "In fact, you just missed her. I'm meeting her later in the press area."

"Guess she didn't want to march with us, huh?"

"It's nothing personal. Wait until she meets you— then you can get paranoid."

"Oh, Donna, give her a break," Samantha interjected. "There must be hundreds of lesbians here who aren't marching with us. Look over there—I see some now." She patted Margaret's arm. "I understand Arden, I think. It's very different for people like you and Donna, who came out so young. When you're older, and you're in the real world, it's hard. Give her some time. She'll find her own way."

"I know. I'm not pressuring her—I want her to be comfortable. Donna's the one who's pushing her."

"Well, Donna's pushy."

"Ain't that the truth," Donna crowed, flexing her biceps. "Margaret, have you seen Alice and Laura? We passed them about half an hour ago."

"No. Who were they marching with?"

"They were standing in line to buy hot dogs. Can you believe they're still meat eaters?"

"And where's the rest of your clan?"

"Kay's at work, Maureen won't come because she says it's too white bread for her, and Lucy didn't feel like getting up at dawn. I think Lucy will regret it, too—I'm having a pretty good time."

"I know. Doesn't this demo seem different from the ones we're usually in? I mean, normally it's kind of grim. But this one—it's like a party."

"That's mainstream politics for you," Donna replied with distaste. "I mean, look at the massive support this thing's getting. Everybody here wants the ERA to pass, but they'll be okay even if it doesn't. It's not the same with lesbian rights, or 'Take Back the Night', or keeping Cook County open. The issues we work on are closer to the survival level. That's why today feels like a picnic—it is."

"I agree with most of that, but I do think we'll all be in serious trouble if the ERA isn't ratified." Samantha pushed her bushy hair away from her eyes. "Right now there's not much standing between us and the 1950s. I remember the 1950s and believe me, they weren't *Leave it to Beaver*. It was a horrible, repressive time, and I for one would sleep better if there was something in the Constitution to stop us if we go that way again."

"Damn, I wish I'd gotten that on tape!" Margaret pulled her recorder out of her backpack. "Samantha, can you repeat that?"

"Never you mind."

"No, really. You were so vehement. It was a great quote. Please."

"The great moments happen only once," she said primly. "I would think you'd have learned that by now."

Margaret stuck the recorder in Donna's face. "Donna, what'd she say?"

"I don't know, something about Mickey Mouse or Clutch Cargo or someone."

Samantha slipped her arm through Margaret's. "I'd repeat if for you, but I don't remember the exact words, and you know it would sound fake the second time around."

"Maybe you're right." Margaret slung the recorder over her shoulder. "Obviously I'm going to have to go to strangers, since I can't get any good quotes from my friends."

Margaret was amazed at the power of the large green "Media" card dangling from her neck to provide her with instant access to women's private thoughts and feelings. Everyone was eager to talk, and it seemed they had all read the same briefing book. With the loudspeaker booming in the background, dozens of women described their motivation: hope for their daughters, redress for their mothers, and for themselves, simply an equal chance. Not much to ask for, it seemed to Margaret.

This unanimity made good politics, she supposed, but not particularly good copy. She took her recorder backstage. The few rally organizers who had time to talk seemed harried but exultant. The speakers, too, veterans of so many issues and actions, looked pleased and excited as they chatted, paced, and thumbed through note cards, awaiting their five minutes in the sun. Margaret briefly interviewed a number of them, picking her way carefully across the cluttered platform.

"Hey, watch it!" she yelled at a heavy-set man wielding a stubby microphone. He had stepped back abruptly and elbowed her in the chest.

"Sorry, hon," he mumbled, and trundled past her, followed by the rest of his TV crew, bound together with electronic umbilical cords. In the space they vacated, she saw Lillian Green gratefully drop into a folding chair and stretch her long legs.

Margaret paused. Clearly the woman relished these few seconds of solitude. On the other hand, if Margaret didn't grab her, one of the other reporters roaming around the backstage area certainly would. She darted to her side.

"Well, hello." Lillian squinted up at her.

"Hi. Margaret Osborn, with *Feminist Times* —"

"In Chicago," she finished the sentence. "Yes, I remember. Have a seat." She took a leather case from her purse and shook out a long brown cigarette. "Want one?"

"No thanks. I didn't know you smoked," she said foolishly, as if they were friends of long standing.

"One of my many character flaws." She pinned Margaret down with a level, blue-eyed gaze. "So how are you doing these days?"

Margaret blushed, thinking of their last meeting. "Much better, thanks."

"Let's see. You were . . . writing a book. How's it going?"

"You have an excellent memory."

"A necessary tool of the trade. But don't change the subject."

"I've kind of put my book on hold for awhile, since *Women's Words* went out of business. By the way, I wanted to thank you for warning me about that."

"Yes, I got your note."

"So, how's your book doing? I mean, is it selling well and all that?"

She waved her hand, leaving a trail of smoke. "I'm sure it's doing fine. I should probably keep track, but I don't. I have assistants, accountants—an entire cottage industry. The whole thing seems to mushroom up when you're not looking."

Margaret was unsettled by her candor. "You sound pretty dispirited."

"Oh, not at all. I think the size and spirit of this march are wonderful. The momentum gathering around the ERA is very exciting. American women are speaking their strength, and the legislatures must listen. Are you getting all this?"

"Yes." Margaret scribbled madly.

"Good. Now, as for my mood, perhaps I'm just running out of steam. I'm pondering a new project, in a new direction. You don't need to write this down."

Obediently, Margaret clicked her pen closed and turned off the recorder. "What kind of project?"

"Well, it's still a bit fuzzy, but my idea is to travel around the country and simply talk with women. Not lecture them, which is what I've been doing, but sit down with them, over cups of coffee, in laundromats, on porch swings, in CR groups, and ask them questions."

"Like what?"

"How they see their lives. How well the movement is serving their needs. What they want from the movement, what direction they'd like to see it take. What changes they envision for their own futures. How far they're willing to go." Lillian gave Margaret a sidelong, almost shy glance. "Then I'd take all that information and put it into a book. How does it sound?"

"Gosh, I think it sounds great." She winced. She hadn't said "gosh" since she was twelve years old.

"But?"

"Well, it seems to me that anyone could ask those questions. But no one can do what you do for the movement. So even though it would be an important project, I wonder why you'd have to be the one to do it."

Lillian stubbed out her cigarette in a metal Sucrets box she pulled out of her purse. "Because I want to know the answers. And no one would ask the things I would. So even if someone else wrote the book, I would still be left wanting to know more. And that's one longing I can do without." She shaded her eyes and peered out to the podium. "I'm up in a few minutes."

"Should I leave and let you prepare?"

Lillian ignored her. "Tell me something, Margaret."

"What?"

"Do you think that women might not talk to me frankly because of who I am?"

"No. I think you're easy to talk to. In fact, if you want me to be perfectly honest—"

"Please do. I don't have time for anything less."

"I think you're so open that it's kind of weird. You're blunt. A lot of people are blunt. But there's an unguarded quality about you that's very unusual."

"That's because I have so little left to hide." She laughed, although Margaret did not see the joke. "Anyway, I do want to pursue this project. I need it. Raw data, raw energy—it's so easy to lose touch." Lillian rose and patted her on the shoulder. "Well, I'm on. Go interview Ellie. She's always wonderful."

"Hey—good luck," she called after the departing figure. Lillian waved, but Margaret couldn't tell if it was meant for her or for the cheering crowd.

Now, that was a strange conversation, Margaret mused as she sat in Lillian's vacated chair and listened to her speech. It was certainly no interview, although Lillian had given her a quote, as she might give someone a kiss with no thought of romance. More intriguing was the glimpse Lillian had offered of her strange, striated world.

One night, many years later, Margaret received a phone call. It was from a woman she admired, a woman who headed a nonprofit organization to which Margaret had often donated time and money.

The organization had been offered a chance to publish an op-ed piece in a major newspaper. It was a wonderful opportunity. But the woman was not a writer. She was calling to see if Margaret would write the piece. Unfortunately, it would have to be finished by the end of the week.

Margaret felt like crying. She wanted to stamp her feet and yell. Some childhood tantrum that she had never indulged was trying to burst its way out of her now. Because the fact was, she would love to write the piece. She believed in the organization, and she would enjoy seeing her byline in this particular newspaper.

But there was no way she could write it by end of this week, or the end of next week, for that matter. There was no way she could write it at all.

Margaret was busy, so busy that she did not have time to eat or read or hold hands or talk on the phone, so busy that her nights were crowded with wild, snarling dreams about all the

*obligations she should be fulfilling instead of twitching on her
bed in her feverish half-sleep. Yet this op-ed piece was important.
And how much time could it take, after all?*

*She had just opened her mouth to respond when, suddenly,
these words marched across her brain: Lillian Green would say
no. Margaret saw them very clearly, in italics, 12 points tall. She
closed her mouth with a bewildered little snap, like a fish.*

*"I know this is an imposition," the woman said. "But you're
my first choice. We wouldn't want anyone else to speak for us."*

*"I'm sorry," Margaret replied, and her voice actually broke.
She cleared her throat. "I can't do it."*

*"I hate to press you, but there's really no one else. If you can't
write it, we'll have to tell the paper no."*

*"I'm truly sorry," Margaret repeated like an automaton. "I
would like to, but I can't."*

*Margaret did not write the piece. The organization had to
decline the newspaper's offer. And some strange things
happened: The women's movement did not die. The
organization Margaret believed in continued to thrive. The
woman she admired continued to call her. Margaret wanted to
phone Lillian Green and demand, "Why didn't you tell me
sooner?" But of course Lillian had told her. Margaret hadn't yet
learned how to listen.*

As the afternoon waned, Margaret picked her way to the
elevated press platform. From a distance it had beckoned like a
serene oasis, promising a wider perspective than the lunging
heads and shoulders that are all a short person sees of a rally.
Now it didn't look so friendly. It bristled with men posed in
aggressive wide-legged stances, their cameras aimed at the
stage, battery packs strapped around their waists, long-nosed
microphones sniffing the crowd.

She knew the quarry they were seeking. They were hunting
the truth, but it would elude them again as it always did.
Instead, they would bag their own version of reality, and take
it home to be butchered, packaged, and marketed on the air
waves, so altered that no one who was present today would
ever recognize it.

Still, there was a chance. In the far corner of the platform
she spotted a crew comprised of women dressed in white.
Perhaps they were recording the story that Margaret saw, the
story that would never make it to the six o'clock news, the
story that every woman here was creating with her life. She

hoped so. Margaret considered climbing over there and talking to them, maybe interviewing the tall blond woman behind the camera. But she would have to squeeze past a lot of people to reach her, and Arden was due any minute. Maybe she would run into her again some day.

Late that afternoon, women trooped back onto the bus for the trip home. The driver was still wearing her "ERA Yes" button, now joined by one that said "59 cents." Joan stood next to her, checking off names.

"Oh, bus marshall!" Margaret sang out.

"What is it?" Joan said irritably.

"I believe we have two lost souls trying to sneak aboard." She pointed to the end of the line, where Samantha and Donna stood waiting.

"Relax, Osborn. They traded seats with Kathy and Mary Ann. For some reason they thought it might be fun to ride with us."

"Who are those people?" Arden asked.

"They're friends of mine, Samantha and Donna."

"Are they the ones who live with all those other women?"

"Yes. Don't get nervous, but I think they're here to check you out."

"I'm flattered." She slipped a comb from her purse. "What if I don't pass?"

"Don't worry. The job is yours as long as you want it."

"I love it so far."

"Uh oh, bad sign," Donna announced in a stage whisper. Margaret jumped. She didn't realize they had boarded so quickly. "Hi, I'm Donna. You must be Arden. We've heard so much about you." She pumped Arden's hand.

"I've heard a lot about you, and about you too, Samantha." Arden waved the two women into their seats. "I understand I'm to be examined today."

Samantha raised her eyebrows. "Feisty! But we just want to get to know you—you're not on trial. Margaret, what awful things did you tell her about us?"

"Just the truth."

"That's bad enough." Samantha dug in the pockets of her white overalls. "Lifesaver, anyone?"

"Yeah. My throat is killing me. All that chanting, I think." Donna handed the roll to Arden.

"All that chain-smoking is what I think," Samantha said.

"Could be."

Joan tumbled into her seat as the bus slowly gathered speed. "So what did you think?" she demanded, her Irish setter eyes gleaming. "Wasn't it wild?"

"It was a good demo," Samantha pronounced. "You should be pleased."

"Yeah, I am. What about you, Donna?"

"The entertainment was good. I'd give the refreshments a C-minus."

"Donna likes to sound cynical, but in her heart she's a big softy," Margaret explained to Arden.

"There you go again, being size-ist," Donna complained. "Isn't being a softy bad enough? Do I always have to be a *big* softy?"

"You are a big, beautiful woman, and you should be proud of it," said Samantha, who in fact expended some effort on keeping herself small and trim. "Joan, you should have seen her. She was chanting her head off. I think it took her back to her days as a high school cheerleader."

"I was only in the Pep Club," she muttered. "It was different."

"I was in the Pep Club too," Arden consoled her. "Don't feel bad. Not everyone can be born with a fully developed feminist consciousness."

"Thanks, Arden."

"See? Isn't she wise?" Joan beamed as if she had invented Arden.

"You're the wise one," replied Arden. "I really admire what you do. I think it's about time for us to get more involved, don't you, Margaret?"

"Maybe you will, but Margaret won't," Joan interjected.

"What's that supposed to mean?" demanded Margaret.

"Nothing bad. It's just that we're all one of the troops. You're like . . . Bob Hope."

"Thanks a lot!"

Joan clapped her freckled hands to her face. "I didn't mean it as an insult, Margaret."

"How else could I take it?"

"I only meant that you have a different job. We can all do the basic activist stuff. You have to report on the campaign and keep the rest of us informed and inspired."

"While we do all the labor," Donna clarified.

It was true, Margaret thought: Not for her the weary, gritty, hand-me-down work of righting wrongs. She had marched in the streets; she would do so again. But her best contribution had always been rolled out of a typewriter. That was a given, like gravity, or feminism itself. She could not stop to ask herself whether it was enough.

"I thought the second wave started with a book," Arden declared. "Isn't that why they call Betty Friedan 'the mother of us all'?"

"True enough." Samantha pawed through her backpack and passed around a thermos of cold water. "We definitely need our writers. We need everyone, and everyone's talents, from old burn-out cases like me to young firebrands like Miss Joan here. I really believe that. We need our sisters and our lovers. Even our new additions." She gave Arden's knee a motherly pat.

"'An army of lovers shall not fail,'" Donna quoted Rita Mae Brown.

"Yeah! That's what I mean about this march." Joan flung her arms wide. "You could just feel it, the power of sisterhood. We owned the town today. I only hope we can do it again the day of the vote."

"When is that?" Margaret asked.

"I don't know yet. Hey, Margaret, read us some excerpts from your interviews. I didn't get to hear a lot of the speeches."

"Really?"

"Sure, I'd like to hear a few," Donna said. "And I do mean a few."

"Okay." Flattered, she shuffled through some pages. "Here's one from Addie Wyatt. 'Sometimes I wish my eyes hadn't been opened to the pain, the hurt, the longing my sisters and I suffer as we struggle to be free. Sometimes I wish we could just sleep securely in our slavery. But we are awake, our eyes are open, and we've got to free the last bastion of slaves, who happen to be American women.'"

Samantha whistled. "Heavy. She's an impressive woman. Who else do you have?"

"Um . . . Karen De Crow. 'It's an embarrassment and a disgrace that a nation which considers itself a leader in human rights doesn't give equal rights to half its population.' Oh, here's one you'll like. It's from Wilma Scott Heide. 'Feminism affirms women in a way that no institution in our society or the world yet does. It also affirms men as potentially human in ways that are not yet true.'"

"Pretty damned good," said Joan.

"Listen to this," Margaret interrupted excitedly. "We were talking about lesbian feminism, and she said, 'In a patriarchal society, it's a miracle when any woman can love a man.' Later I asked if she'd like her daughters to be lesbians, and she answered, 'If they're qualified.'"

Samantha laughed. "That's one thing I noticed about the rally. I haven't seen so many straight women in one place since my first wedding."

"Your first wedding!" Margaret's head whipped around. "Were you married twice?"

"Oops."

"When was this? How long were you married the second time?"

"Never you mind."

"Why are you so secretive, Samantha?"

"I'm not. I just don't like to dwell on everything every little minute like you do. Why are you so nosy, anyway?"

"I can't help it."

"Arden, I hope you don't let her dig around in your business all the time."

"I like her curiosity," Arden said with dignity, "and I trust her."

Margaret squeezed her hand and wondered—guiltily and belatedly—if their jokes about straight women sounded scornful to Arden, or hurt her feelings. She would have to ask her tonight, when they were alone.

But they were not going to be alone, Arden informed her that evening as she guided the old Honda toward Lill Street.

"Why not?"

"I'm going to stay downstairs. I need to sleep tonight."

"You can sleep at my house."

Arden slid her hand under Margaret's leg on the cool vinyl seat. "No, I can't. I haven't yet."

"I won't lay a hand on you. I promise."

"Well, I can't make the same promise."

"Good." Margaret leaned toward her, wishing Arden's car didn't have a stick shift. "It's been rough, being with you all day and not being able to touch you. I'm not trying to pressure you, Arden. I just want to be close to you."

"Well, I'd love that too, but I've got to get some sleep. I can feel my brain cells extinguishing in little puffs, like exhausted light bulbs."

"Okay, I'll tell you what. Get a lot of sleep tonight, and rest up tomorrow while I'm at the bookstore. Then tomorrow night I'll make you dinner, and we can have a long romantic evening. What do you say?"

"Sorry, I can't."

"Why not?"

"I promised Joe I'd go out with him tomorrow night. I've hardly seen him in weeks."

"What? You're going on a date with Joe?" She stared at Arden. Headlights flashed in her eyes like crazy impulses.

"Oh, Margaret, it's not a date. We're just going out to dinner, and then we're stopping in to see some friends afterward."

"I can't believe this." It infuriated her that Arden was so calm.

"You know I've lived with Joe for years. Naturally we have old friends and old habits and things we like to do together. Why does that upset you?"

"I just have a feeling he's going to try to turn this into a date—you know, he'll be so charming, and make sure you have a wonderful time and all that."

Arden laughed. "I don't think he'd sink that low. Anyway, what if he did? I have the perfect antidote: I'm in love with you."

Margaret took Arden's hand. "Arden, you're so sweet, and I can be such a jerk sometimes. I'm sorry."

"You don't have to apologize."

"I hate that you have this long-standing 'we' that doesn't include me. And that you have to keep me hidden from your old friends. I'm not asking you to renounce your entire past. It's just that I want you everywhere in my life, and I want you to feel the same about me."

Arden pulled into the dark garage and turned off the engine. "Margaret, it's true that right now there are places you can't go with me, but that's going to change. I can't instantly transform myself into Super Dyke. You've opened so many doors for me, but at the same time I can hear other doors closing. Do you understand what I mean?"

"Yes."

"Will you wait for me?"

"You know I will."

"I *don't* know. Maybe you can remind me once in a while."

"I'll remind you right now, if you'll come upstairs with me for just a minute."

"Oh, no. Once I set foot in there, I won't be able to leave."

"I know. That's what I'm counting on."

"You're cruel."

"Okay. How about if I sneak into your bedroom and kiss you goodnight."

"Forget it. Kiss me goodnight here."

"In the garage?"

"Take it or leave it."

I'm not really alone, Margaret told herself later as she studied the shadows on her bedroom ceiling. Next door to her, Charles slept. One floor below, Arden's heart beat. Beneath that, Deborah lay curled against Paul.

And at this very moment, all across the Midwest, an army of lovers was taking off their wilted whites, plumping up pillows, turning down sheets. The Stepford Wives, the Continental Bankers, Lillian Green, the woman behind the camera—all of them sinking into sleep together, dreaming of a new dawn.

THE QUEEN OF FUN

It was September twentieth, the end of summer, and
Arden's birthday. She was thirty years old.

"Happy birthday, sleepyhead." Margaret gazed down at
Arden as she lay on her back, chestnut hair feathered across
the pillow, face wiped clean of experience. "I've never slept
with such an old woman."

"And you never will, if you don't shut up." Arden groped
for Margaret's pillow.

"Don't throw that!"

"Give me one good reason."

"Open your eyes and I will."

"In a minute."

"No, now."

"Why did I have to get involved with Miss Assertiveness
Training," Arden grumbled. She pried open one eye, then the
other. "Breakfast in bed! Why didn't you tell me you were
holding a tray?"

"I wanted to surprise you."

"Well, it worked. I hate surprises, but this one is nice." She
reached for the tray. "This looks delicious. Coffee, juice,
grapefruit, and my favorites, hot blueberry muffins. Where did
you get these?" Arden pulled back the sheet, and Margaret
slipped into bed next to her.

"I baked them last night, while you were out with Joe.
Then I warmed them up this morning."

"Did you actually break down and buy white sugar?"

"No, I got some from Deborah."

"Such a little *hausfrau*. I love it." She handed them each a cup of coffee.

"Arden, is it true you hate surprises?"

"Mmm hmm. Why?"

"Joe once told me you loved them."

Arden stirred milk into her coffee. "When was this?"

"The day of Deborah's wedding. He asked me to hide the Dom Perignon and not to tell you, because you loved surprises."

"Oh. What he meant was, 'I just spent our household money for the next three months on some champagne that no one appreciates but me, so please don't tell Arden because she'll make me take it back.'"

"And I thought he was being so generous."

"He probably did too. Joe has never understood the difference between 'want' and 'need.'" Arden broke open a muffin and watched the steam escape. "That's one reason why I don't accept money from my mother. When you live with a man who has a spending problem, it's best not to have too many funds available."

"Why don't you keep it in a separate account?"

"It doesn't matter if he can't get to the money himself. I'm such a pushover that if he's in trouble I'll bail him out." She buttered the muffin and offered half to Margaret. "I know it doesn't really help him for me to clean up his messes, but I can't seem to stop myself. Are you getting disillusioned yet?"

"With you?"

Arden nodded.

"No, of course not. I like every new thing I learn about you."

"So far."

"Arden, I'd have to discover something really terrible to change my mind. Saving Joe from himself doesn't even come close. Besides, I like hearing about your idiosyncrasies."

"Well, that's good, because God knows what humiliating things my mother will tell you tonight."

"I hope she does." Margaret wanted to hear all the stories—silly, charming, embarrassing. She wanted to see the streaky pastel photographs, the jerky black and white movies. She wanted Sallie to give her the gift of Arden's childhood. "Are you excited about her visit?"

"Yes. I haven't seen her in months, since . . . well, I guess not since her birthday, last January."

"You two always get together on your birthdays?"

"Yep. On my birthday she comes here. On her birthday she flies me to wherever she is. Last year it was Santa Fe." Arden turned to her, rattling the dishes in her lap. "Margaret, I can't wait for you to meet my mother. You'll love her."

"Yes, but will she love me?"

"Of course she will, because I do."

"Have you told her about us?"

"Not yet." Arden slid the tray onto the floor and drew her knees up to her chest. "I'll tell her today, when I get her alone for a few hours."

"Maybe—" she hesitated. "Maybe you shouldn't."

"Margaret, that's so unlike you. Usually you want everyone to wear a sandwich board."

"I know, but with parents it's too risky. I don't want you to get hurt."

"Don't worry. My mother won't be like yours."

"I thought I could predict my parents too, and you know how that turned out."

"Margaret, do you ever think that if you had been, well, paying more attention, you might not have been so shocked?"

"What do you mean?"

"I get the impression that your family wasn't big on expressing emotions."

"That's true."

"So it stands to reason that people who like things to be tidy and proper and controlled would be horribly uncomfortable with something as improper and emotional as lesbian love."

"I guess you're right. I never thought of it that way."

"Well, my mother likes impropriety. It's her bread and butter. Besides, she always taught me that my life was my own."

"I just don't want you to lose her."

"If I can't tell my own mother who I am, I've lost her already."

Margaret leaned against Arden. "How did you get to be so wise?"

"It comes with age."

"Then I have something to look forward to, since I'm much, much younger than you are."

"You have a lot to look forward to. Let me give you a little preview." Arden pushed Margaret down on the bed and kissed her.

Delighted with Arden's unusual display of initiative, Margaret was about to make a joke about how spunky Arden must be feeling on her birthday. She was surprised to discover that she was unable to speak. Instead Margaret found herself clinging to Arden, panting so hard she felt light-headed.

They were both wearing nightshirts, and the thin layers of cotton between them suddenly seemed intolerable. For the first time, Margaret understood how lovers could rip each other's clothes. With shaking hands she pulled off Arden's shirt and then her own.

"What's happening?" Margaret murmured hoarsely.

"Don't you know?" Arden replied teasingly. "We've done this before."

"Not like this." Margaret had never felt so frantic. She wanted to touch Arden everywhere, but she could not stop kissing her. Her whole body felt bruised with desire. She pressed hard against Arden and realized that the trembling she felt came not from herself but from Arden. Then she, too, had been swept up in the surprising, sudden intensity.

"You're so wet," Arden crooned in her ear, but Margaret was beyond being able to respond in words. From now on the only answers she could give were in her ragged gasps, her urgent cries, the mounting tension of her body. It was a language that Arden could translate with perfect accuracy.

As Margaret stepped out of the shower, she heard Arden shouting, "Come in here! You've got to see this."

Margaret grabbed a towel and padded into the bedroom, where Arden was lingering over a second cup of coffee and clutching the weekend's book review section.

"Look." Mesmerized, Arden pointed to the page.

Margaret bent over her shoulder. "A review of *The False Spring*. Wow, that's great."

"Keep looking."

"'... Graced with a lively and sensitive translation by Arden McCarthy,'" she read aloud. "Arden, you're a star! Congratulations." She hugged her.

"Hey, stop dripping on my paper. Can you believe this? No one even notices the translation unless it's bad."

"Well, someone noticed this one. The *New York Times*, no less."

"I know." With a visible effort, Arden tucked away her grin. "Maybe I shouldn't be so excited. After all, they are the mouthpiece of the patriarchy."

"Of course you should be excited." Had she taught Arden this, to doubt her own accomplishments unless they received the feminist stamp of approval? "You should be proud. I'm proud of you."

"You're right. I am proud." She leaned over the paper and studied it closely, as if the inclusion of her name might have been a typographical error.

"I'm surprised no one from your office called."

"Well, Cyril's on vacation, and the others probably think I'll be in today."

"Don't they know about Cyril's 'no work on your birthday' policy?"

"It may not be uppermost in their minds. You're the only one who thinks my birthday ought to be a national holiday."

"I do." Margaret pulled a clean t-shirt from the cardboard dresser. "I think banks should be closed and parks should be open, and we ought to have fireworks or a parade. And your mother should get a medal or be made a saint or something for introducing you to the world."

Arden laughed as if she had just invented delight. "Please! Saint Sallie. And you not even a Catholic. But I'll tell you what: when you get home tonight, I promise there'll be a parade."

"What kind of parade?"

"You'll see."

"Arden —"

She closed her lips and pantomimed turning a key in a lock.

"Okay. You can be one stubborn woman."

"And you are a smart woman to know when to give up." Arden leaned against the wall and clasped her hands behind her head. "I could get into this, lounging in bed while everyone else works."

"Sloth becomes you." Margaret pulled a worn leather belt through the loops of her best jeans. "Well, do I look okay?"

"For what? Has Deborah instituted a dress code?"

"To meet your mother. She'll be here when I get home."

"You look perfect." Arden patted the bed beside her. "Sit with me for a minute. You don't have to be nervous about tonight, Margaret."

"What if she doesn't like me, or she doesn't like our relationship?"

"It's her loss. But she will like you. Anyway, this isn't the general inspecting the troops. It's just a little family get-together. We'll all have dinner downstairs, and then sit around while I open fabulous presents from my loved ones."

"Sounds like fun. Well, I hate to leave you looking so sexy and tousled in my bed, but I've got to get to work."

Arden grinned at her. "Think you can still walk?"

"I'm not sure. But I loved this morning." Margaret kissed her goodbye. "Enjoy your day off. I'll see you later for the parade."

Margaret walked briskly home from work that evening. The high, unending daylight of summer was over. Long shadows reached for each other across the quiet suburban streets, soon to merge into suede-soft dusk.

She increased her pace as she caught sight of the house. All the windows were open. In Deborah's apartment a filmy white curtain flapped in the breeze, waving a demure welcome. Arden's stereo was playing and the thumping bass reached out to her like a heartbeat. In the driveway stood a smart, white Lincoln Continental. The Queen of Fun had arrived.

Margaret bounded up the stairs to Arden's apartment. Through the milky glass door she saw Deborah and Paul sitting on the couch, Paul's fingers on the back of her neck tapping absently to the beat of Stevie Wonder.

"Hi, you two."

"Hey, babe," Paul answered affably.

He must be in one of his macho moods, she thought. Normally she would not allow a man to call her babe, but somehow with Paul she didn't mind.

"Where have you been, young lady?" Deborah demanded.

"At the bookstore. Elaine was a little late, and then it took her forever to get out of her work clothes. Where is everybody?"

"Guess we don't count anymore," Paul complained in his rumbly voice.

"Sure you do. But I meant, you know—Mom."

"She and Arden went to the kitchen."

"To feed the baby," he snorted.

"Now, Paul, we all have our own funny habits. Not everyone has to clean their records with a special velvet cloth each time they play them, for example."

"Yeah, and listen to what happens when you don't." He jerked his thumb at the stereo, which sounded fine to Margaret.

"Arden's been dying to introduce you." Deborah patted Margaret's hair into place.

"She's been running to the front porch every five minutes to look for you," Paul concurred. "Good thing Joe's not home yet, because that shit drives him nuts."

"Joe's been dishing it out—" Deborah began.

"—so it's time he learned to take it. I know, I know," Paul finished wearily.

"Do you think I should go upstairs and change first?" Margaret smoothed her shirt into her jeans.

"You're not asking for her hand," Paul laughed. "Just go in and meet the woman. Here, give me that." He reached for her backpack.

"Did Joe ever get hold of you yesterday?" asked Deborah.

"No, why?"

She shrugged. "I think he wanted to know what you were getting Arden. Is it in here?"

She nodded.

"Can I show Paul?"

"Sure, but it's wrapped."

"Not with gift paper from Lucia's Books, I hope."

"You can take it out of my salary."

Arden and her mother sat across from one another, elbows resting on the white wooden table as they leaned into their murmured conversation. A glass of red wine stood forgotten before each of them.

Sallie had Arden's fine, clear eyes. Her hair, straight and smooth, cut just below the ears, must have once been that same chestnut color. Now it was turning gray, as if it had been dusted with a fine coating of ash.

She looked young, much younger than Margaret's memory of her own mother, with her tired eyes and permanently worried expression. Sallie was wearing a white jumpsuit with a soft red leather sash. On her feet were matching red leather pumps, and her lips and nails gleamed with the same vibrant color. Square rubies glinted in her earrings.

"There you are!" Arden bounced out of her chair. "I've been telling my mother all about you." Proudly, protectively, she took her arm. "Mom, this is Margaret. Margaret, this is my mother."

Margaret offered her hand. "Nice to meet you. I've heard a lot about you."

Sallie rose and shook hands warmly. Margaret had to look up to meet her eyes. "My daughter seems to think you're the best thing since sliced bread."

"Mother!" Arden exclaimed, blushing.

Sallie laughed, a funny, tinkly sound for such a tall woman. "Well, it can't be a news flash, can it?"

Arden steered Margaret to the corner of the room, near the refrigerator. "And this is the parade I promised you." She pointed to a small black dog, her head buried in a bowl from which emanated loud gobbling noises, her furry plume of a tail waving like a metronome set to *allegro*.

"She's cute, but she's not much of a parade."

"That's her name, Parade. Mom never travels without her."

"How did you come up with that name?" Margaret asked Sallie.

"Everywhere she goes, she's like a little dog parade. You'll see."

"You guys?" Deborah stuck her head in the doorway. "Paul and I are going downstairs to make the salad. We'll start bringing the food up when the boys get home."

"Want some help?"

"No thanks, Margaret. You can be on clean-up duty."

"So." Sallie studied her as she sat next to Arden. "You're the young woman who has sparked such a big change in my daughter's life."

"You McCarthys get right to the point, don't you?" Margaret braced herself.

Sallie smiled, revealing large handsome teeth. "I've learned there's no advantage to being indirect. And why bother? You're a writer; you know about subtext."

"I guess so."

"Well, I can't say I'm overjoyed about this new direction of Arden's. Love is difficult enough as it is. But for the moment, my daughter's happy and glowing, and I can only see that as a good thing."

"Thanks for saying that."

"I have to believe we're on this planet to enjoy ourselves and to give pleasure to others. What other reason could there possibly be? Besides," she lowered her voice confidentially, "I think every woman falls in love at some point with a woman friend."

"You do?"

She nodded soberly. "I know I did."

"You're kidding! Who was she?" Arden demanded.

"I don't know if you remember her. Theresa McAlister."

"The lady who lived downstairs from us?"

"That's the 'lady.'" Sallie giggled. "She was younger than you are now, honey."

"Rub it in, Mom. So what happened?"

"Nothing. We never talked about it, certainly never acted on it. But I'm sure that's what it was, love." Sallie stared into her wine glass as if she might find her friend in the tiny, inverted world that shimmered there.

"She was married to that brute, I can't remember his name. He was in the Air Force. They got transferred after a couple of years, and I never saw Theresa again." She tossed her head back, and Margaret could see a young Sallie, shaking long hair away from her face as she laughed across a kitchen table with Theresa. "Arden, I'm surprised you remember her at all. You were only about eight when she moved in. Your dad had been gone three years."

"Do you think if she had lived there longer you two might have gotten together?" Arden asked.

"Oh, no. I was a good Catholic widow. I would have had to spend every waking moment in confession just for thinking about it. This was the 1950s!"

"There were lots of Catholic lesbians in the fifties," Margaret pointed out.

"Yes, but they were outlaws. They *had* to be outlaws in those days. I guess it's different now. I wouldn't be surprised if more and more women don't have affairs with their girlfriends, the way the world's changing."

"Mom, can you imagine us having this conversation when I was a teenager?"

"Oh, God. I would have died." Sally dropped her head in her hands. "Margaret, I suppose Arden's told you that I was pretty provincial back then."

"Provincial?" Arden repeated. "How about puritanical? Straitlaced? Completely paranoid?"

"All of the above," she agreed. "Poor Arden—timing has always betrayed you. You were born too late to really get to know your daddy, and you grew up too soon to enjoy the kind of life I could give you now."

"You did fine, Mom. I don't have any complaints."

"I know, honey. I just wish I could have made things easier for you, that's all."

"I think you did a good job," Margaret volunteered. "Arden turned out to be terrific."

"Yes, she is a treasure, isn't she." Sallie smiled at her daughter. "I'm glad you appreciate her. Now, don't get me wrong, girls. I think this is probably just a phase for Arden. But then, I guess every love affair is just a phase. Why else would we need romance novels?"

"Who says we need them?" Arden teased her.

"You may not, but millions of women do. And we say thank God for that, don't we, Parade?" She patted the little dog, who now leaned against her legs under the table. "Because we like to have fun, don't we? And money helps."

"I see," Arden said soberly. "So fun is the one thing that money *can* buy." She and Margaret snickered.

Sallie looked at them, one eyebrow raised. "Private joke?"

"Mom, it's a line from the Beatles. Not exactly private."

"Well, whatever. Believe me, I've lived both ways, and it's much easier with money than without it."

"We'll keep that in mind," Arden said drily. "After today I have to admit I'm enjoying yours."

Sallie beamed at her, then turned to Margaret. "Arden says you girls are quite taken with one another." She tapped a long red fingernail on her front tooth. "I like that. Maybe I'll use it in one of my books. Of course, a man would have to come along and rescue the heroine in the end."

"I hope you aren't counting on that for me, Mom."

"Oh, darling." She giggled. "People can't truly rescue one another. We can only distract each other. Don't you know that?"

"I don't even know what you mean."

"There she is!" a deep voice boomed out. Joe crossed the kitchen in two giant strides. "The lady of the hour!" He enclosed Sallie in an enthusiastic hug.

"Happy birthday, kiddo." He gave Arden a peck on the cheek. "Sorry I'm late. It sure is nice to come home to two such beautiful women. Okay, two and a half." Joe squatted and reached his hand out to Parade, who retreated further under the table. "It's been a long time since we were all together."

Margaret did not exist in this room. She was surprised he didn't sit in her chair, mistaking it for an empty one.

"So what have you ladies been up to today?"

"Oh, you know, girl talk," Arden replied coolly. "Clothes, recipes, overthrowing the patriarchy, things like that."

"Very funny." Joe leaned against the counter, ankles crossed, hands shoved deep into his pockets. Margaret thought he was striving for a casual look, like the models in those catalogs he studied, but his edgy voice and anxious eyes gave him away. "Can you believe the things she says these days?" he asked Sallie. "Kinda makes you miss the old sweet Arden we used to know, doesn't it?"

"Joe, you're looking good," Sallie replied diplomatically.

"I've been better."

"No doubt. But you look handsome as ever."

"Thanks, Sallie. Glad to know looks still count for something to some women."

"Well, I'm going to take Parade for a walk now." Sallie tucked the dog under her arm and pulled a leash from her red leather bag. "See you kids later."

Arden waited until she heard the front door close before she wheeled around. "What is your problem, Joe? Do you get off on upsetting my mother?"

"Sallie's tough and stubborn, just like you. She's not so easily upset."

"You want Mom to play referee? Is that it?"

"Do we have to discuss this in front of *her*?" he whispered furiously, flipping a hand in Margaret's direction.

"Why not? It's about her, isn't it?"

"Maybe I'll go see if Deborah needs any help." Margaret sidled toward the door, but Arden caught her hand and pulled her back.

"Look, Arden, I came home tonight in a good mood, ready to get together with everyone and celebrate your birthday. But you had to blow it with that crack about the patriarchy. Do you hate me so much that you have to jab at me every second?"

"You know I don't hate you. I only said it because I was mad that you were so rude to Margaret."

"Rude?" He turned to Margaret as if to enlist her in his defense. "What did I say?"

"Exactly. You made a big show of ignoring her. It's childish to try to get back at me by hurting Margaret. It only makes me feel closer to her and more alienated from you."

"And I suppose your sophomoric jokes are mature?"

"All right, we're both acting like jerks. But let's see if we can keep it under control while my mother's here. Okay?"

"No, it's not okay. You're always droning on and on about your *feelings*," he sneered. "All I hear is how important it is for you to *feel* whatever it is you *feel* with Margaret. Well, what about my feelings? Am I supposed to stuff them in the freezer just because your mother dropped into town?"

"I'm asking you to change your behavior, not your emotions. Can't you see you're making everyone uncomfortable?"

Uncomfortable was an understatement, Margaret thought. She, for one, was sweating.

What exactly was the issue here, anyway? How to behave in front of Sallie? Of course, Margaret cast her vote with Arden, but she could see Joe's side too. As Sallie herself had said, what was the point of dissembling? She would sense the tension beneath their veneer of civility, and with the boldness she shared with her daughter would probably call them on it. Poor woman, expecting to stop in for a celebration, and finding herself in the middle of a revolution instead.

"I'm so sorry if I'm making everyone uncomfortable." Joe took a few steps closer until he towered over Arden. A twisted blue vein coursed down his neck like a tiny river of rage. "I'm fighting for my life here. You'll have to excuse me if I can't do it in a gentlemanly manner."

"Since when was it so crucial for you to have me in your life?" Arden glared up at him, arms folded tightly across her chest, fingers digging into her own skin.

"Since the first time I held you, eight years ago."

"Until the last time you held me, three years ago."

"Is that what this is about? Sex? I can fuck you till your eyes fall out if that's what you want."

"The fact that you can even say that proves you've never had any idea of what I want, in bed or out."

"And whose fault is that? Am I supposed to read your mind?"

"I hate like hell to interrupt this, folks." Charles' smooth voice made everybody jump. "But I'm coming in and I think you should know we can hear you downstairs." He stepped gingerly into the kitchen and set a large salad in the refrigerator. "Now, it's Arden's birthday, dinner is ready, and

Sallie will be back any second. So let's all get ourselves under
control, shall we?"

No one moved. Joe's bright blue eyes bored into Arden's.
Margaret stood transfixed with embarrassment.

"Shall we?" Charles repeated more emphatically, grasping
Joe's arm.

Joe shook him off. "This is my house. I'll go when I'm
good and ready." He stared at Arden for a few more seconds.
"I'm not through with you," he said bitterly, and stalked away.

Arden sank into her chair. "It's timing, just like Mom said."
Margaret came up behind her and squeezed her shoulders. She
patted Margaret's hand dismissively. "These problems have
been simmering for months. Why is he freaking out now?"

Charles turned a chair around and straddled it. "You and
Joe always fight when Sallie's here."

"I know. Why is that?"

"Beats me."

"Maybe you were right," Margaret suggested. "Maybe he
wants your mother to get involved because he thinks she'll be
on his side."

"Wrong again, short stuff." Deborah marched in,
brandishing a large dish of steaming lasagna between two
purple oven mitts shaped like tropical fish. Paul followed,
carrying a bowl of broccoli, a loaf of Italian bread, and a pair
of tongs, which he kept clacking in Deborah's ears. "Paul,
grow up," she squealed, trying to protect her ears with her
shoulders. She set the lasagna on the stove and smacked him
on the rear end with one of the fish.

"What's your diagnosis?" asked Charles.

"I think birthdays are hard for divorced couples." Deborah
clicked the oven on warm. "I mean, here's this happy occasion
that he usually shares with Arden, and now there's someone
else in his place. I know he vacated that spot, but still, it's got
to hurt. So he acts like an asshole. That's what people do
sometimes when they're in pain."

"What are you suggesting," Margaret bristled, "that Arden
should spend the rest of her life babying him?"

"I'm suggesting that since you're asking some restraint of
him, you two might exercise some yourselves. The goo-goo
eyes, the gravitating toward each other like she's a compass
and you're the North Pole—give it a rest. Maybe it will help
the atmosphere in here."

"I get it. Our relationship is okay with you as long as we don't flaunt it."

"Margaret, put your switchblade away," Deborah said mildly. "You know me better than that."

"God, everyone's so uptight tonight!" Arden shoved her chair back roughly. "Where's my mother? Why isn't she here yet?"

"She's downstairs, graciously allowing us all to get our shit together before she joins us," Paul replied. "Why don't I go see how Joe's doing, and maybe we can get rolling here."

"Don't bother, I'm ready." Joe had traded his business suit for a pair of faded jeans. His sleeves were rolled up, his tie removed, his curly black hair still damp from the comb. He looked altogether smaller. "Sorry, Arden." Joe studied his black polished loafers, then looked up at her with a charming, sheepish grin. "I don't know what gets into me sometimes. Maybe you should call an exorcist."

"It was my fault too. I could have been a little more sensitive."

He gave Margaret a light, buddy-buddy buff on the shoulder. "No offense. It's, you know, nothing personal."

"That's okay, Joe." She considered joining the general humility-fest, but what would she apologize for? Loving Arden? She felt as if a huge wave of contention had crashed in, drenching them all. But when the wave receded, everyone else was calm and dry, and only Margaret stood on the shore gasping for breath. She had yet to figure out the tides on this strange little planet.

"I'll go get my mom." Arden slipped behind Joe, giving his arm a brief caress as she passed. "She loves these happy endings."

After dinner, Margaret and Joe stood hip to hip at the chipped white porcelain sink. From the living room they heard shreds of conversation, an occasional shout of laughter.

"That must be Sallie, holding court," Joe guessed, taking a plate from Margaret and rubbing his dish towel around it in squeaky circles.

"She's a good storyteller. Have you ever read any of her books?"

"Once, a long time ago. I didn't see what was so special about it. The main characters got married in the end. Big surprise." He chugged down a glass of ice water.

"Maybe I should read one."

"What for?"

"Oh, I don't know. Just to get to know her."

"I don't think she writes that kind of book. They're all the same, basically. She calls it her secret recipe."

"But she's so successful." Margaret squirted in more detergent.

"Yeah, I know," he said wistfully. "Rich and famous."

"So she must be good at it. She couldn't get that popular from following a recipe."

"Maybe it's not a recipe. Sallie often says things she doesn't mean." His back was turned to her as he fumbled in the freezer. "She believes them at the moment, but later she changes her mind. It doesn't matter to her anymore if she makes a mistake." With an emphatic clunk, he set a fresh glass on the kitchen table.

"What do you mean?" She glanced at him warily. Was this some kind of strategy in their intermittent war? But he was guilelessly polishing up Deborah's serving bowl, one dish towel in his hand, another folded over his shoulder as if he were about to burp a baby.

"I don't mean that she's dishonest. She's . . . flighty. She might say something because it has a nice ring to it. Next day she realizes she doesn't feel that way at all, but she simply thinks 'Oh, well—next time I'll know better.'"

"What's wrong with that?" Margaret asked.

"Nothing, I guess. I suppose if you've got Sallie's kind of money, you can believe anything you want."

"You keep saying that. How rich is she?"

Joe enunciated each word clearly. "As rich as you could ever want her to be." He gulped some more water. "And Arden could be too. Someday she will be."

"So if Arden didn't want to, she wouldn't need to work."

"Not a day. She could pay off all our debts in a minute and do whatever she wanted for the rest of her life."

Margaret submerged the last pan. "But Arden values her independence. She's not interested in material things."

"No, but she likes going to concerts and plays. And she loves to travel. We used to take three-day weekends all the time." He gave her a sideways glance. "Margaret, don't take this the wrong way. I know you can't afford to live the way Arden and I used to, and Arden doesn't make enough to pay your way, even if you'd let her. But can't you tell she misses it? How long do you think you can keep a woman like Arden interested if all you can offer is political rhetoric and meatless spaghetti?"

"I don't think that's any of your business."

"You're entitled to your opinion," he replied cheerfully. "Arden still confides in me, don't think she doesn't. You can't change the habits of a decade in a few months."

Margaret didn't respond. Her heart was a stone in her throat.

"Are you finished with this?" Joe took the pan from her hands and patted it dry. "Hey, I didn't mean any offense."

"You never do, do you?"

Joe gulped the rest of his water and wiped his hand across his mouth. "Come on out before they finish the cake, Margaret." He pulled the clean dish towel off his shoulder, wadded it up with the damp one he'd been using, and dropped them both onto the table. "I can't wait to give Arden my present."

Absently, she reached for his glass to wash it out. The sharp citric odor told her it was gin he had been drinking all night, not water. Why should she care, Margaret asked herself as she dried the glass and put it back on the shelf. Yet the discovery alarmed her.

This guy is dangerous, she realized with such clarity that it sent a chill skittering down her back. Maybe Arden did confide in him. Maybe they were still close in ways that Margaret couldn't fathom and could never replace. She pictured the dark nights she shared with Arden, lit only by the fire between them, and she knew he was bluffing. But 'maybe' was a small word. It could always find someplace to hide.

"It's about time you joined us." Arden grinned from her vantage point on the couch between Sallie and Charles. To their right, Joe hunched in his chair, elbows on his thighs, hands hanging idly between his knees. In front of them, the low glass coffeetable was crowded with plates, forks, wine glasses, and a small stack of wrapped gifts. Margaret sat on the floor near the large overstuffed chair in which Deborah cuddled with Paul, despite her admonition that everyone else refrain from public displays of affection.

Margaret's entrance seemed to galvanize Joe. "All right!
Time to unwrap the presents," he announced. "Here, take mine
first."

Carefully Arden opened the small velvet box. Her eyes
widened, one eyebrow shot up. Slowly she lifted out a heavy
gold necklace with a small diamond hanging from it. A soft
"Oh!" of appreciation escaped from Sallie.

"It's beautiful," Arden began, "but it's, well, it's awfully
fancy."

"You're worth it."

Margaret felt her face flaming red.

Deborah bolted upright in her chair, eliciting a startled
grunt from her husband. "Joe, you are such a bastard."

"What do you mean?" he asked innocently.

"You know damn well what I mean. Arden, open
Margaret's present."

Charles and Sallie exchanged glances, as if they foresaw the
evening's outcome.

Arden tore the wrapping paper off and opened the box.
Before she could remove the gift, Joe stuck his hand in and
yanked it out.

"Well, would you look at that. Another necklace." He
looped it casually around his fingers. The delicate gold chain
looked even smaller against his big hand.

Margaret had imagined trailing her fingers lightly across
Arden's skin as she explored the texture of the necklace,
following its liquid form as the chain rested in the V-shaped
indentation below her throat, tracing the line of her collarbone
out to her smooth shoulders, which at the end of summer were
brown and freckled as two country eggs. She shuddered now
to think that Joe might have entertained the same images as he
selected his gift.

"You knew Margaret was giving her a necklace," Deborah
accused. "You asked me yesterday."

"So? Now she's got two. Although this one looks kind of
flimsy," he added, tugging at Margaret's chain.

"Put it down, Joe," Charles ordered in a perfectly flat voice.

"What's that, Charlie?"

"I said put it down." Charles looked exactly the same as he
always did, with his taffy-colored hair, his mild blue eyes, his
hands folded calmly in his lap. But in his cheeks flamed two
identical circles of red.

"I might have expected that from you." Joe dropped the chain into some cake crumbs on the littered table. "So what's it going to be, Charles? Which side are you on?"

"I don't see that I have to take sides."

"Sure you do. We all do. The personal is political, right Margaret? So let's draw the lines. Where are you going to stand, Charles, with the boys or the girls? Or do you think you can flit back and forth forever?"

"Joe, shut the fuck up," Margaret exclaimed.

"Ooh, don't frighten me, Butch."

"Can it, Joe," growled Paul. "You're going to go too far."

Joe grabbed somebody's wine glass from the table and downed it. "Things have already gone way too far around here. I want to know where every person in this room stands."

"Get a grip on it!" Deborah's voice lashed with scorn. "I'm not going to let you spoil Arden's birthday."

"You stay out of this, Stern. I already know whose side you're on.

"Hey, don't talk to my wife like that. I'm warning you."

"You're warning me?" Joe gave a bark of laughter that made Parade look up from her nap. "I warned *you*! I warned you when that bulldyke first moved in here, and now look what's happened. You think your woman is off-limits?"

"That does it." Paul stormed over to Joe and pulled him to his feet. "You want to know the score, Joe? Let's count it up. You've spent a lot of bucks just to be hateful. You've hurt Arden. You've embarrassed her mother. You're insulted the rest of us. It's a clean sweep: you've pissed off everyone in the world who gives a damn about you."

Joe stood swaying. With a sigh of disgust, Paul let him go, and he dropped into his chair, clutching the arms for balance. Finally he spoke in a low, hoarse voice. "Maybe things have gotten a little out of hand tonight. Probably everyone's right and I'm wrong, as usual. But let's cut to the bottom line. Arden, which necklace do you want?"

"To tell you the truth, I don't want either one anymore. But if you force me to choose—"

"I'm forcing you," Joe interrupted.

"I'll take Margaret's," she said firmly.

"You'd keep this," he lifted the chain languidly on one finger, "—instead of this?" He hefted his necklace, making the diamond sparkle.

"Some things that can't be bought with money, Joe."

"Forgive me for butting in," Sallie began, "but since everyone else is going to hate themselves in the morning, I might as well get into the act."

"Go ahead, Mom."

"I've known three of you since you were babies. Paul and Joe, of course, I've known for many years. And it's always astounded me how this group will take the most private issue and throw it on the table for everyone to examine and dissect."

"We have this sort of ecosystem here," Deborah explained. "We try to talk things out so nothing will upset the balance."

"But you're making a bad mistake this time. Sexual jealousy—Joe, I'm talking to you—is like a horrible bout of the flu. You feel utterly miserable, but it passes quickly. And it's so unimportant."

"Easy for you to say," he muttered.

"No, it's not. I've learned this the hard way, by going through it. Just as you're suffering over Arden. Just as Arden suffered over you."

"Oh, so now we're even, is that it?"

"No, Joe, not at all. What I'm saying is that the six of you have something rare and wonderful here. You're not kids anymore. You're not going to find friends like this again. Don't destroy it over something as trivial as who sleeps with whom."

"I'll tell you one thing, " Joe declared, "I won't live like this. Arden, you better start reading the want ads. You can't afford this apartment if I move out."

Arden closed her eyes briefly and pinched the bridge of her nose. "Look, it's been a rough evening. We're all upset. You've—we've all been drinking. Why don't we call it a night and discuss this another time?"

"I understand," Joe replied with exaggerated sweetness. "You're in a hurry to get upstairs with your girlfriend."

"Cut it out," Charles said wearily.

"Hey, Arden, you know what?" Joe snapped his fingers. "Maybe I'll stay here and you can move out."

"Could we drop the subject?"

His eyes glittered as if he had a fever. "No, really, that's a good idea. Why should I have to leave? You go."

"No one's going anywhere, Joe," Arden replied evenly.

"Sure you are. I'll give you till the end of the month. Maybe even two months. But I want you out by Christmas, or at least New Year's. Start the new year clean." He swept his hand above the coffee table and made a "whoosh" sound.

"Forget it."

"Use your head, Arden. There isn't a single law in this state that protects a homosexual's right to housing. Isn't that true, Margaret? And we don't even have leases. You're out of luck. A few words from me to Mrs. Rogers, and it's furniture on the sidewalk time." Joe looked astonished, as if someone else had made those words issue from his mouth.

"Think about what you're saying!" Margaret felt a sickening lurch of *deja vu*. This was a nightmare, and she had dreamed it many times before. "You can't be serious."

"Oh, but I am."

Arden turned away, as if the sight of him were painful. "Joe, I am begging you to drop the subject."

"Nope. Too late. No can do."

"Jesus Christ!" Paul spat out. "I don't believe you, man. You'd make Arden move because she's got a new gig?"

"It's not *that* she's fucking. It's *who* she's fucking."

"That's not the point and you know it."

Joe laughed, a chilling sound. "Of course you wouldn't think so. You don't have the balls. Everyone knows Deborah cracks the whip in your family."

"Shut your mouth!" Charles leapt to his feet.

"Calm down, Charles. I'd be upstairs packing if I were you."

Sallie spoke in a quiet, hypnotic voice that drew everyone's attention. "You know, Joe, I go to a lot of parties. I see a lot of belligerent drunks. You're not even very good at it."

"What's your point, Sallie?"

"Excuses like 'I'm sorry' and 'I was drunk' and 'I don't remember' can only go so far. Once you cross a certain line, they don't work anymore." She pierced him with her clear, hazel eyes. "You're teetering right on the edge of that line, my friend. Be very careful."

"I'm not the one who needs to be careful here. It's the gay community that has to watch its step."

"Okay, I've had it." Paul reached for Deborah's hand. "Come on, honey."

"You two don't have to go," he declared expansively. "You're safe. I've got nothing against you."

"Listen to yourself!" Margaret urged. Her own voice reached her like a bad long-distance connection. "You try to come across as a big liberal, but you don't think twice about using your white male heterosexual privilege to get your way."

"That's what it's there for."

"Would you really want Arden back on those terms—knowing that she was with you because you threatened her, and not because she wanted to be?"

"I don't care about the terms. I just want her back, and I'll make it right with her later."

"Some things are inherently wrong. You can't make them right. Don't you get that?"

Deborah put a restraining hand on her shoulder. "Don't waste your breath, Margaret. Look who you're arguing with. This drunken fascist isn't Joe."

Joe blinked at Deborah, trying to focus. "How would you know?"

"Because the Joe I know wouldn't threaten to get his best friends evicted."

"If this is what my best friends *do* to me—" and his voice cracked—"then I might as well be alone. I am alone, anyway. Nobody here is on my side."

"You're not alone," Arden said.

He shook his head. "It's too late. You're moving out, and so is your girlfriend, and so is Charles. The party's over."

"Joe, for the last time, I am not leaving, and neither is anyone else."

"Why? Give me one good reason."

Arden glanced at her mother. "Because I own this house."

"Since when?" he demanded, amidst the exclamations of the others. His face looked waxy.

"Since today," Sallie answered. "I gave it to her for her birthday."

"Last year you gave her a sweater," Deborah wailed.

Sallie laughed, her surprising girlish giggle. "She's thirty years old, and I wanted her to have a little security. Little did I realize how much she'd need it."

"What about Mrs. Rogers? How'd you get her to sell?"

"She's a sharp lady. She got a very good price."

"And I told her she could live here as long as she wanted," Arden added.

"Did you tell her how much garbage she can put in the cans?" asked Deborah.

"Congratulations, Arden," said Joe leadenly. "I guess money buys more than you thought, huh."

She ignored him. "Listen, I'm tired. If you guys don't mind, let's save the rest of these gifts until tomorrow."

"I think you should throw them out," Deborah exclaimed.

"Maybe I should exchange mine," Charles mused. "I got you a necklace."

Arden groaned. "Do I have an ugly neck or something?"

"Just kidding."

"Darling, would you like a hand with these dishes? If not, Parade and I will be on our way."

"Mom, don't you want to stay? It's such a long drive to your hotel."

Sallie rolled her eyes, a mannerism Margaret recognized. "Stay here, with this *menage*? Lord, no. How about if you come with me? You know I keep that sweet apartment at the Drake."

"No thanks," Arden said with a shy smile. "I'd like to spend my first night here in my new house."

Sallie glanced at Margaret. "Of course you would. Silly me. Well, goodnight all."

"Come on, I'll take you to your car." Arden slipped her arm around her mother's waist. With matching strides they walked to the door, while Parade marched behind them.

Wordlessly, the others picked up plates and glasses and filed into the kitchen. They left Joe alone in the living room, head cradled in his hands. Charles washed the dishes as they all chattered about the evening's events.

"Cool it," Deborah whispered dramatically. "Here comes the landlady."

"Very funny." Arden picked up a dish towel from the table.

"Put that down," Paul ordered. "You're the birthday girl. You don't have to clean up after your own celebration."

"Look, it's my party—"

"And she'll dry if she wants to," Deborah finished.

"Deborah, some things are real," Arden said wearily. "You can't fix them with a joke."

"I know that. Do you think I enjoyed this evening?"

"Sorry." Arden patted her arm. "I'm kind of in shock."

"It's okay."

"And I'm worried about Joe." She twisted the cloth painfully. "How's he going to face himself tomorrow? We'll all have each other. He'll have nothing."

"Except a mammoth hangover," added Charles.

Deborah pulled the towel from Arden's hands and threw it to Paul. "You can't spend the rest of your life like you're in a three-legged race with him."

"Arden, you know I love the guy," Paul said, "but he was way out of line tonight. Sure, he'll be miserable in the morning. He should be. That's how you feel when you trash your best friends."

"So I should just let him suffer?"

"Do you try to protect the batterer from the remorse he'll feel the next day?" Margaret demanded.

"You can't stop him from suffering," Charles advised. "You can only stop him from learning from it. Let him take the rap, for once."

Arden shook her head. "Everyone told me things would change the minute I hit thirty, but I never thought I had to take it literally."

"You were wrong." Deborah hooked her fingers around Paul's belt and tugged him toward the doorway. "Good night. We're going now."

"Get some sleep," said Paul.

"Or whatever." Deborah winked lasciviously at Margaret.

"Charles, stick around." Arden held up a bottle. "There's a little bit left of this fine red wine that Joe bought God knows where for God knows how much. Let's finish it off."

"Sounds good to me."

Margaret raised her glass. "Here's to Arden: famous translator, new home owner, and not bad looking, either. Happy birthday, baby."

"I'll drink to that and raise you one." Arden clinked her glass with the others. "Here's to us: the almost-exiled gay community of Lill Street."

"Arden, I don't think you've ever declared yourself before," Margaret said proudly.

"I've declared myself to you."

"I know, but not to the larger sisterhood." She patted Charles' hand. "I mean that word generically."

He grinned at Margaret. "Sure you do. Well, here's to Arden, for joining the club."

"And paying her dues," added Margaret.

"Wait! I have another toast," he said. "Here's to the Queen of Fun, who proves that money can't buy love, but love stories can pay a lot of bills."

"Oh, let's broaden our horizons." Arden spread her arms. "Let's drink to all the things that money can't buy."

THE FALSE SPRING

Joe was sick with shame for three days after Arden's birthday. Finally he emerged from his room gaunt, subdued, and pink-cheeked, as if, having neglected to shave during his seclusion, he had regenerated the tender skin of a boy. He went to each person and apologized humbly, earnestly explaining why his ugly words could not possibly represent his true feelings.

The odd thing was, Margaret believed him. He was not a bad person; he had simply reacted badly to a difficult situation. Charm had failed to win Arden back, so he had tried force. Under the same circumstances, Margaret thought she would have behaved differently, but who could be sure? Desperation was a strange accomplice.

Now it was Sunday morning, not yet eight o'clock, and Joe was on the phone. "Are you awake?" he asked Margaret in a strange, solicitous tone.

"Barely. What's up?" Thinking it was Arden calling, she had run into the office to answer the phone. Now she could feel her hair, wet from the shower and still unbraided, starting to soak the back of her t-shirt.

"Um, you have a visitor."

"In your apartment?"

"No, I'm downstairs, at Paul's place." Joe's voice grew faint and then strong again. Margaret guessed he had turned to glance at the visitor. He continued, "She wants to know if it's too early to see you."

Margaret chuckled at his grave, courteous demeanor.
"Well, I appreciate the service, Joe, but you don't have to be
my doorman. Why don't you just send her up?"

"I think you better come down here."

"Why? Who is she?"

Joe hesitated. "It's your mother."

Margaret sat down, hard. She could feel the cool metal
chair pressing against her spine. She could hear her heartbeat
crashing in her ears. She reminded herself to breathe, as if it
were a chore she had meant to do earlier. "Tell her—" she
began, and ran out of words. Margaret passed a hand over her
eyes, and when she put it down her face felt hard. "You can tell
Anne Osborn she's not too early. She's too fucking late."

"Margaret, no," he said gently. "I'm not going to tell her
that. Now take a few seconds to get it together, and then come
down here and meet your mother. If you're not down in three
minutes, I'm coming to get you."

"It's not your decision, Joe," she whispered furiously, as if
her mother could overhear them. "You don't know anything
about it."

"I know a second chance when I see one, kiddo. Now get
down here."

It took Margaret forever to descend the two flights. For
one thing, her legs had turned into some dense, inflexible
metal. And for another, she didn't want her mother to hear an
eager clatter as Margaret closed in on the one woman she had
loved the most.

As she passed through the empty kitchen and living room,
Margaret wondered where Deborah and Paul were. Probably
out for a morning walk, or hiding in their bedroom. She could
hear voices on the front porch: Joe, charming and polite, and
her mother, sounding nervous. Good. Then Margaret was not
the only one whose hands were shaking.

She stopped to take a deep breath before she reached the
porch. Margaret told herself she would not rush. She would be
dignified. She would be cautious. She would find out what the
woman wanted and respond judiciously.

Silently, Margaret pushed open the screen door. "Mother,"
she said.

Anne wheeled around. Her gray eyes were wide, startled.
Her brown hair was pulled back into a bun, with feathery
wisps already escaping. She looked smaller than Margaret
remembered. In her hands was a copy of *Feminist Times*.

"Magpie," she exclaimed, and held out her arms.

It was the cruelest thing she could have said. That word, that family nickname which no one else ever used, broke open the world for Margaret: the world of her childhood, the world of family connections, the world that she had lost when she found herself as a lesbian.

"Damn you, Mama," Margaret cried—another infant word, dredged up from who knows where inside—and found herself sobbing in a breathless, helpless way, so fiercely that she had to lean against the splintery wooden wall.

Instinctively Joe reached out to Margaret, but stopped himself when he saw Anne moving toward her. Head down, he walked swiftly across the porch and into the house, letting the screen door slam behind him.

"Maggie, I'm so sorry," Anne murmured repeatedly, hugging her tightly. But Margaret would not yield. Her elbows remained pinned to her sides, her hands covered her face. Her arms had held beautiful women; they would never hold someone who hated love. Margaret stood motionless until she could stop crying and step out of her mother's embrace.

Anne handed her daughter a tissue from her purse and kept one to wipe her own eyes. "God, I've missed you," she declared in a choked, fervent voice. "Letting you go like that was the worst mistake I've ever made."

"You didn't 'let me go,'" Margaret replied acidly. "You cast me out. There's a difference."

Anne bowed her head. Margaret couldn't see her face, but she could see her chin trembling, and she thought her own heart would shatter. "Mom, I'm sorry. I don't want to be so mean."

"I don't blame you." Anne spoke rapidly, as if each word burned her mouth as she spoke it. "I know that what we did must have hurt you terribly."

"It did. Why did you *do* it?" Margaret demanded, her voice involuntarily falling into a childhood cadence. "You abandoned me. You exiled me from my own life. How could you do that to your own daughter?"

Anne glanced around the porch, and without a word, both women moved in unison to the swing. As they sat down, Anne snapped her purse closed and set it on the floor, a prim, familiar gesture that Margaret hadn't thought of in years but recognized instantly. Anne turned to her daughter. "You don't know how often I've asked myself the same question. Since the moment it happened, I've never stopped asking myself." She paused, a thoughtful look on her tired face. "It destroyed me," she concluded simply.

"It destroyed you!" Margaret exploded. The jolt of anger that shot through her body made the swing jump. "What about me? You chose to do it. You were the fucking parent!"

"You don't understand," Anne insisted quietly. "My life stopped that day. The family I thought I had, the person I thought I was, the man I thought your father was—all gone. Your life has moved on. You live in this beautiful house. You write for this intriguing newspaper. You have new friends like that handsome man who seems to think very highly of you."

Margaret sighed. Might as well get it over with. "He's not my boyfriend," she stated evenly. "He's my girlfriend's ex-lover."

"I know. He told me."

"Joe told you that?" Margaret glanced at the copy of *Feminist Times* lying on the swing between them. It occurred to her how much her conservative mother must have hated every word, how difficult it must have been for her to call the paper 'intriguing.' "What did you think of *Feminist Times*?" Margaret couldn't help asking.

Anne gave her a direct, level gaze. "You must know I don't understand anything in there. But some of the writing was quite good. I wish I could tell which articles you wrote."

"All of the quite good ones," Margaret replied, and they both laughed. The laugh dissipated quickly in the still morning air, leaving the two women staring at one another unprotected.

"Well, anyway, you seem to have survived," Margaret said flatly. "You look good, pretty much the way I remember you."

Anne winced. "Oh, I survived. I still get up in the morning, I still make breakfast, I still go to work. But I stopped growing that day. Your father and I, we both turned some kind of corner."

"Yeah, well, I turned some kind of corner too." Margaret looked out across the yard and studied the familiar street. She couldn't believe she was sharing this view with her mother. "So what made you decide to come here?"

"Your father's had a stroke." Anne laid a restraining hand on Margaret's arm. "Don't worry, he's fine. It was just a tiny one; he didn't have to stay in the hospital long. But it was a wake-up call. It shook us both up pretty badly."

"And the first thing he said was, 'Let's go find Margaret?'" she asked sarcastically.

"As a matter of fact, it was something like that."

"So why isn't he here?"

Anne smiled, and unwillingly Margaret joined her. "You know how he is."

Yes, Margaret knew how he was. Throughout her youth, the consoling, the disciplining, the arranging of their family's emotional life had always been her mother's responsibility. She guessed the great wake-up call hadn't changed that. "How did you track me down?"

"I always knew where you were. Jane told me."

"And you never called me? You never read my letters? You never once tried to get me back?" Margaret's voice broke, and she turned her face away. She couldn't afford to let herself be so vulnerable again.

"Darling, you can't know the kind of loss I've been living with."

"Your loss!" Margaret spat. "I can't believe this. You boot me out of the family, you never speak to me again, and you have the nerve to whine to me about your loss. Exactly what the fuck did you lose?"

"I lost you," Anne said quietly. "You."

Both women fell silent. The still street had come alive while they were talking. Women pushing strollers passed by in pairs, caught up in their laughing conversations. Bicyclists rolled past effortlessly. From up and down the block came the patient, papery sound of leaves being raked.

"Does he want to see me?" asked Margaret.

"He does."

"When?"

"That's up to you."

"I don't know if I can forgive you. Either of you."

"I know." Anne clicked open her purse, pulled out a pad and pen. "And I have to live with that. With what I did to my daughter—to both my daughters." She wrote a few lines, tore off the page and handed it to Margaret. "Here's our address and phone number. Call me when you get ready." She grasped Margaret's hand. "And Maggie, if you possibly can, please make it soon. We've lost so much precious time already."

"I will if I can. I can't promise anything, Mom." Margaret looked at her shyly. "So, are you okay? I don't mean about this, but otherwise?"

"Fine. And you?"

"I'm okay too." Margaret sighed with the frustration of having so much to say and so much standing in the way of communication. "I have a lot to tell you. One of these days," she concluded lamely.

"One of these days," agreed Anne sadly, and she rose.

"Hey, don't forget your paper." Margaret tucked *Feminist Times* under her mother's arm.

"Don't worry, Maggie," she solemnly replied. "I will never forget anything of yours again. I promise."

Margaret stood on the porch steps as her mother crossed the street. Their old station wagon was nowhere to be seen, and she wondered which car her mother would climb into. "Mom!" she called as Anne unlocked the door of a small blue Ford—the car of a woman who had no children.

Keys in hand, Anne turned toward her.

"Tell Daddy—tell him I'm glad he's okay."

"I will, Magpie."

Margaret watched her mother drive away, clutching tightly the piece of paper that had the power to bring her back.

Margaret recounted the visit in detail, first to Arden and Deborah, then to Joan, then to Samantha and Maureen. She wanted to call everyone she knew and tell them the news, but she was too busy.

She had received a phone call asking her to meet Lillian Green at a downtown hotel. Margaret spent hours preparing for her interview.

"Thank you for coming over." Lillian sat in an old-fashioned barrel chair with her back to the window, immune to the drama of the street and the sparkle of Lake Michigan beyond. She was wearing a tailored white blouse, soft with age, and a pair of baggy jeans. Her long legs stretched in front of her and crossed at the ankles. On her feet were old white gym socks, worn thin at the heels. Margaret was touched by the sight of them. Here was a woman whose face was known to millions, and still she wore these homely socks.

"Thanks for inviting me." Margaret put her tape recorder and reporter's notebook on the round table between them.

"So, Margaret, what have you been up to since last we met?" Lillian asked in her unhurried way.

She considered telling Lillian about last week's miraculous reconciliation with her mother, but it seemed too personal. And Lillian had probably forgotten all about that embarrassing afternoon when Margaret had acted like an idiot. At least Margaret hoped she had. "Nothing new. I'm still writing for *Feminist Times*, and I work in a bookstore part-time."

"Did you ever finish that book?" Lillian asked with genuine interest.

"Well, no. I kind of got off the track, and never got back on."

"It's difficult with a project of that magnitude. Of course, sometimes we grow out of our own ideas, no matter how wonderful they were to begin with."

"Yeah, I guess that is what happened." Margaret stared at this woman with her short blond hair and her blue eyes that seemed to see right through her. "I never realized it before."

"In that case, I wonder if you'd be interested in a new adventure?"

"Adventure?"

"Yes." Lillian pulled a leather-covered pad from her briefcase and flipped through a few pages. "Didn't my assistant brief you?"

"She set up this meeting. I figured it was for an interview." She tapped her notebook with her pen.

"So it is. A job interview. Perhaps Carol assumed you knew."

"Oh! I didn't know. I didn't bring a resume or anything."

"Oh well. It's probably better this way." Lillian glanced down at her pad. "Do you remember the conversation we had at the ERA rally in June?"

"Yes, about a project you wanted to do, and how tired you were." Margaret faltered. Perhaps that was a tactless thing to say. Lillian did look weary, aged as her clothing.

She laughed. "That's the one. I see you remembered all the highlights. Do you recall the specifics of the project, or shall I refresh your memory?"

"No, I remember. You wanted to travel around to ask women how they feel about the movement and where they want it to go. Then you'd write a book about it."

"Exactly. My publisher has just given me the go-ahead as well as a nice advance. Now I'm in the market for an assistant. That's where you come in."

"Me? I thought you had an assistant."

"I do, but I need Carol to run things in New York. My life's gotten so complicated it requires a full-time coordinator just to keep the threads untangled. But this—this would be simple." Lillian smiled, an inward smile at a vision Margaret couldn't share. She didn't see how running around the country talking to strangers would be simple. "Besides, Carol doesn't have the qualifications for this job."

"What are they?"

"I want someone young, but not too young. Someone who's committed to the movement but not overly ambitious. Someone bright, articulate, energetic. Someone who's still got a little fire left."

"Gosh," said Margaret. So much for being articulate.

"And I want someone who's a lesbian."

"Why?"

"Because I'm not. But outreach to the lesbian community is essential. No matter how enlightened we straight women are, sometimes a lesbian perspective sheds a different light."

"I'm very flattered, Lillian, but why me? You must know a hundred women like that."

She nodded. "New York is full of them. But I don't really want a New Yorker. You've got a lot of the Midwest in you. Of course, I know young women in other places. I'm asking you first because I happened to be heading for Chicago when I heard from my publisher. So if you're not interested, please don't do it for the cause. Joan of Arc I do not need."

"I understand. What exactly would this job entail?"

Lillian rose and opened the window. Traffic noises floated up to them from ten stories below. She lit a long brown cigarette and began to pace. "There's nothing glamorous about it. Basically you'd travel with me and do all the things I don't want to do. You'd organize the material I collect, make travel arrangements, set up interviews. Sometimes you'd go on the interviews with me, other times you'd be back in the hotel room typing up the notes from yesterday." She stopped. "I hate to ask you this, but you do type, don't you?"

Margaret smiled at her discomfiture. "I'm a writer, remember? Of course I know how to type."

"That's another thing." Lillian resumed her long strides. "You wouldn't be doing any writing. Oh, maybe a few letters now and then, but nothing substantial. What it boils down to is I'd be having all the fun, and you'd be doing all the drudgery that makes it possible. I want to be clear about that, because I don't want to paint too rosy a picture."

"Don't worry, you're not."

"But keep in mind that you'd also be meeting a lot of wonderful women. And you'd get to be intimately familiar with the raw material long before it comes out in book form." She mashed out her cigarette. "How does it sound so far?"

"Pretty good."

"Wonderful. Now, on to the nitty gritty. You'd be living in hotel rooms, most of them not as nice as this one. We'd have separate rooms, of course. But you'll undoubtedly learn more than you want to know about my private life, and naturally I'll expect that to remain private. I'll extend the same courtesy to you."

Lillian paced faster, hands clasped behind her back. "Of course you'd be spending a lot of time with me. And I'm warning you, I can be impatient and crabby. When I'm involved in a project, I get obsessed; I'm an inveterate blabbermouth. I'll ask your opinion a thousand times and then I won't listen to you. I'm sure Carol will be glad to confirm all this if you give her a call.

"Let's see, what else? I smoke, I eat meat, I won't be around drugs. I have a terrible weakness for chocolate. If I'm engrossed in the work I may occasionally ask you to get some for me, since I don't dare keep any available. On the other hand, sometimes I'll offer to go out and pick up a nice tofu loaf or whatever it is you crave. Not very often, though."

Lillian dropped into her chair. "God, I'm exhausted. I hope you accept the offer, Margaret, because I don't know how many times I can give this job description without becoming truly depressed."

"That was no ordinary job description. It sounded more like a marriage proposal."

Lillian laughed. "I suppose nine months on the road together is a marriage of sorts."

"Nine months!"

"Give or take a month. Oh, Lord, I just realized I haven't even mentioned payment. Your expenses would be covered, of course, and your fee would be eight thousand dollars. Is that a problem? You look upset."

"The money's great. It's the time—nine or ten months."

"I realize you'd have to give up your jobs, but perhaps you could sublet your apartment."

"No, it's not that. I . . . I'm seeing someone."

"Oh." Lillian sighed, closed her leather-covered notebook and tossed it onto the table. "Then you have a classic dilemma." She studied Margaret in her kind, impersonal way. "Well, I'm not going to lobby you, but here are my thoughts, for what they're worth. I've been in this struggle a long time, and I'm terribly proud of all we've achieved. But there are very few things I can put my hands on and say, '*This* is something I accomplished.' This book will be one of those things.

"And Margaret, this project could be so important. I believe in leadership, but this is a mass movement. Let's check now and then to see where the masses want to go. I think it will be thrilling. Why not be a part of it?"

"You ought to give up this line of work and get into sales."

Lillian smiled. "What profession do you think I'm in now?"

Margaret stood and faced the window, watching the painfully slow progress of a tiny white sailboat across the vast lake. After a moment she turned toward Lillian again. "I'm really excited that you asked me. It would be a fantastic apprenticeship. But I have to figure a few things out before I decide. Can I have some time to think this over?"

"I'd like to get started in about a month, and there's a lot to do before we hit the road. So I'll need your decision in two days. After that, I'll have to give this pitch to a wonderful young woman I met in Iowa City."

"Fair enough."

Two days, Margaret repeated to herself as she kicked at the browning tufts of grass in Grant Park. All around her, petulant breezes sent dead leaves scuttling across the sidewalk. Dun-colored pigeons squabbled over invisible crumbs. Pedestrians hurried past, wrapped tightly in their own worries. Margaret kept her hands in her pockets, her eyes on the ground.

Why did life always work out like this? Why couldn't Lillian Green have made her offer after Margaret and Arden were an old established couple? Or why couldn't Margaret have met Arden after returning from her journey through the feminist heartland with Lillian?

Perhaps they didn't have to be separated. Maybe Arden could take time off from her job and travel with Margaret. She could afford to do it if, just this once, she would accept some money from Sallie. But Arden had always been so adamant that she did not want to coast on her mother's income. And what would she do on the road for nine months, trail behind Margaret like some kind of wife?

No, she could not ask Arden to give up her career, her friends, her new house, her financial principles, all for the dubious benefit of staying close to Margaret. She was embarrassed even to have considered making such a request.

On the other hand, nine months wasn't that long. Surely she'd be able to see Arden a few times along the way. And they could write to each other, long romantic letters, which someday Margaret would bind into a beautiful notebook and present to her as a gift. It would be hard to be apart for so long, but Margaret thought they could manage it. Arden was smart; she would understand. This was only a journey Margaret was taking; Arden was her home.

By the time Margaret stepped off the el that evening, she had convinced herself that everything would work out. Certainly *Feminist Times* could get along without her. There were plenty of other aspiring journalists ready to bleed for the cause. Deborah would be angry, but she would get over it. As for Arden, she was bound to encourage Margaret to grab this opportunity.

Excitement clanged in her chest. She leaped over a pile of fallen leaves. This was the right thing to do, and this was the right time to do it—now, while she was young and totally devoted to the movement. Never again would she be so fiery, so fearless, so faithful. Never again would she be twenty-four.

"Here you are," exclaimed Arden as Margaret burst into her apartment. "I've been trying to call you all afternoon to see how your interview went."

"It was incredible." Margaret was breathless. "Come on up and I'll tell you all about it."

"Why don't you stay down here? Joe's out for the evening, and I'm building a fire. First fire of the season."

Margaret described her afternoon, fighting a strong urge to get up from the couch and pace as Lillian Green had done. "So what do you think? Pretty amazing, huh?"

"Definitely. I'm so proud of you." Arden squeezed her knee. "It must have been very difficult."

"What must have been difficult?"

"To turn her down. I know how much you would have loved that job."

"Arden . . ." She swallowed hard. "I didn't turn her down."

"You mean you agreed to go?"

"No, I told her I'd let her know. I wanted to talk it over with you."

"I don't understand." An uncertain half-smile crossed Arden's lips. "What is there to discuss?"

"Well, you know, what you think about this and everything." Margaret cleared her throat. Why did her vocabulary always desert her just when she needed it most? "I mean, do you think I should do it? Could we stand to be apart for so long? Would you wait for me?"

"Wait for you?" Arden repeated incredulously. "While you spend a year meeting the most fascinating women in America? No, I don't think so." She looked away from Margaret and stared at the fire. "This is a joke, right?"

Margaret would have given anything to say yes, but it was too late. She had spoken the words; she could not call them back.

"Arden, please, let's talk about this rationally. I don't want us to have any misunderstandings."

Arden stalked to the fireplace. She grabbed the poker and began to stab at the logs, sending clusters of sparks hissing into the chimney. "Neither do I. But when you tell me you want to pack up and leave, that's not very subtle. It's a difficult gesture to misunderstand."

"I don't want to leave you, Arden. I just want to take a trip, to do a job. It's not the same thing."

"It feels like it to me."

"We're only talking about nine months. Maybe eight."

"Maybe ten. And maybe a year. Maybe forever. You don't know what's going to happen. Margaret, I've barely known you for nine months. Don't you think you're asking a lot?"

"Arden, this is a once in a lifetime experience."

"And what am I?"

Margaret wrung her hands. "You are too. Look, if the situation were reversed, I would wait for you."

"I wouldn't ask you to."

"You don't know that. If a chance like this suddenly dropped into your lap, you don't know how you'd respond."

She whirled toward Margaret, angrily brushing tears off her cheeks. "A few weeks ago, Cyril asked me to go to Geneva with him next summer for a two-month conference of international publishers. It's a big honor. But I said no, because I couldn't stand the idea of leaving you. I didn't give it a second thought."

"You shouldn't have done that."

"I see that now."

"No, I mean you shouldn't have assumed it wouldn't work. You should have given me the benefit of the doubt and at least talked to me about it. I thought our love was bigger than that."

Arden dropped the poker into its wooden stand and threw herself into a chair. "I thought this was going to be different too. You kept promising me it would be. But I've been here before. This is romance Vietnam style—search and destroy."

"What do you mean?" Margaret knelt by her side.

"You find me, you change my life, and suddenly the thrill is gone and you're off to a new crusade. The *blitzkrieg* lover."

Margaret sat back on her heels, astounded. "Is that really what you think?"

"I was fine before I met you. I was safe. I didn't feel a thing. Then you came along and opened me up like some stupid, trusting little flower. And now you want to leave. You know what you are, Margaret? You're not the *blitzkrieg* lover. You're the *lozhnia vesná*, the goddamned false spring."

"I am not! It's not that way at all."

"Then how is it that you've lost interest in me so quickly?"

"I haven't lost interest in you. I love you." She grasped Arden's hands. "Look at me. This thing, this job offer, came out of the blue. I went there expecting to interview her for the paper, remember? It's a coincidence that it happened to take place now. Just plain bad timing."

"Well, maybe," Arden relented. "My mother has always said I'm cursed with it."

"Come and sit next to me. Please. I can't talk to you when you're all folded up against me like that." Margaret tugged her to the couch. "Arden, I'm sorry. I would never have brought the subject up if I'd known it would hurt you like this. I should have just told her no."

"Why didn't you?"

"I guess I was greedy. I thought I could have you and the job too." She smoothed a lock of Arden's hair into place. "But I was also thinking about our future. I don't want to be a bookstore clerk all my life. And goddess knows, *Feminist Times* barely hangs on from month to month. So I was thinking that this job could open some doors for me. I want to be someone you're proud to be with."

"I'm upset, Margaret. That doesn't mean I'm ashamed of you." She laughed harshly. "God, this reminds me of what

Sallie used to say when I misbehaved. 'I love you, Arden, but right now I'm not proud of you.'"

"My mother used to say that too, only without the 'I love you' part."

"Didn't she ever tell you that she loved you?"

"Not often. She didn't even say it yesterday, after all that's happened."

"Tonight was the first time you said that to me." Arden spoke in the husky, intimate tone that Margaret was afraid she'd never hear again.

"Arden." Margaret pressed her face against Arden's neck. "I'm not going. Forget about Lillian Green. Forget about the job. Forget I ever mentioned it."

"I can't do that," she murmured.

"Try."

"No. I don't want you to give it up because I had a tantrum. Let me think about it. Talk to some of your friends. I'll talk to Deborah."

"Can't I talk to Deborah too?"

"Maybe. After I do."

"You drive a hard bargain."

"I'm just warming up."

Arden was right, Margaret reflected the next day as she retyped copy at the newspaper office. She did need to talk to someone. Improbably, she pictured her mother: she would know what to do. It was thrilling to think that she could pick up the phone right now and call Anne. But Margaret really couldn't consult her about this life decision—not when the woman knew nothing about Margaret's life since the day she graduated from college. Who could Margaret find to talk to in the middle of the day? Deborah was off limits, Alice would be asleep, Joan would be sparking somewhere like an errant bolt of lightning. Luckily, Margaret knew a place where someone was always home.

She found Samantha bent over the sewing machine, stitching up a new pair of bright purple overalls. Kay napped on the ancient sea-green couch, a black cat curled on her stomach. The two women were surrounded by glossy plants so profuse they threatened to crowd out the sunlight.

"Have a seat while I finish this seam." Samantha said. "How did the editing collective let you escape their clutches on such a fine afternoon?"

"They don't keep tabs on me anymore."

"Oh? Why not?"

"I must have passed some kind of secret test. Ever since my little blow-out with Letitia last spring, they've treated me like a human being."

"Maybe it's because you've stopped treating them like keepers of the sacred torch."

"Maybe. How can Kay sleep through that racket?"

"You know her, she can sleep through anything, especially when she's working nights. I have to wake her soon, anyway. The kids will be coming home from school, and she likes to pretend she's conscious when they're around."

"Must be rough."

"There! Another fine example of fashion for the discerning feminist." Samantha turned off her sewing machine. The silence dropped on them like sudden rain.

Kay sat up abruptly, sending the cat skittering away. "What's wrong?"

"Nothing. I just stopped making noise."

"Oh." She rubbed her eyes like a child. "I was dreaming. . . Hi, Margaret. When did you get here?"

"Just now."

"What's up?"

"She has yet to tell us," Samantha replied. "You sit there and rest, Nurse Nightingale, while I make us some tea."

"She was a lesbian, you know." Kay yawned.

"Who was?" asked Margaret.

"Florence Nightingale."

"Oh, yeah. I've heard that."

Margaret described her dilemma while Samantha absently scratched the ears of a cat who was winding figure eights around her ankles.

"The good news is, you've got two positive things happening here. They're not necessarily mutually exclusive," Kay said dubiously. "Would Arden wait for you, do you suppose?"

"I asked her that. First she said no, then she said she'd think about it. But even if we did wait for each other, things would change between us after such a long time."

"Monogamy is an outdated patriarchal notion anyway," Samantha reminded them sharply.

"Samantha, you only say that because you're not in love," Kay accused. "You'd change your tune pretty quick if you were."

"Too true. Margaret, didn't you tell us Arden does some freelance work? Maybe she could go with you, at least for part of the time."

"I thought of that." Margaret fingered the faded brocade on the chair arm. "But Arden's pretty tied up with her job and the house and everyone in it. I don't think it would be fair to ask her."

"You mean you're afraid she'll say no," Samantha corrected her.

"Maybe. Anyway, if what we have is real, it will still be real in nine months, right?"

"That's what Ann Landers would say," Kay agreed earnestly.

"No, no, no." Samantha tilted her head and gazed at Margaret intensely. Margaret was reminded of an elementary school teacher who was sure her student knew the right answer, if only she could muster the courage to say it. "I could see that happening in a year or two. But now, after such a short time together? Don't bullshit yourself, Margaret. You'll break her heart. I'm not saying you shouldn't take the job, but let's be realistic about it."

"It's not only a question of what I feel or what Arden feels." Margaret gestured excitedly and sloshed tea on the table. "There's also the issue of what would be best for the movement. Am I giving the most I can by living a righteous lesbian life, loving Arden, and writing my articles? Or could I make a greater contribution by joining forces with Lillian Green? Although I guess anyone could do what I'd be doing for Lillian's project."

"She asked you to do it." Samantha discreetly slipped a napkin under Margaret's cup. "Besides, anyone could love Arden too. I think she's pretty cute myself."

"I know what you mean, Margaret." Kay leaned toward her, a holy light in her blue eyes. "I ask myself the same thing all the time: Would I be helping my kids more by going to a meeting tonight and trying to advance the revolution, or by staying home with them? I want to raise feminist children, but I also want to create a feminist world for them to live in. It would be real nice if other people would do that work so I could concentrate on my kids, but it looks like that's not going to happen."

"What's not going to happen?" demanded Lucy as she strode into the room with her spiky blond hair bobbing.

"Oh, Lucy, I'm so glad you're here!" Samantha hopped up and gave her a hug. "Margaret has a problem and I know you can help her with it."

"Uh oh. Hope I don't disappoint anyone here." Lucy blushed and played with the fringe on the end of her long lavender scarf. Margaret and Kay looked at each other with raised eyebrows. "What's the problem, Margaret?"

Lucy listened soberly to Margaret's recitation. "I think I can help you," she said slowly. "If you trust me."

"Of course I trust you."

"Okay." She went to the window, gently pushed aside tendrils of hanging ivy, and released the belts that held open the heavy, old-fashioned drapes.

"What are you doing?"

"Trust, remember?" Lucy repeated the performance at the other windows. Dusk fell in the room. "I'm creating a space where you can listen to your feelings. They'll always give you the right answer."

Margaret wished Maureen had come home early instead of Lucy. With her crystalline understanding of politics and ethics, Maureen could have instantly identified the correct decision. Then Margaret would be on the el now, instead of sitting in this dark room about to undergo a seance. "Lucy, I don't go in for this kind of thing. Thanks anyway, but I know what I feel. I feel confused. I need to think it through."

"You need to *feel* it through," she replied imperturbably. "Just relax. Take your shoes off."

"Lucy—"

"Don't be such a baby," Samantha ordered. Margaret removed her shoes.

"Good. Now. Close your eyes, and try to empty your mind of thoughts."

"What for?"

"You live too much in your head. I want you to live in your heart for a few minutes."

"I can't get rid of those pesky thoughts," Margaret announced after a brief effort. "Maybe we should try this another time."

"Margaret, picture your thoughts as a bunch of thin white fibers. Can you do that?"

"Uh huh."

"Good. Now picture all those fibers spinning themselves together into one white thread. Do you see it?"

"Yeah! Amazing."

"Now imagine a piece of black velvet. Gently place the white thread on the black cloth. The thread's safe, you can see it easily, you can pick it up any time you want. Got it?"

"Got it."

"Good for you. Okay. Take a deep breath and exhale it slowly. Now, picture yourself on an airplane. You're sitting next to Lillian Green. She looks exactly the way she looked yesterday. You look exactly the way you looked yesterday. What are you talking about?"

Margaret squinted in the dark. "We're talking about . . . tomorrow. The women we're going to meet. The questions she's going to ask."

"And how do you feel?"

"Excited. Nervous. Strong."

"What are you nervous about?"

"I know I can do it, but I have to prove myself to her. And what if I don't like the job, or I don't like her? What if Lillian Green is an asshole? She sort of hinted that she was."

"What then?"

She imagined Lillian Green barking orders at her, ignoring her suggestions, breezing out the door with some male companion while Margaret sat up the rest of the night transcribing interview tapes in a scummy hotel room. She shrugged. "I can handle it. She's one of the leaders of our movement. It will be fascinating to learn how she thinks, even if she does turn out to be a jerk.

"Besides, the project itself is exciting. I can see it now: the voices of all those women turning into piles of paper, the paper gathering into a book —" She opened her eyes and blinked at Lucy, a pale figure in the dark room. "I can't believe this shit works!"

Lucy smiled. "It's nothing magical, just a way of focusing your imagination. There are many kinds of knowing. They don't all rely on information."

"Sounds pretty mystical to me."

"No, just matriarchal. Trying to relearn the wisdom that all women had before the rule of men."

"Well, whatever. It's doing the trick."

"Glad to hear it. Now, close your eyes again. Let your vision wander for a moment. Can you see Arden?"

"Of course." Her image was clear, immediate, tangible. Margaret envisioned her glossy hair, her hazel eyes sparkling with intelligence, her wide candid smile and the deep parentheses that framed it. She could almost inhale her powdery scent.

"Okay," Lucy said gently. "Now picture yourself next to Arden. You're sitting in your living room, on one of those fat pillows. What are you talking about?"

Margaret saw herself, short, wordless, unforgivably young. Doubts sprouted around her like mushrooms. What would she and Arden discuss in the months to come, when their love was no longer a constant source of wonder?

What did she have to offer such a complex, accomplished woman, a woman who could break down the walls of language? Daily Margaret struggled to write words that would be read by a few hundred people in a city of millions. Daily she worked to prepare for a revolution that might never arrive.

"Keep looking," Lucy's quiet voice urged. "Tell me what you find."

Margaret squeezed her eyes shut until streaks of red shot through the black. She pictured the future stretching endlessly in the house on Lill Street. She saw that she was not in it. She pictured the long, strong stamina of love. She saw that she did not have it.

Margaret counted her courage and came up short. She could not stay, could not risk letting Arden see inside her, only to find there was nothing there. She would go off with Lillian Green.

Her shoulders sagged. Her head sank into her hands.

"What's the matter?" Samantha clicked on a lamp.

"I guess I saw how the story ends."

"You're going."

"Yes. Can you believe I could do something like this to Arden?"

"Margaret, this job is custom made for you." Lucy glanced at Kay, who had dozed off again in the darkness. She lowered her voice. "How often do you think you're going to get an opportunity like this?"

"You're right. I just can't stand the thought of hurting her."

"It'll be tough, I know. But Arden's not a sure thing. She's not an outfront lesbian, and she still lives with that man. A few months apart may be just what she needs."

"You don't know her."

"Maybe we're all underestimating her," Samantha suggested. "If she loves you, she'll want you to have this chance."

"You're the one who said I'd break her heart."

"I can be mistaken, you know. Besides, hearts do heal. Arden's an adult. She's probably had some practice at it."

Lucy pulled the curtains open. Margaret was surprised that it was still light outside.

"When do you meet with Lillian Green again?" Samantha asked.

"I have to call her tomorrow with my decision." She sighed. "I feel sick."

Samantha reached across the table and patted her knee. "Never you mind, Margaret. This is right. You know it. Everything will work out for the best in the end."

"Do you really believe that?"

"Generally speaking."

"Well, generally speaking, I have to go. I start work at six. Listen, thanks for everything."

"We'll see you before you leave town, won't we?" Samantha asked.

"Count on it."

Deborah stood in wait behind the counter of Lucia's Books, her dark eyes narrowed like a cat's. "You son of a bitch," she said flatly.

The words struck Margaret like a blow to the chest. "Deborah, do you think that's fair?"

"Oh, *I'm* being unfair? What about you?"

"You don't know what this is like for me. You don't know how I feel about her."

"Maybe not." Deborah glanced around the store, lowered her voice to a hoarse whisper. "But I know how she feels about you, and I can't believe you'd put her through this. For a fucking job! When did you become such a big careerist?"

"We're only talking about nine months. It doesn't seem like too much to ask for Arden to support me, or you either. I'd do the same for her. Or for you."

"Does that mean you've definitely decided to go?"

"Yes."

Deborah bit her lip as she rang up a sale. "Look, it sounds like a fabulous job. I agree. I just don't want you to hurt Arden."

"And you think I do?" She flung her jacket onto the peg and shoved up the sleeves of her sweatshirt.

"No, but I think you're going to." Deborah sat on one of the tall stools and immediately hopped down, too agitated to sit still. "Margaret, you don't know her. She's vulnerable right now. We all agree it's time for this thing with Joe to be over, but it's still hard for her. Arden's gone through a lot of changes to be with you. You can't just say, 'Keep my side of the bed warm, honey, I'll be back in a year.' She needs something solid, and that was supposed to be you."

Margaret wanted to shake Deborah by the shoulders and yell, "Can't you see *I'm not solid?*" But while she was framing her response, Deborah plunged ahead.

"I mean, isn't there something exciting and challenging you could do here?" she pressed. "Do you have to go on this *fekakteh* odyssey?"

"What the hell does that mean?"

"Just what it sounds like. Crazy. Fucked up."

"What's crazy about it?"

"It'll take you away from here, for starters!" Deborah grasped her arm, as much to steady herself as Margaret. "Look, I know I can be a little overzealous about Arden."

"Yeah. Sometimes I think you're in love with her yourself."

"But can't you see that we don't want to lose you?"

"Why should you lose me? I'm just going on a trip, for christ's sake."

"Because even if you come back, things will never be the same."

"Deborah, you're one of the strongest people I know. I can't believe you're afraid of a little change."

"Well, I am. I hate change."

"You said it would change everything if I got involved with Arden, remember?"

"It did, didn't it?"

"Yes, but we all survived."

"You swore you'd be careful with her feelings, and now look what's happening."

"You don't understand!"

Deborah clutched a handful of curly blond hair. "That's right, I don't. You're the one who's so good with words. Why don't you make me understand?"

Margaret faltered. "I can't. Deborah, if you trust me at all, trust that in my own way, I'm doing what's best for Arden."

Deborah leaned back against the counter, arms folded across her chest. She examined Margaret for several long seconds. Finally she nodded curtly. "Maybe you are."

Neither one spoke. The cow bell on the door clanged jarringly in the silence.

"Okay. Right." Deborah scanned the aisles, counting customers. "You can reorganize Science Fiction tonight. And if you find the feather duster, you might give it a workout. I think Elaine threw it away when I asked her to dust last weekend." She slung her big leather book bag over her shoulder. "And Margaret."

"What?"

"Write a job description for your replacement."

"All right. Deborah, I really loved working here."

"Maybe you can re-up when you get back, unless you're too big for your britches by then."

"If you think you're being kind by not telling me what's wrong, you're not," Arden said quietly. They were in her living room, sitting stiffly on either end of the couch. "Was it something I said, or did? Something I didn't do?"

"Please believe me, Arden, it's not you. It's me. I wouldn't want you to be different in any way."

"Then why are you leaving me?"

"I'm not leaving you. I'm just—leaving."

"But why?"

Margaret closed her eyes against the pain in Arden's face. "Because I can't be what you want."

"But you *are* what I want. Don't you think you should let me be the judge of that?"

"I can't give you what you deserve."

"What do I deserve that you don't have?"

"Everything."

Arden threw up her hands and gave a short, bitter laugh. "I'm lost. I can't follow this at all. Are we speaking the same language?"

"Arden, this doesn't have to be an ending. I'm just taking a journey. It may be a long one, but it's only temporary."

"I know you, Margaret. You're a runner. If you leave here, you'll never come back."

"Is that an ultimatum?"

Arden smiled sadly. "No, a prediction."

Margaret took a risk. It was a risk she would never have dared in her careful, guarded, constructed life if not for all the craziness that was suddenly the norm: meeting Lillian Green, and loving Arden, and losing her family, and creating a new one, and her book dying, and her mother returning, and everything that had seemed solid and immutable now shifting like a fleeting shape glimpsed out of the corner of an eye.

Margaret turned to Arden and held out her hands. "Then come with me," she said. "Take a leave of absence, or quit your job, or pack up a trunkful of Russian manuscripts, but come with me."

"Yes," said Arden. "I will."

WHAT SHE KNOWS NOW

Arden's prophecy came true, of course: Margaret never did return to Lill Street. Other goals, other urgencies got in the way. For three months, Margaret and Arden traveled with the enormously tolerant Lillian Green, lugging piles of Arden's incomprehensible manuscripts from state to state. But Arden could not bear their discursive, disconnected life on the road, and Margaret could not bear to give it up. After long nights of hopeless tears and anguished talks, Arden went home, and Margaret went on with Lillian to the next town.

Margaret's nine months of travel turned into twelve, followed by another year in New York working for the famous feminist, and still more years there on her own. That decision, to leave Chicago and follow Lillian Green, has made all the difference. Margaret first broke into print with a series of light-hearted magazine pieces about her adventures on the road with Lillian. Indeed, she has dined on those stories, and the assignments they led to, for years.

And yet, just as she cannot resist poking a sore tooth with her tongue, so Margaret cannot stop herself from wondering what might have been. What would her life be like if she had chosen to accompany Arden back to Lill Street? If Margaret knew then what she knows now, could she have kept Arden's love? And what, in that case, of all the experiences Margaret has had since that wrenching separation— the articles she's written, the people she's known, the woman who is waiting for her decision right now?

Margaret laughs when she catches herself thinking like this. She realizes that no one could have stayed with her in those days.

Her earliest loves were bursts of passion interrupting wastes of caution. It took her years to explore the topography of the heart.

Margaret stares at the picture of herself on Lill Street and shakes her head. She has barely a cell in common with that young, long-haired woman who was so sure of the future, that fervent face trapped in the flat, shiny universe of an aging photograph. Hard to believe that, despite everything, the little planet of Lill Street continues to spin contentedly in its orbit.

Arden and Joan have been together now for more than ten years. They live in the big house on Lill Street, happily and noisily, with their two daughters. Joan serves as business manager for The Hunger, the chic and successful catering service started by Samantha and Lucy. Arden does most of her translating at home, working from the office she built on the fourth floor after Mrs. Rogers moved away.

Deborah and Paul still live in their old apartment. She continues to manage Lucia's Books; he is a partner in an engineering firm. Deborah is considering buying the bookstore to ward off the panic she feels at her daughter's imminent departure. Everyone has warned her against this, but no one holds out much hope.

Charles lives not far away, in a small house he rents with his partner Armand. He is the head librarian now, and hates it, having to devote too much time to management chores and not enough to the work he enjoys. Summer Sundays find Armand on the front porch of the house on Lill Street, sharing the newspaper with Deborah, Arden and Joan, while Charles and Paul stand in the oil-spattered driveway and continue their futile tinkering with the '65 Mustang Paul bought over his wife's objections.

As for Joe, he is the surprise. He lives in New York, just two blocks from Margaret. They run into each other around the neighborhood, and sometimes go out for coffee and bagels on Saturday mornings.

He is a Wall Street lawyer, silver-templed, chummy with people whose names Margaret curses when she comes across them in the newspaper. It's only business, he tells her. You can't take it personally. Besides, he reminds her, she should be pleased by his success: five percent of his income goes to worthy causes. His accountant, a woman Margaret once dated, insists on it.

Still, if she can put all that aside— and it astonishes her that she can— he is good company. They rarely reminisce, and when they do, they argue about the details. But there is something comfortable between them, something unspoken, like two immigrants from the old country who do not need to compare accents to recognize one another.

Last month Joan and Arden came to New York for a visit. The three women stayed up late, traded stories, laughed until their cheeks hurt. Margaret loved every instant of it. And when the night ended, she only smiled at the whisper of nostalgia that rippled the air as Arden followed Joan into the bedroom and closed the door behind them.

Margaret knows now what she didn't know then. She knows that her best words won't trigger a revolution. She knows that it is time to go home. She knows that in a minute she will call Gwen and say yes.

She knows a last chance when she sees one, and she is seeing one now.

The fact is, Margaret rarely thinks anymore in terms of revolution. Instead she thinks of education, of reformation, of doing what one can do. Sometimes she grows indignant at younger women, so cavalier about the rights that cost blood to secure. Sometimes she gets angry at her contemporaries, because they turned from CR groups to self-help groups, because they grew tired, because they gave in.

But at other times she experiences a wave of overwhelming pride in women everywhere. She does not entirely trust this emotion; it reminds her of the trembling, wet-eyed patriotism that overcomes aging Legionnaires as they salute the flag.

Still, the strangest things can set her off: the name of a woman director at the end of a good movie; the sight of the local lesbian mothers' group pushing their strollers through Central Park; the multi-hued faces of women writers peering back at her through a bookstore window. At these times Margaret feels: it was all worth it. I helped make that possible.

She knows it is not enough. But she is not yet finished.

Other Books from Third Side Press